THE FORBIDDEN TEARS SERIES

RULED BY FATE

SAM WITHROW & AMELIA PINKIS

FRESH INK
PRESS
LLC

This is a work of fiction. Names, characters, places, and incidents are products of the author's imagination or are used fictitiously and are not to be construed as real. Any resemblance to actual events, locations, organizations, or persons, living or dead, is entirely coincidental.

FRESH INK PRESS
Cape Coral, Florida

CONTENTS

ACKNOWLEDGMENTS

Many thanks to my family and friends for their support throughout this decade-long quest. A special shout out to my husband Jim, who has stood by me, supported me, and read ad nauseam. You are the brightest star in my universe. To my daughter Loryn, never stop reaching for the stars. Dreams do come true.

Sam

This book is dedicated to Natalie. You are my light. To my children, Anakin, Auden, Arianne, and Adeline, and my husband Alex – you can achieve anything you set your minds to. I love you.

Amelia

CHAPTER ONE

The Fox and the Phantom

"Farewell, happy fields, where joy
forever dwells: Hail, horrors, hail."
John Milton, Paradise Lost

The golden quiet of the woods was interrupted only by the sound of feet rhythmically pounding the trail. White shoes flashed against the dark path as the girl ran in silence, crunching fallen leaves into the earth, each fleeting step echoing in the idyllic stillness of nature.

A trilling, high-octave wail blasted through the air, frightening birds from their branches as the latest pop hit declared that the singer didn't want to go to Heaven without raising Hell.

She careened forward and stumbled over a rock, dropping her phone in the process. She spat a lock of hair and a good quantity of leaves out of her mouth as the song continued to blare at top volume.

"Well this was always going to happen," she muttered, groping around on the path until she found her phone. She'd made the mistake of letting her best friend, Sherry, use it a few months back. When it was returned, she discovered her alarms and ringtones had all been changed to hilarious effect. Siri wouldn't stop calling her *"Sexy Beast,"* and she hadn't figured out how to change it back yet.

She glanced at the screen and groaned. It was her therapist. Again. He probably wanted to have another conversation involving the phrase, "So tell me again about this… *light.*" That was the thing she hated most — the weighted pause before the last word. It made therapists sound almost… patronizing.

She closed her eyes as she answered and tried to inject as much level-headed cheerfulness into her tone as she could muster. "Hi, Dr. Rogers. How's it going?"

"Hello, Brianna. I'm glad you picked up. How are things going with you?"

Another classic therapist move — answering a question with a question.

"You missed your last two sessions," he continued. "I was getting worried."

"Oh, no need to worry. Everything's fine." She yanked off her shoe to remove a pebble, immediately falling backward off the decaying log she'd used as a seat. A blanket of moss cushioned the fall and her hand landed in something she very much hoped was tree sap.

"Brie? Are you there?" Dr. Rogers' voice crackled through the phone.

"Yes, yes, I'm here!" she said, popping up again. "I'm sorry for missing our appointments. I was just, um… packing, you know. Super busy with the move."

The move had been a constant source of discussion for the last few months. She remembered the day she'd told him, the way he'd paused in surprise beside the office aquarium, staring at her intensely, unaware that he was tragically overfeeding his fish.

"So, you're sticking with your decision? You're taking a step back from therapy?" he asked. He'd never say she was quitting. He'd never say she was walking away. Words were weapons, and he handled his with the greatest of care. It was a trait they didn't have in common.

She tensed ever so slightly, wiped her hand on some leaves, then walked determinedly down the trail. "I prefer to think of it as a graduation."

There was a long pause before he spoke. "Brie, let me be frank with you." She heard the familiar creaking of his chair. She could picture exactly how he was leaning back and steepling his fingers to make his point. "I know you keep saying you're 'cured,' but as I keep trying to tell you, grief is a journey, not a destination. There is no 'cured.' And the fact that you insisted for so long that what you saw was real—"

"I know it wasn't real," she interrupted flatly. "It was a grief manifestation. Something my brain invented to deal with the tragedy. I accept that. I accept that there was nothing supernatural about the accident. I accept that the man who came to save me wasn't real. Just like I accept that instead of dealing with me himself, my dad hired you."

Silence.

She cast a quick look to the heavens, cheeks flushing in shame. The man didn't deserve her anger. The truth was, he'd been nothing but supportive ever since her father had decided he no longer knew what to do with her or her insistence that beasts made of shadow had attacked her mother and a man made of light had driven them away. Dr. Rogers had been patient and kind, and he never once said she was crazy, which she very much appreciated. Especially considering how often she wondered if she was.

But it had been years, and she was done rehashing the past. She wanted to look forward.

"Look, I'm fine," she said, preempting his attempts to push the party line. "I've done everything you've suggested. I kept diaries, journaled my dreams, considered yoga—"

"Are you going to the waterfall again?"

She flashed a look up the trail before glancing suspiciously at her phone. *What number am I thinking of?*

"Brie?" he asked.

"No, I'm not going to the waterfall," she said quickly, covering the receiver as her heart hammered away in her chest. "Haven't you been listening? I'm done with all that. I'm at home now — packing. I'm listening to the soothing sounds of a South African rainforest on YouTube and considering getting an emotional support animal. A dog. Or maybe a ferret. I hear they come in ferret."

There was a scarcely audible sigh. "You know I'm only asking because—"

"I know why you're asking," she interrupted, "and I'm fine, really. Now I promise I'll check in when I get to Virginia, but this line is full of static, and I'm going through a tunnel—"

"Wait, I thought you were—"

She hung up quickly, biting at her lower lip.

That could have been handled better.

She slipped her phone into her pocket and continued down the trail.

A few minutes later, she cleared the last of the trees and pulled in a deep breath, letting the mist from the churning water whisper gently across her face. The sunlight bounced off the water and dazzled her eyes for a moment before she quietly spoke. "Hi, Mom."

She never felt close to her mother at the cemetery. But here in the woods, in her favorite childhood spot, the place they were headed when she died, Brie felt her presence.

She settled cross-legged on a smooth, flat stone overlooking the falls and gazed over the tranquil scene. Splashes of water chimed sweetly below her. Time ceased to matter, as though the world stopped at the entrance of the forest, like all the problems that plagued her on the other side had simply melted away. As she watched, a silver fox loped out of the underbrush and cocked its head, studying her. Brie was taken aback — the creature had one green eye and one blue. She stared, astonished, unable to believe it would venture so close. Just as she was about to move, it winked.

"Did you just wink at me?" she asked incredulously. "*Can* foxes wink?"

Sherry is never going to believe this.

The fox almost seemed to smirk before skittering away into the trees.

"Did you see that, Mom?" she whispered, waiting a moment for an answer she knew would never come. She shook her head as though to dispel the curious incident, deliberately not thinking about how many similar and strange things had happened to her in these woods.

"Sherry can't wait for me to get to Virginia," she continued softly. "She's all excited about some guy she met named Mike. And she swears I'll love my new place. She went on and on about 'cottage vibes.' You know me. As long as there's a bed and a coffee maker, I'm fine."

She went silent, watching the play of water over the rocks and checking the treeline for overly friendly woodland creatures before continuing. "I don't know how Dad will deal with both of us gone.

I'll try to come home as often as possible to take care of him, but you know how busy the first year of this job is supposed to be."

She reached for the chain that had been placed around her neck on that terrible day. There hadn't been a single moment that she'd taken it off. Not *ever*.

"I miss you, Mom. All the time."

She brought the pendant to her lips and kissed it gently before tucking it back under her shirt. It wasn't until she'd risen to leave that she turned around with a passing thought.

"Mom, since you're up in heaven, do me a favor, would you? If you ever see that 'guardian angel' guy again? Cameron? Punch him in the face."

With a last look at the lovely waterfall splashing into the pool below, she inhaled a deep breath of warm, fragrant air and started to run home.

She didn't see the palm-sized golden glimmer, near-indistinguishable from the sunlight, tuck itself away behind the trunk of a pine as she ran off.

She never saw it. It made sure of that.

◆　　◆　　◆

It was another half hour before Brie arrived at her apartment, red-cheeked and gasping for breath. She hung her keys on the hook by the door and made straight for the refrigerator to down a pro-tein-laced tropical fruit amalgamation Sherry once told her was indispensable for her electrolytes. She generally made it a practice to do as Sherry commanded, assured that her best friend's pen-chant for storing vast amounts of pseudo-useful information would see her through.

She wandered into the living room, making a mental note of what had yet to be packed. There wasn't much. Although she'd been there a year and a half, she'd never fully moved into the place. Aside from a series of sun-bleached photographs, a rapidly decaying Ficus tree constituted one of her only attempts to nest. She stroked one of the lank, yellow leaves before fetching a glass of water. The little tree shuddered pitifully as she poured it in.

"There you go, little one," she whispered encouragingly. "You've got this." She'd read online that houseplants lived longer if you talked to them. After a moment of indecision, she poured in the rest of her fruit smoothie as well.

Couldn't hurt.

She checked her phone — two voice messages. She put it on speaker.

The first was from Sherry.

"Darling! You need to get here already. You know what happens when you're not around to rein in my genius designs. Sidenote: Is there any such thing as too pink? I'm looking at an ottoman that would, in the wrong hands, be frankly shocking."

Brie grinned, rolled her eyes, and started putting the few personal items that decorated her living room into a cardboard box. Sherry was in the middle of another interior design project, and Brie knew her opinion wasn't required. Her best friend was merely looking for an excuse to go full-magenta on some poor, unsuspecting home decor as she deconstructed, then reconstructed her apartment into something resembling an eccentric *Vogue Home Edition* centerfold.

"I can't wait to see you, girl. Call me the second you get into town!"

Brie clicked on the next message.

"Hi, Brie. It's your dad."

She almost dropped the picture she'd taken off the wall.

"I was hoping… I was just wondering if you could stop by. You know, on your way out of town. We… I haven't… Well, just come on by if you can."

She looked down at the picture in her hand. It was one of the few she'd taken from her dad's house when she'd moved out, and the image had long since been seared into her mind. It was the simplicity that captured her most. The same photograph could have been hanging in a thousand other happy homes, and this one just happened to belong to her. It was a family portrait—one of their very first. Her mother and father were holding their newborn baby, gazing adoringly at the tiny bundle as she reached up a hand to them in return.

She loved this photograph. It was a perfect moment, frozen in time. Her throat grew thick with emotion. She wrapped it carefully in several scarves and sweatshirts and placed it at the top of a box, determined that it would not break in transit. Then she decided to save the rest of the packing for later and headed for the bath.

One final bath. I don't even know if the new place has a tub.

She turned on the faucet and waited for the water to warm up, considering her reflection in the mirror. It was no wonder it was so hard for her father. She'd always been the spitting image of her mom. They shared the same long, chestnut hair, the same wide-set green eyes, and the same mouth, slightly upturned at the corners, as though always on the edge of laughing. She'd even inherited her mother's dancer figure, though none of her inherent grace.

She let out a quiet sigh, her father's voicemail still ringing in her ears. Considering the level of complexity and nuance her therapist had delighted in heaping on every situation, the way Brie saw it, the problem was rather simple: After the accident, she'd gotten help. Her dad hadn't.

In the quaking aftermath, as she had wrestled with the flickering memories of angels and death, her father sank into a kind of unremarkable depression that left him wandering around the house with a bottle permanently affixed to his hand. For a long time, she'd resented him. Bitterly. She was the one who'd been in the car. She was the one who'd had half a windshield pulled from her chest. She was the one who'd been sentenced to weekly therapy sessions in the years that followed. But as time progressed and the relationship deteriorated, she'd come to realize an important lesson: it was impossible to resent a person so truly, incurably sad.

She looked after him instead, watching as he buried himself in work and neglected everything else. She secretly restocked the refrigerator and made deals with the electric company to have his bills forwarded to her new address. She took the slow route through nursing school so she could care for him, watching Sherry graduate ahead of her and move out to Virginia, escaping the little Atlanta suburb they'd been so anxious to leave since they were children. Anger was replaced with acceptance, even if that acceptance slowly chipped away at her heart.

She understood when he didn't show up at her graduation. She understood when he forgot appointments and birthdays. She understood when he couldn't teach her how to drive. *He* was less understanding when Sherry taught her instead, and they plowed into her neighbor's mailbox. But understanding didn't make it any easier.

The truth was, she missed her father desperately, and she'd give him that precious photograph in a second if it meant he'd never touch another bottle of vodka again.

Her bath was ready.

She added a few drops of lavender oil and slipped beneath the water, letting it quiet her mind and soothe her muscles, still aching from her run. This was the one good thing about the apartment.

Though it was lacking in other areas, like basic insulation and structural support, it had come with an improbably-sized bathtub. She'd taken one look and leased it on the spot.

She relaxed back into the tub, gazing up at the crack in the ceiling that looked like Saturn. She'd spent many nights just like this, letting her mind wander as her eyes focused on that one inconsequential thing. It had become a kind of solace. The little apartment had afforded her a bit of space from her father without leaving the town entirely. It had given her just enough room to stay sane — just enough independence to feel like she wasn't wholly, irrevocably stuck.

She closed her eyes and luxuriated in the water. She wondered if she'd miss it. She wondered if she'd ever find herself wanting to move back.

"You've got to work those buns if you want to lose them!"

The trance broke, and her eyes drifted slowly upward to where her neighbor had started his nightly routine of calisthenics and self-loathing. She rolled her eyes and slipped under the water. The instant she submerged, the world vanished, and the noise quieted to a gentle hum. A sense of nostalgia washed over her as she opened her eyes beneath the warm water. There had been many nights when she'd sat just like this, counting the seconds to see how long she could stay under, sometimes wondering what would happen if she decided not to surface.

Those were the earliest days. Things are different now.

It was good that she was leaving. How long had she cocooned herself in this place — this apartment, this town — trapped in some stagnant shrine to the past? Most people would have packed up and moved away years ago. But she'd only lost one parent. She still had a tether.

Come on, you know that's not the only reason.

The water rippled around her fingers as if on cue, and her pendant drifted up in front of her eyes. It shimmered in the dim light, delicate filigree metal encasing a strangely beautiful opaline stone, hovering in perfect stillness beneath little waves.

No, it wasn't the only reason. And it wasn't the only tether. She wasn't just leaving the town. She was leaving all of it. The road they'd been driving, the cemetery she hated, the falls where she secretly jogged almost every morning to offer her mother a bashful hello. She'd be leaving the story — the idea that everything that happened was real.

I used to call it a memory. When did I start calling it a story?

With a little frown, she reached out in front of her, touching the tips of her fingers to the glinting pendant. How could she leave when she couldn't even take off the necklace? She could picture it as clearly as if it had happened yesterday. The way the angel had reached out his hand to touch the pendant before pulling back and telling her, "Don't *ever* take it off." A surge of anger swept through her. How could she pack up the car when she was still bound to the promise of an angel who didn't really exist?

Her jaw clenched in determination, and without stopping to think about what she was doing, she reached behind her neck and unclasped the delicate chain. Rather than sinking, the pendant floated strangely away from her, hovering just out of reach.

Suddenly, a crack like thunder snapped across the room, whipping through the air and sucking the color out of everything. She sat up with a jolt. At least she tried, but she couldn't break through the surface of the water. Bewildered, she put one, then two palms to the surface and encountered a barrier as hard and clear as glass. She made a fist with one hand and banged against it, but it wouldn't budge, and the sound of her struggle merely echoed back around her.

What the hell?

Again and again, she tried to break through to the surface. Again and again, she was held in place as though by an enormous, warm force.

Is this an earthquake? That must be what this—

Beyond the surface, a black, oil-like ribbon snaked its way to the crack in her ceiling, then spiderwebbed outward, quickly filling up the whole room. She let out a waterlogged shriek, and the lights went dead above her, pitching the cozy room into sudden darkness. The scent of lavender was gone, and the tub itself had chilled to such a degree she thought she must be having a seizure, though her body thrummed with the warmth she could not explain. She clawed at the porcelain edges, trying to hoist herself free.

Except, she couldn't.

This isn't an earthquake.

Suddenly, a warm pulse rippled through the room like a wave. It trembled the edges of the bathtub and rattled the sink against the wall. The faster it spread across the length of the ceiling, the faster the shadow retreated back, repelled by the strange, warm energy. Another muffled scream ripped through her lips, emerging only as bubbles as the floor buckled and shook. Her neighbor was still exercising in the apartment above her, seemingly unaware of the deadly struggle going on just beneath. She could hear his feet rhythmically pounding her ceiling. Though it couldn't have been more than thirty seconds, she felt herself running out of air.

I have to get out of here. I'm going to drown.

Her head was spinning. Another few seconds, and she was going to black out.

There was a soft nudge against her fingers like a friend tapping for attention. Her eyes flew back to the water, only to see a tiny flicker of gold drifting in the evening light.

She instinctively reached for it and looped the pendant's chain around her wrist.

At once, the room steadied. At once, that inexplicable pressure disappeared. A second later, she burst through the surface in an explosion of bubbles and spluttering gasps. When she opened her eyes, the world had returned to normal.

The lights flickered another moment, then went steady. Her neighbor's aerobics music pounded through the ceiling above her, shaking occasional bits of plaster from the walls.

She took a second to catch her breath, then clasped the necklace around her neck and snatched the drain plug out of the water.

No. I'm not going to miss this place at all.

Brie stood, shivering and wrapped in a towel, looking down at her bathtub.

What the hell was that?

Her nurse's training kicked in, and she patted herself down, checking for injuries. Two fingers on the inside of her wrist told her her heart was racing, but that was to be expected. She wiped off the mirror and checked her pupils. Normal. Frustrated, she resorted to checking the tub itself, running her hands over the inside of the ceramic vessel, looking for what, she couldn't say.

When she started to shiver so hard her teeth chattered, she gave up and headed to the bedroom. She put on some black yoga pants and a sweatshirt over a strappy bra she had to wrestle to put on.

A gift from Sherry. Her wardrobe had long ago fallen victim to her best friend's sartorial sensibilities. If Brie ever hinted that she wouldn't mind something a bit more practical, she'd be met with a stunned look and the affirmation that "Beauty is pain, Brianna. Stop acting brand new." As a result, her closet was better stocked with more fashionable items than she'd ever have chosen if left to her own devices.

She pulled in a faltering breath, trying to shake past whatever had happened in the bath as she packed what remained into boxes, bracing for an emotional response that never came. Perhaps she was merely spent. The seismic shudders in the tub had scared her, and there was only so much someone could give before survival instinct took hold. But if she was honest, she supposed Dr. Rogers was right; her walls were too high and too strong to allow for any true intimacy, even with her own home. She was okay with that. She had her studies, her best friend, and the constant repression of severe trauma to keep her company.

And her plant.

It was a lonely thought — lonely enough that it made her self-conscious, even though she was standing by herself in a now barren living room. The emptiness seemed to close around her, and she suddenly decided she couldn't stand to be in the place for another second.

She packed the boxes into her trusty silver Suzuki and went back into the apartment for a final look around to make sure she hadn't missed anything. After a moment of consideration, she doubled back at the last second and wedged the dilapidated Ficus under her arm.

"You know what? I think you're bouncing back."

CHAPTER TWO

The Ambush

It was a ten minute drive to her dad's house, but Brie stopped by her landlord's place first to drop off her key, then by a favorite family restaurant to pick up takeout on the way. She drove the streets on autopilot and realized this was the last time she'd be able to do so for a long while. Geography and spatial orientation were not among her strengths. She relied entirely on her phone's maps and navigator to get her to and from every new destination. She winced at the realization that she'd likely spend the next several months perpetually lost. For the first time, she felt a pang in her heart at the prospect of losing the familiar.

She turned onto her dad's street and rolled to a stop by the curb. The grass needed mowing. She hadn't had a chance to do that this past week. She wondered if she should call the boy who lived next door, maybe see if she could pay him a little each month to keep the place looking decent, assuming her dad didn't frighten him off.

The old Chevy was out front, with grass growing underneath, parked in the spot farthest from the house. The area nearest the front door, where her mom's Buick sedan had always parked, remained empty. Brie and her dad never spoke about it openly, but they both knew never to park there. It remained a shrine, as though she were going to come home any day now.

Brie walked up the cracked cement path to the porch with her sleeping bag in one hand and a takeout bag in the other, raising a finger to ring the bell. She hesitated. Part of her wanted to fetch the spare key from below the potted geraniums and let herself in. A stronger part realized this wasn't her home anymore and hadn't been for some time. She rang the bell.

Her father answered the door in bleary confusion. "Brie? What are you doing here?"

She offered him an uncertain smile, suddenly regretting her impulsive decision to come.

"Hi, Dad. You called me, remember? Asked me to stop by before I left? I thought maybe I could spend the night. We could catch up."

He continued to stare in silence, and she shifted awkwardly on the porch.

"Can I come in?" she finally asked.

He blinked twice, then took a step backward, opening the door. She heard the bottle clink against the doorknob before she saw it. She chose to ignore it and walked into the house.

It had been a while.

Nothing had changed, not since that day. Things had been occasionally cleaned, but nothing had been moved — not one chair rearranged, not one painting rehung — since her mother's death. There were no photos of life after that fateful day. It was a house locked in time. And it was a mess. Bottles and pizza boxes littered the floor. Takeout containers and unopened mail piled up in corners. Cobwebs occupied every corner of the ceiling.

A pang of guilt shot through Brie's heart.

If this is how he's coping now, what will he be like when I'm gone?

He returned to his place on the couch, where the cushions had worn to his imprint years ago — one depression from his elbow, another one for his thigh. She had the sad thought that the couch knew him better than anyone living.

"So, you're off tomorrow then, huh?" he said, slurring the edges of his words.

He set the half-empty bottle on a side table, a little too hard. She moved a pile of papers and perched on the chair beside him, watching as he turned back to the television as if she wasn't there. As if he couldn't bear to look.

"Yes, I'm off tomorrow. Did you open the shop today, Dad?"

"Don't you worry about the shop or about me. It's handled, little missy."

She set down the bag she was carrying on the coffee table. "I brought your favorite. Pastrami on rye and vegetable soup." She tried to keep her voice light and playful, searching his face for any hint of affection, any sign that coming here had been a good idea.

"I'll eat when I'm hungry, Brie."

Her heart sank. "I'm going to get some water. Do you want a glass?"

"I'll take some ice." He shook the vodka bottle in her direction.

She tried not to react and went to the kitchen.

Her eyes were naturally drawn to the crack on the island where she and her mother had accidentally chipped the tile sword fighting with wooden spoons. And there was the place where they'd made pancake batter together with cinnamon and bananas. And there was the place where her dad had accidentally burnt her fifth birthday cake, and they'd all laughed.

Stop it, she told herself. *You know where this leads, and this is hard enough as it is.*

She filled one glass with water, the other with ice, and made her way back to the living room. Her dad hadn't moved. He took the glass from her hand and poured it high. Too high.

She sat down to sip her water and watched him discreetly. When had his face become so weathered? His cheeks so sunken? His clothes seemed too big for him, and he suddenly reminded her of a small child.

She cleared her throat. "Dad, have you reconsidered my offer?"

"To move to Virginia with you?" He took a swallow of vodka and wiped his chin before turning his attention to the wrapped sandwich he pulled from the bag. "No, thank you."

"Well, maybe you could plan to visit a few times?" she pressed hopefully. "Come see where I'm living? Who knows, maybe Virginia will start to grow on you."

"I am never leaving my shop, Brie, and I am never leaving this house."

She fell silent, ducking her head so he wouldn't see her lip quiver or the years of emotion clouding behind her eyes. Her only solace was that she wouldn't cry. She hadn't cried in years. She didn't even know if she could.

She recovered herself and retrieved her sandwich from the bag. They ate in silence, watching mindless TV and avoiding eye contact.

Just like old times.

After a while, she yawned and realized her foot had fallen asleep. The grandfather clock struck ten. She got up and paced downstairs a few times before circling restlessly back to sit on the arm of the couch. She cleared her throat softly. "I'm a little tired, and I was thinking I'd sleep in my old room if that's alright."

His eyes never left the screen. She tried again.

"I was going to try to get an early start. I don't want to wake you."

He gave her a curt nod. "Goodnight, Brie."

They sat inches from each other, yet worlds apart. "Goodnight, Dad."

She turned and walked to the stairs.

I love you.

With a feeling of profound fatigue, she trudged up the stairs, threw her sleeping bag onto her childhood bed, and fell into an exhausted, dreamless sleep.

She didn't see the little shimmer of golden light float to a corner of her room and settle in for another in an endless series of watchful nights.

She never saw it. It made sure of that.

"Mine eyes have seen the glory of the coming of the Lord…"

Brie woke the following morning to the dulcet tones of Johnny Cash singing "The Battle Hymn of the Republic." She blinked in confusion, then groaned.

I'm never letting Sherry borrow my phone again.

She splashed some water on her face and rolled up her sleeping bag, casting a final look around the room. It was frozen in time, just like the rest of the house. A child's room, filled with neon nail polish and old paperbacks she'd long outgrown. The room of a child who had started out with great purpose then lost her way.

She tiptoed downstairs as quietly as possible to find her dad asleep on the couch, right where she'd left him. She put down her things, eased the empty bottle out of his hand, and put it in the empty takeout bag along with all the trash she could fit. She disposed of it silently in the kitchen and brewed a pot of coffee. She put out an empty mug on a saucer for her dad, then filled a glass with water and placed it on the coffee table with two aspirins, where he'd see it as soon as he woke up. Another childhood routine. One she no longer questioned.

She picked up her bags and turned to leave, then hesitated and came back.

After another parting look, she gently kissed her father's forehead, whispering in the quiet room, "I love you, Dad."

A second later, she was walking out the door to her car and turning the key in the ignition, suddenly anxious to get to her new apartment and her new life as quickly as possible.

She told Siri the address and asked for directions, which it started disseminating straight away, as though she couldn't be trusted to get out of her own driveway. The street rolled away beneath her, but when she looked around for a final glance at her house, she was surprised to see her dad on the porch, staring at her with a fathomless expression.

She rolled down the window quickly, thinking something might be wrong. "Dad?"

He stood there for a moment, then held up his hand in a gesture she hadn't seen since she was a child. It was sign language — all fingers extended except the middle and ring, which were pointed down towards the palm. *I love you.* They used to make it all the time. Her throat tightened, and she held up her hand in reply, offering him a tentative, hopeful smile. He returned it tightly, as if his mouth had nearly forgotten how, then more naturally as he gave a little wave.

"Good luck," he mouthed.

She nodded, then accelerated away, driving off towards her new life.

♦   ♦   ♦

Alright. This is good. Don't worry about him. You'll call and check up on him. You need to DO this, Brie. You need to move forward and live your life. This is a good thing. Onwards and upwards. A new chapter, new possibilities, a brand new—

A light flashed on the dashboard, and her newfound momentum suddenly paused.

Out of coffee. Out of gas.

She bit her lip, slowed to a stop, then reluctantly veered off the main road and towards the nearest gas station, vowing to edit this bit in later memoirs of her life.

After this, things will be good. Right after this.

After two stops at Texaco and Starbucks, she was back on the road, latte in hand, feeling significantly more prepared to meet the challenges of the day. Hours passed as she listened to music and let every single car pass her while she stayed in the slow lane, as far away from large trucks as possible, opting to take frontage roads and backcountry routes whenever available. Call it a trauma response, but she had a thing about oncoming traffic and avoided large, fast-moving highways whenever she could.

She stopped in Charlotte to grab a quick bite and ate in the car.

"Siri? How much further to Yorktown?" she asked her phone.

"*It is four hundred forty-six point four miles to Yorktown, Virginia,*" Siri answered.

Brie nodded before clarifying, "And how long will that take?"

"*The remainder of your drive is five hours and seven minutes, Sexy Beast,*" came the reply. Brie paused mid-chew and silently reminded herself to figure out how to change the settings on her phone before any of her new colleagues heard that.

She threw out the chocolate cupcake that had come complimentary with her meal and got back on the road. After the accident, two of her childhood loves had disappeared for good: her love for speed and her chocolate frosting addiction. It had never tasted the same.

Before long, pines reached skyward, interspersing themselves among the ancient oak trees as the road began to wind in earnest. Towns became fewer and farther between. She drove past giant slabs of limestone jutting from the earth, lovely groves of apple trees overlooking little vineyards, and actual amber waves of grain. Before she knew it, she passed the *Welcome to Virginia* sign and let out a little whoop of excitement.

"See that?" she asked her plant. "We're nearly there. And *you* wanted to stop for tacos."

The plant received this with its signature stoicism. She patted it all the same.

"I know you have your doubts, but you'll see. I have a good feeling about this place. It's a prestigious hospital, you know. I'm sure Sherry had to bat her eyelashes at somebody over there to convince them to hire me, or I don't know if I'd ever have been accepted fresh out of school." She took another sip of her now-cold dregs of coffee and looked firmly at the road ahead of her before whispering to herself, "I think Mom would be proud."

When it happened, they were just off Highway 311, near Madison County.

The plant was stubbornly disintegrating, and she was playing with her necklace while vowing to broaden her social circle when the pendant suddenly glowed red-hot.

"Ouch!" she exclaimed, looking down to see what could possibly be on fire. She stared in shock for a split second before yelling,

"Ow — OUCH!"

The car itself was forgotten as she let out a screech, clawing frantically at her chest and trying to remove the metal sizzling against her skin. A simple chain, yet it seemed strangely reluctant to come off. She braced her knees against the steering wheel and attacked the thing with both hands, lifting it over the crown of her head.

The second she did, everything changed.

A burst of cold air hit the back of her neck, chilling the entire car. The windows crackled as ice slowly formed a thin film, obstructing her view. She looked around in confusion, her breath clouding suddenly in front of her.

That's when she saw it. Through the ice, there it was — the monster from her nightmares, in the middle of the road.

Oh, my God...

Acting on nothing but instinct, she dropped the chain back over her head and swerved to avoid the creature, only to let out a piercing scream as three more winged horrors swooped down on her, attacking the car on all sides.

One ripped the trunk door clean off and scrambled its way inside. As she whirled around to look, still screaming, the car drifted for a second before hitting the curb exactly wrong. Her forehead hit the steering wheel with a sickening *crack,* and she went limp.

Then, all at once, the image shifted.

The world turned upside-down as the car flipped twice and landed on the roof, leaving her floating in and out of consciousness, the necklace hanging precariously from her hair.

Memories splintered. The picture began to fade.

There was a flash of white, a hellish noise, and an impossible creature dissolving into thin air. Like nails on a tortured chalkboard, shrieks ripped through the once peaceful woods. More flashes of light, a muted hiss, then quiet. A sudden, breathless quiet.

The sound of footsteps.

It felt like hours but must have been minutes later when a pair of strong, gentle hands slid under her head and shoulders, lifting her from the car as though she were as light as a child's toy. The moment they touched her, nothing else mattered. The dizzying chill vanished, and the sun filtered warm through the trees. It felt like Christmas morning when she was five. She felt protected and loved, wanting for nothing. The hands settled her onto the street with infinite care.

Her eyelashes fluttered open, and she found herself gazing up into a pair of bright blue eyes. Eyes that looked exactly the same as they'd looked five years ago.

"Hello, Brianna. I told you we'd meet again."

Brie took a few shallow breaths, staring up at him in bewilderment, near-blinded by his beauty, stunned senseless by that perfect, impossible visage.

She punched him in the face.

Then she passed out cold.

CHAPTER THREE

The Savior in the Woods

The dreams always came in fragments, like shards of a mirror, reflecting her past in incomplete, cutting splinters of memory.

Her mother, smiling with tears in her eyes.

The way their hair had floated around them, weightless, as their car flew from the cliff.

A monster with its hand inside her mother's chest.

A blue-eyed angel staring in shock as her pendant glowed white.

But this time, the angel was speaking to her, calling out her name.

"Brianna… Brianna!"

She opened her eyes and found herself staring into those pools of ocean blue again. The eyes that couldn't exist. The eyes she'd conjured with her own imagination. This couldn't be happening. Several doctors and all her friends and family had been telling her for years this could not be happening.

She blinked, hard. When she opened her eyes again, he was still there, still holding her by the side of the road.

Still bleeding from his nose.

She said the only thing she could think of. "Where the hell have you been?"

Looking back on it later, it wasn't the most pressing·question. *Were you just throwing lightning bolts? What the hell attacked my car? Is there a radioactive half-life on spontaneously combusting jewelry?* Those all might have been more on the money. But in a strange way, she had been expecting this. A part of her felt like she'd been waiting for it all these years. No matter how many hours she'd sat in therapy, no matter how many false promises she'd made, or mantras she'd repeated at the ceiling, trying to fall asleep.

Cameron.

When he'd told her his name and asked for hers, she'd been cradling her mother's lifeless body in a forest much like this one. She'd held his name like a talisman for years before giving up and moving forward as though it was all a hallucination.

But she'd never truly believed it.

In her heart of hearts, she'd always known it was real.

"It's a long story. Which I will tell you," he added quickly, seeing the look on her face. "But for now, let's get you taken care of. How's the leg?"

She couldn't move it. She couldn't begin to move it.

"It's fine," she said through gritted teeth. "How's your face?"

He went perfectly still for a moment as if he'd never considered such a thing. A tiny line creased at the center of his forehead, then his lips curved up in the unlikeliest of smiles. "It hurts."

A small trickle of blood slowly traced down his chin. Blood that shimmered when blood shouldn't, emanating a soft, curious glow.

Problems for Brianna's NEXT therapist.

They stared at each other, neither one speaking a word, until there was a small explosion behind them, and they both turned to watch as fire slowly engulfed her car.

"I hope you've updated the insurance," he offered, trying to keep things light. "What are all those things in the back? Anything important?"

She lifted a trembling hand and tried to rub the clouds of soot from her cheeks, succeeding only in making herself look like a chimney sweep from the seventeenth century. "Just my life's possessions."

"Oh." He shot her a bracing look as if trying to remember a script from a past life. "Well, you know what they say about material possessions—"

"It's just stuff, right?" she interrupted bitingly. "It's all replaceable?"

His face went blank. "I was going to say you should treat them with care."

With a sound like a dying whale, the car roof collapsed in on itself, emitting another puff of smoke. She turned slowly from the rubble to look at him, narrowing her eyes.

Perhaps it's best if you don't say anything.

She tested her limbs. Three out of four. Fewer than she preferred, but she'd make it work. She struggled to sit up and made some decent headway before a sharp, stabbing pain made her gasp and sink back to the asphalt with a defeated whimper. There was no part of her that didn't hurt. She was scraped, cut, bruised, and likely broken in several places. She swore her hair hurt.

That's when she spotted what was left of her phone, lying on the ground in several pieces.

"The next town is twenty-two miles away," she said in misery, remembering the last road sign. A wave of hopelessness swept over her. "And these woods are full of raccoons."

He pursed his lips, following her gaze.

With spirals of acrid smoke curling around her, she honestly didn't know what the worst part of this situation was: that she had wrecked her car and lost all her possessions, that she would probably never make it to her new home in Virginia, or that she was stranded on the side of the road with a man or hallucination she had recently sworn to disavow for all eternity.

Probably the shadow monsters. Remember the shadow monsters?

…On second thought, DON'T think about the shadow monsters.

It might have seemed impossible, it might have seemed like the only thing in the world she should care about, but there was only so much a person could handle before they simply shut down. She consciously put the terrifying creatures out of her mind.

At any rate, they weren't new. She had seen them before.

"Twenty-two miles," she muttered again, shoulders dropping with a helpless sigh.

He hesitated a moment, tensing as if he'd heard the entire parade of despairing thoughts. Then without any warning, he scooped her up as one would a small child. "Then we'll have a lovely walk."

◆　◆　◆

For the next twenty-two miles, Brie's imaginary angel carried her effortlessly down the road, along with the only bag that had managed to escape the crash and the blast radius of the ensuing pyrotechnics. Mercifully, it was her backpack. Inside it, her wallet, a change of clothes, and a bottle of water had all escaped the ordeal unharmed. The water was apparently of premium importance. He'd insisted she take a few sips before he took off at a crisp pace down the road.

As he walked, she stole glances at him, trying to examine him without being noticed.

Well, he's certainly real.

She was pressed against his body, which was every bit as solid as her own. The warmth of him, the beat of his heart, the rhythmic breathing. He was steady. Everything about him was steady. He hadn't even blinked when her car exploded.

My car.

An alarming thought occurred to her. *Maybe I'm dead.*

Oh, she hoped not. Her poor father. He couldn't lose his wife *and* daughter like this, so many years apart. It was too cruel. She had to be alive, if only for his sake.

She decided to put it to the test. As discreetly as she could muster, she lifted a hand, preparing to strike herself across the face. Most people might try pinching, but she figured things had escalated several levels past that point. Her eyes closed as her palm flew towards her face, but an inch before contact, it abruptly stopped, hovering in the air, halted by some unseen force. She stared in alarm as a throat cleared softly above her.

"Brianna?"

She looked up slowly, only to see him staring back down at her with an indecipherable expression. It might have been exasperation, but the twinkle of amusement in his eyes gave it away. "This is real."

She nodded once, deciding to put the matter to rest.

"How did you get here?" she asked suddenly, squirming to see him better, head swimming with concussed questions. "We're pretty far from civilization. Did you drive?"

"Drive," he repeated, amused by the idea. "No, I didn't drive."

She looked around at the seemingly endless woodlands. "Where are we?"

"About fifteen miles inside the boundaries of Hanging Rock State Park."

"Hanging Rock," she repeated. "Oh, good. I was worried you'd say something ominous."

She was silent another moment before the questions poured out like a flood. "How do you know where we are? What's the nearest town? Why don't I feel worse? I'm pretty sure I'm supposed to be feeling worse. Am I in shock? Are you a hallucination? You have to tell me if you're a hallucination, you know. It's in the rules. Like asking if someone's a cop."

She paused. Then for good measure, though it seemed unlikely, she asked, "Are you a cop?"

He looked down with another amused expression that seemed both genuine and quite out of place, considering the circumstances. "Yes."

She blinked in shock. "Yes, you're a cop?"

"Yes, to all of it. All five hundred questions."

At that point, she began to suspect he was teasing her. She also decided to revisit the idea that she might be dead. With a look of grim resignation, she lifted her hand again, prepared to strike either one of them, only to have him catch it with that disarming mental power once more.

He chuckled. "I will answer all your questions, I promise. First, let's get you inside."

Not good enough.

He glanced at her face and relented a little. "The nearest town is called Eden." He looked back at the road and shifted her slightly in his arms. "And I always know where you are."

They lapsed once more into silence. An unending silence, interrupted only by the distant call of birds and the quiet crunch of gravel under his feet. Those questions ate away at her, pushing their way into prominence as far as her aching head would allow. She cast another secret look at him, gauging his resistance, preparing to relaunch the interrogation.

But there was a chance he sensed this, and there was even a chance his miraculous powers extended further than she thought. For no sooner had she opened her mouth, than a wave of fatigue came over her, slowing her breath and making her eyelids suddenly, irresistibly heavy.

Less than a minute later, she fell into a dreamless sleep.

By the time Brie opened her eyes, they were in the lobby of the tiniest motel east of the Mississippi. To her surprise, when her mysterious protector put her down, she was able to stand. In fact, aside from a deep tingling sensation, as though it had fallen asleep, her leg didn't hurt at all.

She tested her weight on it three, then four times.

How is this possible?

Her adrenaline had started to ebb away, and exhaustion loomed, but she registered the shock of the teenage girl manning the front desk. Upon catching a glimpse of herself in a mirror on the opposite lobby wall, she immediately understood the clerk's expression. It looked like she'd been through a war. Her cheeks were smeared with soot, her hair was a tangled mess, and every inch of her clothing was ripped and singed.

That said, she wasn't the person who'd caught the girl's eye.

At least I'm not the only one who thinks this is absurd.

The girl's eyes had swept straight past the crash victim to the man standing behind her — the one studying a brochure about local hiking trails with intense fascination. Under the harsh glow of the fluorescent lights, against a backdrop of knotty pine-paneled walls, he looked even more ridiculously out of place than he had on the side of the road. As though he was taking a brief respite from heaven to enjoy the local scenery and inhale the aromas of Pine-Sol and black mold.

Brie reclaimed her backpack.

"Bad day in the woods?" The girl's name tag identified her as Lucy.

"You could say that," Brie answered flatly, rummaging around in the bag. She produced an ID and slid it across the counter. "Just the cheapest room you have, please."

One with a shower.

The girl nodded and began typing, though her attention remained elsewhere. "Didn't seem to rough him up too much," she murmured under her breath.

Brie opened her mouth with a cutting reply, but her savior beat her to it, setting down the brochure and walking up beside her.

"Only my nose," he answered proudly, gesturing to the blood. "It may never be the same."

Brie looked at him, looked at the girl, then grabbed the key off the counter and stomped off towards the stairs, limping defiantly, though it was no longer necessary.

Maybe I am dead. Maybe this is punishment for killing my plant.

Five minutes later, she was in a shower, letting the hot water stream over her and wash away the dirt, blood, ash, and trauma from the past few hours. She raised her head and let out a long breath.

What the hell just happened to me?

She shut the thought down firmly.

Not now. For now, she was going to treat herself with a bit of kindness and care. And that meant focusing on nothing but the water — the sweet, wonderful, warm water.

Water that started to run cold.

She sighed, shut off the faucet, and toweled off. Thank goodness she'd had an extra set of clothes in her backpack, or who knows what outdoorsy, flannel monstrosity she'd have been forced to purchase from what passed as a gift shop in this place. She slipped on some white cotton shorts and another of those too-strappy yoga shirts Sherry kept impulse-buying for her.

Oh, God. Sherry.

She needed to call her. She needed to call her dad. She needed to call the police, or the fire department or some government agency to tell them about the heap of rubble that now constituted what remained of her first and only car. The thought caught her off guard, and the image of the trusty car turned into a burning mass of metal, brought a lump to her throat.

She gripped the sides of the sink and sucked in a deep breath.

Keep it together, Brie, she thought. *What would Dr. Rogers say? Acknowledge the feeling without endorsing it.* She considered this another second, then shook her head. *Therapists.*

She took another few deep breaths and raised her eyes to the mirror. She pinched her cheeks to put a bit of color back into her face and combed out her long, dark hair as best she could before sweeping it into a high ponytail with a hair tie she'd managed to find at the bottom of her backpack.

Much better.

Now, time to go into the next room and see if my angel has disappeared into thin air again, leaving me to wallow in therapy-supervised confusion for another five years.

She hesitated a moment with her hand on the doorknob, suddenly realizing she was terrified of precisely that. More than the accident, more than all those burning questions, it was the sudden isolation that she feared. To be left alone again. To doubt her own mind.

Whether he's there or not, I'm alive. I'm going to be okay.

She took a steadying breath, then opened the door slightly too fast to be normal.

He was sitting on the bed, surrounded by a bizarre array of foods.

"It's grilled cheese and tomato soup," he declared with a flourish, rising to his feet and crossing to the window. "Your favorite when you don't feel well."

Her face went blank. An ancient air conditioner buzzed beside the window.

"Or that's… that's probably not right." He faltered for a moment, then gestured to a bowl heaped with sour gummy worms. "I also got a few of the sugar insects you like. I didn't know how many might constitute a meal, so I got them all."

He glanced up again, beginning to panic. "There's also cheese?"

Perhaps it was because he'd phrased it as a question, but she crossed over to the bed, took the grilled cheese and tomato soup, and sank amongst the cushions. The gooey triangles had been pre-cut. She dipped one of them into the steaming bowl and took a bite, savoring the taste. "This is perfect. Thank you."

His eyes brightened with a flash of unrestrained delight before he hastened to control himself. It wasn't until she'd gotten halfway through the sandwich that he allowed himself to speak. "You should drink some water."

She lifted her eyes slowly, staring at him.

He blushed, if an angel could blush, but held her gaze. "I'm sorry, I don't mean to press. After a trauma, mortals are always telling one another to hydrate. I've heard it so many times, I just…"

He backtracked quickly at the look on her face. "Or perhaps you'd like to drink from a can? I got all the colors."

Only then did she notice the tower of carbonated beverages in the corner of the room. Unnerved, she put down the plate and crossed her arms and legs, studying him once again.

He looked like a man but was not. He moved like a man but did things no man could ever fathom. He'd carried her over twenty miles through the woods without a second thought, then turned into a five-year-old kid after discovering the vending machine.

"Cameron," she murmured without thinking, saying it almost to herself.

He glanced up immediately, eyeing her with a touch of surprise. "I wasn't sure if you remembered."

She let out a breath of hard laughter. "I remembered."

Despite my very best efforts to forget.

A surge of anger welled up inside her, but she deliberately held it back. Some questions needed answers, and some things needed to be explained. And even though she might very well end up dividing her life into the time before and after she had this conversation, she was damn well going to have it.

"No jokes, no lies, no deflections." She made each command softly, staring him right in the eyes. "My car is gone, my life is in shambles, and I'm sitting with a celestial stranger in some dilapidated motel room. We are past the point of you blowing me off. Do you understand?"

He stared back at her, then nodded slowly.

Here goes.

"What the hell are you doing here? How did you know where I was? How did you get to where I was? Where have you been all this time? Why didn't you ever try to contact me? Why aren't you acting like this is the least bit strange, and—" She huffed in breathless fury. "Are you *smiling* right now?"

He lowered his gaze immediately, keeping his distance from the bed. "I'm sorry," he said softly. "I've thought of you often. I always hoped our paths would cross again. That I'd be able to..." He trailed off, shaking his head. "That you'd be able to see me again."

That I'd be ABLE to see you?

"I've thought of you often, too," she said sharply. "Talked about you, even. In therapy. Because everyone thought I was crazy. Because *I* thought I was crazy. Because my drunk dad couldn't handle my lunatic ravings about an angel chasing off a horde of evil shadow monsters and promising me he'd come back someday." She took a breath, realizing how long she'd waited to yell at this man, if he was a man. "I thought you'd be back to explain what happened. I kept waiting for some kind of..." She fell into silence, hands balling at her sides. "You left a hell of a mess behind you, Cameron. You don't know how hard I've worked to get past this. To get over you."

He absorbed each accusation quietly, then raised his eyes to her again. "I do know," he said quietly. "I know how hard this has been for you. But I didn't cause those things to happen, Brianna. I do not cause tragedy, and I am not responsible for people's choices after tragedy strikes."

He paused again, then looked out the window at the darkening Virginia evening. "If I were, people would have made much better choices, and you would never have felt alone. You would never have been alone. Not for a single moment."

She stared back in stunned silence, at a complete loss for what to say.

In all the years she'd imagined this moment, in all the years she'd spent hypothetically preparing, it hadn't gone anything like this. There had been tears and apologies. There had been lengthy explanations and specific reasons for what had transpired. There had been shouts, curses, and arguing — fire and brimstone, perhaps quite literally.

It hadn't been anything like this. Soft truths, spoken by a saddened angel in a motel room that had gone so abruptly quiet, she could hear each one of their shallow breaths.

He looked at her again and let out a quiet sigh. "You should finish your soup," he murmured. "And have a sip of water. Your body has been through a lot today."

It was a gentle conclusion. At least, that's what he wanted it to be. But she'd waited a great many years for this moment. And somehow, he knew, it wasn't about to end now.

She narrowed her eyes at the eclectic feast in front of her. "Here's my proposal. I'll eat, and you'll answer my questions."

His lips curved in bemusement. "Are you bartering?"

She crossed her arms and raised an eyebrow. "Needs must. What do you say, Cam?"

There was a split second of silence. Then his mouth opened in surprise. "Did you just call me Cam?" he asked with curious delight. "Like a nickname?"

She pursed her lips, refusing to be dissuaded. "Don't try to change the subject."

They stared at one another appraisingly for a moment, each measuring the other's resistance, before she decided to take things up a notch. "I really hope you agree because I probably should eat something. And drink something." A look of pure melancholy swept across her face as she slumped theatrically on the bed, one hand fluttering to her forehead. "You're right about us mortals. Hydration is key."

His lips twitched like he was holding back a grin. Then he tossed her the candy. "Eat a sugar worm," he conceded. "I'll tell you whatever you want to know."

She grinned in triumph and bit off its head. "Why are you here?"

"Start with something easier."

It flew back at her so fast that the food lodged in her throat. She stared back with wide eyes, then swallowed and adjusted her course. "So, you're an angel, huh?"

He hesitated, then decided to allow it. "Not exactly. I come from a place that is neither Heaven nor Hell but somewhere between the two. But your human conception of an 'angel of mercy' is perhaps the best description of what I am and what I do."

Her chewing slowed. "What does that mean?"

"It means..." He gathered his breath. "Have you ever had a relative die?"

She looked at him, expressionless.

"I'm sorry," he amended quickly. "Have you ever had a relative die of natural causes?"

She remembered her grandmother. Her whole family had visited to say their goodbyes when she was nearing the end.

"Yes," she answered. "Grandma Mary. She had cancer."

"Were you there at the end?"

"I was too little. My mother was."

"What did your mother say about Grandma Mary's passing?"

"She said that it was peaceful," Brie remembered. "She said Grandma's pain was gone, and she kept seeing her sister Ann, even though she'd died years ago."

Cameron nodded. "That was one of us."

"What does *that* mean?"

He sighed again, trying to condense a massive amount of information into a digestible story. "I come from a place called Elysium. The beings there, such as myself, exist within a field of energy — the same energy that powers a human life. When humans die, we come to be with them and ease their suffering. We offer them... I suppose you would call it natural morphine. It takes away their pain and sometimes causes hallucinations. Positive hallucinations," he clarified swiftly. "Usually we're mistaken for a family member or loved one who has already passed on."

Brie sat frozen with her sandwich halfway to her mouth.

"When they die, we take their essence to Elysium. Their soul passes to Heaven or Hell, depending on the life they've led and the choices they've made. But their energy stays in Elysium and becomes part of our continuum. The barrier between Heaven and Hell."

She was still frozen. He gave her a wry look. "Any questions?"

"Oh, only about five million." She gave up on the sandwich and pushed the plate away, twisting a gummy worm around her finger as she searched for an innocuous way to start. "You don't... you don't *eat* the energy, do you?"

There was a beat of silence.

"Really?"

It was impossible to tell whether he was exasperated or deeply offended. Quite possibly, it was a little of both. But at the same time, he seemed on the very edge of laughter.

"I tell you that I'm an angel of mercy from a mystical realm between Heaven and Hell, sustained by the life force of everyone on this planet, and you want to know if I *eat* the energy?"

A deflection if ever I saw.

"No, Brianna." He was definitely laughing now, shaking in

silence, struggling to maintain a straight face. "I don't eat the energy any more than a plant eats sunlight."

"Okay, okay, just making sure." She laughed nervously, hesitant to continue. They were quickly leaving "innocuous" behind, but there were questions she needed answered. "So, you're an angel. Sort of an angel. Does that mean there are demons as well?"

He sucked in a tight breath, sensing the rather pointed change in direction. "Demons are what attacked you today. Where I come from, we call them wraiths. I'm not entirely sure why—" He caught himself, lowering his gaze to the pendant. He stared a moment, then lifted his eyes to meet hers, gesturing at the lovely golden teardrop. "Do you remember what I told you about this?"

A shiver swept across her shoulders. She certainly did remember. There wasn't a single detail of that horrible day that she could begin to forget. Her mother had placed the necklace around her neck, had pulled the glass from her chest, and had...

Brie shook her head, refusing to go deeper.

She looked back at Cameron. "You told me never to take it off," she said. She trailed a finger along the chain, trying to remember what had happened in the car. The pendant had glowed, just as it had glowed before the accident with her mother. And it was burning her. Burning her so badly, she needed to rip it off her skin.

But the moment she did—

"Where were you going?" Cameron asked, interrupting her train of thought. She lifted her head abruptly, realizing she'd been sitting there a long time.

"I'm supposed to be moving to Virginia. Yorktown."

"What's in Yorktown?" he asked, head tilted in curiosity.

"My new life." She looked hopelessly around the tiny hotel room. "I got this great job in the same hospital my best friend started working at last year. I'm supposed to be moving into my new place right now. I start in two days, and now I have no clothes, no car, no things of any kind, not even my plant — which, let's face it, has definitely died — and no way to get there. I don't even have a phone. Sherry will be worried sick about me, and I can't tell her I'm alright."

A lump rose in her throat, and she snapped a gummy worm in frustration.

He paused for a moment, then his face set into an expression of resolve. "Then, we'll just have to get you there."

"What?" she asked, sure she'd misheard him.

"This isn't supposed to be your life, Brianna. You're not supposed to be attacked by demons in the woods. You're not even supposed to be able to see me unless I want you to. The only reason you can is likely because of that pendant around your neck. If your life is taking you to Virginia, then that's where we're going to go."

She stared at him, both touched and disbelieving. "We?"

He stared a moment longer, like he'd been asking the same question himself. Then his lips lifted in a gentle curve. "Obviously. I can't very well leave you to fend for yourself until we know what's going on. Not if today was any indication."

She processed this, staring at him, before lifting a hand to touch her pendant. "And this necklace… Are you going to tell me more about that?"

A strange look clouded his eyes. "That isn't my story to tell."

For whatever reason, she believed him. At any rate, she'd had enough to take in for one night. A sudden hush swept over the little room, and she stifled a yawn, realizing she was exhausted.

Cameron noticed immediately. She had a feeling not much escaped his notice.

"You need to rest," he said gently.

She nodded, suddenly too tired even to talk.

Together, they moved the strange smorgasbord to a table on the other side of the room. She turned down the covers and climbed into bed, freezing in surprise when he climbed in beside her.

Uh, okay?

Neither was undressed. Neither was touching. And only one of them seemed to think it was remotely strange. He merely flashed a polite smile and settled beside her on the pillows.

Maybe everyone sleeps together where he comes from? Maybe it's like that scene in Willy Wonka, except everyone is beautiful and eternally young.

"Well, goodnight, Cameron."

He rolled on his side to face her, still touched by that lovely expression. "Goodnight, Brianna."

When it became clear he had no plans to sleep, she turned over in the bed and let the exhaustion of the day wash her consciousness away like the waves on a shore, drifting off to sleep under the watchful eyes of the impossible man who somehow lay beside her.

She had almost managed it — she had nearly floated completely away when another question rose suddenly to the surface. Her eyes opened slowly, wide and fixed. "Cameron?"

His soft voice drifted over her shoulder. "Yes?"

There was a pause.

"Is my mother okay?"

A much longer pause. "Your mother..." He trailed off into silence, his gaze drifting out the window to rest upon the distant trees. "All I can say about your mother is that things happened just as they were meant to."

CHAPTER FOUR

The Angel and the Officer

Brie woke up to a strange light.

At first, she thought it was the sun. There was the same warmth, the same instinctual draw. But it was too close, too powerful, and too *gold*.

She blinked several times in rapid succession, then turned over in the bed to see Cameron sitting on the side of the mattress — head bowed, hands folded, haloed in all that radiant light. Her mouth fell open slowly, and her breathing hitched. It was as if some lovely dream had carried with her into the waking hours. He glowed like a celestial statue in the grimy motel room.

It looked like he was meditating or maybe praying. Certainly, he was communing with a higher power, allowing her to study him in secret delight.

An angel. There is an actual angel in my bed.

She stared at him in silence, lamenting the recent death of her phone and her subsequent inability to immortalize the image in a picture. After only a few seconds of consideration, she realized this must be what Michelangelo was trying to create when he sculpted *David*. Every angle was perfection. Like one of those great artisans had dreamed him to life.

Time and again after her mother's death, she'd fantasized about this man coming to save her from the ruination of her life, but she'd never fantasized about him as a person. Not in that way. It was always an emotional rescue, a grand fixing of all her problems.

Never in all her dreams had they ended up in bed.

With the curiosity of a child, she lifted a tentative hand, tracing the tips of her fingers between his shoulders. He startled and whirled around, the bright glow fading from his eyes.

"What are you doing?"

She froze in panic, then decided to tell the truth. "Looking for wings," she answered shyly.

His lips parted in surprise, before curving up. "No wings. At least, not when I'm like this."

She couldn't tell if he was joking.

He hesitated, looking suddenly shy himself. "Disappointed?"

She warmed and shook her head. She was many things that morning, and most of them were so overwhelming they would need to be processed at a later date. But she was in no way disappointed.

"Come on," he continued, taking her hand. "I want to show you something."

She threw on the sweater from her backpack and grabbed the room key on her way out.

No need to check beneath the bed for errant clothes or possessions, she thought ruefully. She was basically wearing everything she owned. *I wonder if I should have looked into that before I left. Maybe they make traveler's insurance for this kind of—*

She froze the second they stepped outside, blinking in astonishment. Her car was sitting in the parking lot. Not a scratch. Nothing beyond the usual wear and tear that was there before. And on top of that…

"All my stuff," she gasped in amazement, looking at the boxes stacked neatly in the back seat. "How did you—?"

His finger pressed her lips as he glanced towards the motel's front office. "I didn't do anything," he answered casually with a twinkle in his eye. "Just had it towed over this morning."

She turned to face him, beaming with gratitude. "Well, isn't that convenient?"

"It is, indeed."

The unlikely pair shared a quick look, then walked back into the main office to check out. Lucy was there again, this time wearing a low-cut top and a shocking amount of makeup.

Subtle, thought Brie, internally rolling her eyes.

"Was everything to your liking last night? Do you need anything else? Anything at all?" Lucy asked, pressing her arms to either side of her chest as she leaned across the counter.

Utterly oblivious, Cameron rested his hand next to the pile of brochures, then looked up with a wondering expression. "The tree used to make this desk was three hundred fifty-six years old and had over ten thousand children before it was felled by loggers in upper Appalachia."

Lucy straightened up slowly. "What?"

"Everything was fine, thank you." Brie left the key on the counter and grabbed Cameron's sleeve, pulling him almost out the door before reconsidering and turning back. "Actually, do you know a good place to eat breakfast around here?"

The girl blinked, recovering herself. "There's a waffle place down the road."

"Got it. Thanks!"

Brie towed the angel swiftly towards the parking lot, not seeing how the girl stared after them or how she melted into a puddle of hormones on the counter and sighed, lost in the throes of infatuation.

"Do you always do that?" she asked, unlocking the car.

Cameron circled quickly to the driver's side and opened the door for her, staring back with a completely innocent expression as she climbed inside. "Always do what?"

"Never mind."

Ten minutes later, Brie was stealing peeks over the top of an oversized diner menu. If her life hadn't recently been turned so utterly sideways, the scene would have been hilarious. Her guardian angel was attempting to be equally discreet, taking in every corner of the diner, studying every server and patron while holding his menu like a stage prop. He hadn't yet realized it was upside-down.

Maybe he only reads ancient Aramaic.

A waitress came by with the usual, "What can I getcha?" only to stop short at the sight of the angel sitting in the booth. He flashed a smile, and Brie watched the poor woman melt, utterly enchanted.

"Well, aren't you just a tall drink of water," she said, putting a fist to her hip in genuine appreciation.

Cameron went blank, trying to interpret, then answered as best he could. "I'd love one."

Brie snorted into her menu, trying not to laugh.

The waitress, whose name tag identified her as Pam, lifted her eyebrows slowly, then gave Brie an unsolicited pat on the shoulder. "With looks like that, he doesn't need to be a genius, honey."

Brie grinned back widely, handing her the menu. "French toast, please, and the biggest, most irresponsibly sweet coffee you have."

"Coming right up. And for you, mister?"

"Just the tall drink of water, please," he said with another blinding grin.

The waitress pursed her lips, flipped his menu right side up as she collected it, and walked away after giving him a quick pat on the hand. "Anything you want, honey."

Brie waited until she was gone, then folded her hands on the table. "You are utterly ridiculous."

He stopped playing with his napkin, lifting his eyes in surprise. "What do you mean?"

"Okay, aside from the fact that you were delighted by the traffic lights on the drive over and you used all my remaining quarters playing the claw game on the way in here so you could, and I quote, 'rescue the little bear' — *this*." She gestured to his body, tracing a finger up and down. "*This* is utterly ridiculous. Don't you see it? You don't see how out of place this is?"

He frowned. "You mean—"

"I mean your *face*, Cameron. I mean, your perfect, clueless *face*."

There was a slight pause. "I am as I was made. I see nothing ridiculous about it."

Of course you don't.

The waitress returned with his ironic beverage and a fragrant assortment of sugar, carbs, and caffeine for Brie. She gave Cameron an exaggerated wink before walking off again as Brie inhaled deeply, reveling in the lovely scent of cinnamon and maple.

Near-death experiences and supernatural plot twists really make you work up an appetite.

As the delicious chemicals began to work their magic, she considered her companion.

He felt no need to fill silences — that much was clear. He spent an excessive amount of time taking his straw out of its plastic sheath before dropping it into his drink and stirring curiously at the ice cubes, but he never took so much as a sip. He also seemed to be constantly checking the exits, though whenever he caught her looking, he smiled as though nothing was wrong.

He's guarding me, she realized. *He's afraid it will happen again.*

The idea resonated with a sudden pang.

Maybe I should be, too.

The thought stilled her hand halfway to her mouth, and for a split second, she found herself unable to breathe. The memory of the giant shadowy monster ripping its way into her car flashed back with a rush of adrenaline, and the accompanying wave of nerves made her physically sick.

Cameron set down his glass and reached his hand across the table, pressing two fingers against her pulse and staring with sudden concern. "Are you alright?"

No. Absolutely not. I am absolutely NOT alright.

"I'm fine," she replied quietly, staring at her plate. She didn't want to ask. She *really* didn't want to ask. She asked anyway. "Are those things that attacked my car going to come back? It happened so quickly before. I couldn't even..." She looked up at him. "Are they going to find me?"

He sat back in the booth with his jaw set in grim determination. "If they do, I won't let them get anywhere near you."

She pushed her plate forward, having lost her appetite. "But how were they able to find me at all?"

He hesitated, clearly reluctant to say.

She looked at him levelly. "I deserve to know."

He took a deep breath, then nodded. "You're right." His eyes flashed briefly around the diner, assessing the other patrons again before he leaned closer and spoke in a softer tone. "Do you remember what I said about where I come from? How it's sustained by life force energy?"

She nodded quickly, latching onto every piece of information that she could. "Which you definitely do not eat."

He flashed a glance heavenward before saying rather painfully, "Yes, which I definitely do not eat."

He hesitated again, choosing his words with great care. "My people, and the beings from the realms above and below, can see this energy. Like ultraviolet light, it's invisible to you, but it's as clear as day to us. Most people, Brianna, have a life force energy that might seem as bright as a desk lamp." He looked straight into her eyes. "Your light is more akin to a star."

She froze.

"But when you wear that pendant, Brianna, I cannot see it at all."

Her hand drifted up to her necklace, like someone remembering a dream.

"It was burning me," she murmured, pushing through the trauma and putting things together for the first time. "I was taking it off. That's why…"

He nodded slowly, regarding her intently. "It was like cracking the lid off a pot, only to find a supernova inside. It outshone the sun for my kind. And for other kinds as well."

She leaned back, breathing hard. "But that means if it burns me again, if it ever so much as slips off, anyone can find me. *Anything* can find me. Except… you found me in the woods. Even after I caught it, even after I put it back on. So even with the necklace, they'll be able to track me—"

"They won't be able to track you," he interrupted swiftly. "Trust me."

"But... but how could that be?" she insisted, heart racing in panic. "Cameron, I'm telling you, that chain was back around my neck when you got there. If you could find me—"

"I found you because I was already there." He cut her off, his voice hot with an emotion she couldn't identify.

The two stared at each other in silence — a silence neither one knew how to break.

"Excuse me, sir?" Pam walked up beside them, plopping the bedraggled teddy bear from the claw machine on the table between them. "I think you forgot this."

◆   ◆   ◆

Brie paid the bill while Cameron went to the door to check the parking lot.

For supernatural beings trying to kill me.

Next time I ask the universe for a fresh start, I should remember to be more specific.

A few minutes later, they were back on the road. The teddy bear sat on the dash between them — a reluctant prize neither would acknowledge. She wanted to press him for more answers, but she'd never seen that expression on his face, and she'd certainly never heard him snap.

It was somehow more frightening than the thought of him throwing lightning bolts. Every time she opened her mouth to ask another question, her eyes drifted to the bear.

If he believed it would be fine, she would trust him.

If there was ever a time for a leap of faith...

She sighed and gave her magically-repaired phone a nervous glance. She wanted to call Sherry to assure her that she was okay, but she hadn't the faintest idea what to say. How was she going to explain her delay? How was she going to explain the celestial Ralph Lauren model rolling her window up and down in the passenger seat with a look of complete enchantment?

Sherry had seen her through the bulk of her therapy in the months following her mother's death. She'd held her friend together with both hands, wiped all her tears, and listened to all her breathless raving. She'd never uttered a word of complaint. She'd never asked for anything in return.

But Sherry would not understand this.

As if the premise itself wasn't enough to dizzy the mind, the woman absolutely hated anything "spooky" or supernatural. She avoided it like the plague. She wouldn't even read her horoscope.

Might have something to do with the fact that her best friend spent a solid six months insisting her mother had been killed by shadow monsters in the woods.

Brie couldn't think of a single thing she wanted more than to tell Sherry about these new and bizarre developments in her life. She also couldn't think of anything that would devastate her more. She had to keep this to herself. It was the least she could do to protect her friend, who had spent so much time, love, and energy protecting her. That made her solution rather simple.

She needed to lie. Convincingly.

Super. Absolutely my strong suit.

She dialed and took a deep breath.

A moment later, Sherry picked up with a screech. "Where the hell have you been? I was *this close* to calling the National Guard!"

Cameron looked over, trying not to laugh.

"I'm so sorry, Sher. It was unavoidable. I'm on my way now."

"Did you have car trouble or something? Or…" Sherry let out something between a gasp and a shriek of condemnation. "Did you see another fox? I keep telling you, they're wild animals, Brie.

They don't want to be adopted, and you can't chase feral creatures through the forest. No matter how fluffy their tails are."

Cameron glanced over again, but this time, she determinedly avoided his gaze.

"It wasn't a fox," she muttered, sliding a few inches lower in her seat. "I promise to tell you all about it when I get into town in just another few hours. Can you call my dad and let him know I'm okay?"

"Fine, but… *are* you okay? You sound weird."

"I'm fine, don't worry."

Not a lie. I am fine.

Her eyes flashed to the angel in the front seat.

Totally fine.

She could practically hear Sherry roll her eyes. "Text me the moment you get to your new place. Also, drinks tomorrow night after your first day. That is not a request. I'll send you the address. I can't wait for you to meet Mike! You're gonna love him."

"I can't wait to meet him, too. I love you. See you soon."

"Drive safely, you fiend. Love you, bye!"

Brie hung up with a sigh of relief.

Then she turned with the greatest hesitation to the angel sitting beside her. *Verdict?*

He pursed his lips, trying to control his expression. "Foxes, eh?" A flash of mischief danced in his eyes, almost completely obscured by centuries of composure. "They *are* wild animals, Brianna, and not to be trusted. I happen to know this for a fact."

Her knuckles whitened on the steering wheel. "Okay, for one thing, there was a perfectly reasonable explanation for the—"

"I like your friend."

She caught herself suddenly and let out a sigh of relief. "Sherry? Yeah, she's the best."

He nodded thoughtfully, his eyes on the road. "She cares for you deeply," he murmured. "She thinks of you before herself."

Brie nodded along absentmindedly, then looked over in sudden shock. "You know what she's thinking?"

Do you know what I'm thinking?

He shook his head vaguely. "I know what she's done."

A profound silence followed this remark.

"How do you know what she's done?"

His face flushed, and he became suddenly absorbed in the locking mechanism on her glove compartment. "I have a great many powers I find difficult to explain in only three dimensions."

If I had a dime.

She drew in a deep breath and looked back at the road. "We'll have to work on dialing down those little truth bombs. It's bad for my blood pressure."

He shot her a look of alarm, then placed two fingers on the inside of her wrist, feeling for her pulse. "Do you have any basil root?"

Her eyebrows shot into her hair. "Excuse me? Basil—"

"Basil root. To help with your blood pressure."

There was a moment of silence.

"I honestly can't tell if you're joking."

He turned back to the road, looking slightly unsettled. "Neither can I."

For the next few minutes, the two drove in perfect silence, trying to ignore each other and trying to ignore the watchful gaze of the teddy bear on the dash between them. When that silence became too much, too charged with things unsaid, she turned to the radio, fiddling with the dials, finding and rejecting several stations at lightning speed.

After watching for a minute or so, he had to ask. "What are you looking for?"

"Anything classical. Anything soothing."

He cocked his head, then gave the dial a slight touch. Two clear, bell-like soprano voices rang out in perfect harmony, trilling a moment before soaring to even greater heights.

Her heart quickened, and she looked at the radio in surprise. "'The Flower Duet!' How did you…?"

He simply looked out the window. "It's your favorite when things are complicated."

Just like tomato soup is my favorite when I don't feel well.

Her eyes fixed upon him as those words from the diner echoed in her mind. *"I found you because I was already there!"*

Those questions started spinning again, and for a split second, she almost lost that tenuous grip. Who else in the world was having a conversation with their guardian angel? How was it *possible* that a person like him could even exist? Could she even call him a person? Was that right? And why, in the name of Heaven and Hell, was *she* being forced to ask all of these questions?

She stared a moment longer, then turned to focus on the road. "Complicated, huh?"

Better play it on a loop.

Two hours later, the situation had gone downhill.

The sweet balm of the music wore off around the same time Cameron decided it was a good time to start asking *her* questions or "dissecting the mortal nonsense," as he'd called it with delight. She'd tried humoring him. She'd tried leaping from the car. Nothing had worked.

She'd also begun to suspect that his kind didn't need to breathe.

"Why do you say, 'If the shoe fits' when footwear is not the issue?"

"Why do you assign value to shiny rocks?"

"What is meant by the term, 'broseph?'"

"Do you never consider how the hot dog feels?"

"Why are you driving so fast?"

Brie gripped the steering wheel and gritted her teeth, vaguely aware she was doing about sixty in a forty-five zone. Her pulse quickened, and she had just opened her mouth with a rather cutting answer to that last question when she heard the siren and saw flashing lights behind her.

You've GOT to be kidding me.

She let out a curse that made his eyes widen and pulled over to the side of the road.

"Don't say anything, okay?" she hissed. "Let me do all the talking. And don't fiddle around with the window. And don't get out of the car. And don't talk about your bear. Just sit there quietly and let me handle this. It's going to be fine. Everything is going to be fine."

I've got to stop using that word.

"You needn't be afraid," he inserted gently, trying to calm her. "The police will merely hold you accountable for your actions. In the end, it's actually a kindness—"

"I will gut you like a fish."

He decided to sit there quietly after all.

She was fumbling for her license, trying to remember any of the breathing techniques Dr. Rogers had taught her when the cop rapped twice on her window.

She rolled it down with her most winning smile.

"License and registration."

She handed them over and put her hands back on the wheel, bouncing her knees up and down with the manic energy of a Warner Brothers cartoon.

Don't panic, don't panic, this is fine.

Just stay quiet and calm.

And no matter what happens, don't—

"I'm so sorry, officer," she blurted. "I know I was going too fast. I'm just anxious, and in a new town, and frankly, you wouldn't believe the day I've been having. I've been trying not to look at this judgmental bear for miles, and I'm still a little sugared up from the gummy worms. Or maybe I'm just jittery from the car accident? I don't know, but I *swear* I'm not a criminal. I've never even had a parking ticket before. This is completely out of character for me, and if you could just take a second to—"

"You were in a car accident?" the cop asked sharply.

Her mind went blank. "Yes... it was... a long time ago."

Excellent. Great job. Top-notch display of sanity and self-restraint.

He gave her a strange look. Such a strange look that she dug herself in a little deeper. "I've never even been sent to the principal's office."

His eyes strayed a little farther to the angel beside her.

"Neither have I," Cameron volunteered helpfully. "But I've been instructed not to speak."

As Brie rotated towards him with a chilling glare, Officer Mitchell, as his nameplate identified him, leaned in to take a better look. "You've been instructed not to speak?"

Cameron opened his mouth to answer, then paused as if the man might be testing him. He hesitated another moment, then nodded slowly instead, shooting Brie a conspiratorial wink.

She made a silent vow to kill him.

"Gummy worms and bears, huh?" The officer's impassive sunglasses gave nothing away. "Have you two been drinking?"

Fair question.

"Not at all," she replied frantically. "Everything's just a little... I'm moving to Virginia. For work. For my best friend. *With* my best friend. It's a fresh start for me and the plant."

The officer glanced at the withered tree in the back. "And who's your silent friend?"

Cameron was staring with muted defiance, as if wild horses couldn't pry open his lips.

"He's, uh... he's like one of those emotional support creatures?" She couldn't help but phrase it as a question, staring at the officer with wide, imploring eyes. "But neither of us were——"

That's when she accidentally nudged the horn.

Cameron stared in fascination. The cop flinched.

There was a lengthy pause.

"Ma'am, please step out of the vehicle."

Cameron shot her a sideways glance. "I really do think you should keep a supply of basil root in your car. Better safe than sorry."

She shot him a look that could wither flowers before turning back to the cop. "Officer, I'm so sorry. If we could just——"

"Step out of the vehicle."

Her eyes snapped shut as a familiar lump rose in her throat.

How can this be happening? How can things have gotten so far off course? This is supposed to be my new chapter. I'm supposed to be unpacking and having drinks with my best friend. Now, here I am, about to get arrested.

She pulled in a tight breath, already looping the tired mantra.

It's fine. Everything is going to be——

"You don't want her to step out of the vehicle," said a deep, resonant voice beside her.

Officer Mitchell took off his sunglasses. "Excuse me?"

Yeah, excuse me?

Brie whirled around in shock as Cameron calmly leaned past her, speaking with a strange, sonorous affectation, staring deep into the officer's eyes.

"You don't want her to step out of the vehicle," he repeated softly. "You want her to continue on her way. She promises not to drive so fast anymore."

Officer Mitchell's face was a study of conflicted emotions. His forehead furrowed deeply, and he opened his mouth as if to say something before his face suddenly relaxed.

"She promises not to drive so fast anymore," he repeated with a vacant expression.

Cameron shot Brie a stern glance. "She absolutely promises."

She looked back and forth between them like she was at the world's most confusing tennis match, but she caught on. "Yes, I absolutely promise."

The officer nodded vaguely, playing with his sunglasses. "Nice and safe."

Cameron nodded as well, never breaking that gaze. "You want to give her back those papers."

They passed through the open window.

"You're going to have a wonderful day, officer. Surprise yourself. Do something fun."

Officer Mitchell smiled broadly. "I think I'll take my girlfriend to that fancy restaurant."

Cameron inclined his head. "She'll love that. Now, take your hands off the car."

They disappeared, and the conversation came to an abrupt pause. After a few seconds of waiting, Brie chimed in with a hesitant, "Can I go?"

"Of course." The man lifted his hand in an amicable wave.

"Take care now." He was still waving when they eased back onto the road, driving comically under the speed limit.

It was a few minutes before Brie was able to catch her breath.

It was a few miles after that before she managed to speak.

"What the ever-loving hell was that?"

Cameron glanced out the window, having already forgotten the exchange. "Those are longleaf pine."

She sucked in a breath. "I meant with the *cop*, Cameron."

He shot her a quick glance, his eyes twinkling with delight. "I believe that's what they call, *getting off on the right foot*."

She stared a moment, then turned back to the road.

"Brianna, do you get it? It's one of your little idioms."

"That's not what that…" She raised her eyes heavenward for a moment before refocusing on the road. "You know what, Cam? You're right. I'm going to start keeping basil root in the car."

CHAPTER FIVE

Playing House

Thirty minutes later, Brie's phone beeped to indicate they'd arrived at their destination, and they rolled to a stop in front of her new house. It was a modest little one-bedroom, one-bath cottage just off Lakeside Drive... and it was postcard-picture perfect. Tangles of wisteria dripping with fragrant purple blossoms wound their way around the entrance. The weathered white brick arches implied reliable craftsmanship and a well-aged charm. There was a swinging bench on the porch.

It's lovely.

When Sherry had used words like "quaint" and "vintage" to describe the place, Brie had worried it was a cover-up. She was ecstatic to discover that she completely agreed.

Cameron leaped from the car and circled around to open her door. He even offered his hand as she stepped out, which she regarded with suspicion before deciding to ignore him. She grabbed her backpack and wandered to the front door by herself.

It swung open with a loud creak, and she let out a happy sigh. It was everything she could have imagined. Old, without being ancient. Comfortable and unpretentious, and best of all, the entire place was filled with light.

And yet, it's cozy. It's the perfect place to start fresh.

She stepped over the threshold, breathing in the fragrant air.

No baggage. No complications—

"Where would you like these?"

She turned around, then yelped as she saw Cameron carrying an impossibly high stack of moving boxes, heavy enough that even the proudest of men would have used a dolly.

He peeked around the edge. "Are you alright?"

"Are *you* alright?" she countered quickly, rushing forward to help. "You don't have to carry all those, much less at the same time. You're going to break your—"

"Brianna," he interrupted gently. "Where would you like these?"

She stared a second, then gestured vaguely behind her. He walked into the living room and set the boxes down as she watched him in secret, pulling out her phone and dialing.

There was a single ring, followed by a squeal of delight. *"Are you here? Do you love it? I told you, you'd love it. Why are you so late?"*

Brie grinned in spite of herself, aching to see her best friend. "I'm here. I love it. You have the very best taste in all things," she replied, watching as Cameron circled the room. "And I'm late because some cop almost gave me a speeding ticket."

So, I helped brainwash him with my new angel friend.

A baffled silence rang out in reply.

"*You* almost got a speeding ticket?" Sherry exclaimed. "You've never even been to the principal's office. Also, what a jerk. It's a small town. We'll find out who it is and egg his house."

Brie grinned and bit her lip. "Because we're seven?"

"That's right." Sherry's tone shifted. "But seriously, Brie. What are you doing speeding, showing up late, not checking in? What's been going on with you?"

Brie looked across the room at Cameron, who pulled a toaster from a box with a look of childlike perplexity. "Can I tell you at drinks tomorrow? Right after work, right?"

"Nope, that's been changed to a fancy dinner at this restaurant I've wanted to try. And you're not getting off that easy. Coffee. Tomorrow. *Before* work. Something's up. I can feel it."

That bodes well.

Brie fiddled nervously with the phone but couldn't restrain a grin. "It's a date. Alright, I need to go unpack my entire life."

"Do you want me to come over?"

"*No!*" Brie exclaimed, before backtracking quickly. "I mean, I've got this. I'm sure you're still busy anyway, transforming your own place into the envy of the entire neighborhood."

"Careful, flattery will get you everywhere with me."

"I know this well."

"Alright, see you tomorrow. Love you, bye!"

"Bye."

Brie hung up, turned around, and froze. Cameron had put the toaster in pride of place in the middle of the kitchen island and seemed to be building it a shrine out of coffee mugs.

"You really don't know how any of this works, do you?" she asked.

He glanced up with a guilty flush. "Is this not how it's supposed to look?"

She pursed her lips, trying her best not to laugh. It didn't help that his hair was littered with purple petals. It also didn't help that the teddy bear from the diner claw machine was peeking out of his coat pocket.

"It's alright. I'm sure you have other skills."

The unlikely pair unpacked boxes for the next hour or so and explored the house. There was a leak under the kitchen sink, and Brie was fairly certain she heard a squirrel in the attic, but overall, the charm won out over the damage. The place had even come semi-furnished, so she didn't need to worry about buying a bed, couch, or shelves. Instead, she could focus on other things — like the man kneeling beside her with a book in each hand.

"So, why are you just starting this job now?" he asked curiously, placing the books on a nearby shelf. "I thought that you and Sherry were in the same class. Have I gotten that wrong?"

She threw him a quick glance. "I'm surprised you thought anything at all. How do you know we were in the same class?"

His eyes flashed up before returning quickly to the boxes. "You must have mentioned it."

Must have.

"I kind of took the long way around to finish nursing school so that I could stay close to my dad," Brie explained, slowly filling her bookshelves with the contents of her boxes. "Sherry finished a year before me and landed a position in this great hospital up here. I think she pulled a few strings to get me in. They let you finish your clinical rotations and everything, then keep you on afterward. It's very competitive. I was so happy when I got in, but I just…" She trailed off, absently flipping through a novel.

"You're worried about your father," he finished gently.

She set the novel down with a bit too much force. "I'm always worried about him."

He was quiet for a moment, passing her medical textbooks and the odd volume of poetry or music theory before he cleared his throat and spoke up again. "Sometimes, the most inspiring thing a person can see is someone they love taking charge of their life." The two locked eyes. "Following your dream isn't selfish, Brianna, especially when your dream is to help others on their darkest days. By lifting yourself up, you lift all whom you love."

She stared in silence, unable to formulate a response, as he pushed to his feet and started stacking the shelf with her, alphabetizing as he went, correcting each book she placed out of order.

"Do you play the piano?" he asked suddenly.

"Excuse me?"

He held up a biography of Robert and Clara Schumann. "Rather niche reading for someone who doesn't play."

"I used to. My mom brought me to this great teacher when I was little, twice a week for years. I was actually getting pretty good." She caught herself swiftly. "I haven't played much lately."

She took the book from his hands and placed it on the shelf. He threw her a quick glance, then took it out again and slipped it into the correct order.

"I would love to hear you play," he said softly.

Her eyes flashed up, resting a moment on his face. Then her heart started thrumming, and she whipped out her phone again to fill the awkward silence. "Well, in the meantime, Siri, play some Schumann."

He looked at her, puzzled.

"Playing, 'Träumerei, Opus Fifteen Number Seven,' by Robert Schumann."

In a literal flash of light, the angel became rigid as a statue, eyes flickering to the windows and doors as if they might be under attack.

"Is there someone else in the house?" he asked accusingly as if she'd been hiding them all along. "Answer me softly, Brianna. We don't know where they might have gone."

She stared at the back of his head, baffled. "What?"

The lovely notes of the piano filled the air between them.

"Siri, could you turn that down?"

"Certainly, Sexy Beast."

He jumped and whirled around with an almost cartoonishly threatening expression. His hair spiraled messily around him, littering the ground with petals, as his eyes lifted slowly to the ceiling.

There was a moment of silence, followed by some ancient oath. He whispered, "Keep still," before directing a warning towards the ceiling at his unseen foe. "You cannot hide forever."

She blinked, then looked at the device in her hand. "Wait, do you mean—"

"Who was that?" he demanded. "What's happening?"

"It's my smartphone… It follows basic commands."

She waved it innocently between them as he stared warily back.

"You have enslaved it?" he asked stiffly. "It does your bidding?"

She let out a burst of laughter and lifted her hands. "Hang on there, Methuselah. I didn't enslave anything. It's a phone."

His eyes narrowed with suspicion. "I think you should keep it outside."

There was a beat.

"Outside," she repeated flatly. "You want me to keep my phone—"

"It seems overly fond of you. I would feel more comfortable if it wasn't in the house."

There was another pause. Much longer this time.

Then she turned on her heel and headed up the stairs. "I'm going to take a shower."

"I'm serious, Brianna—"

"You want to be useful? Resuscitate my plant."

♦   ♦   ♦

Five minutes later, Brie was still waiting for the hot water.

Perfect house. There had to be something.

The pipes were humming, but no matter how she flipped the dials, the water remained ice cold. After a few more seconds spent shivering impatiently on the tile, she gave up with a sigh and redressed before slumping back into the living room. Cameron was standing not far from where she'd left him, running his fingers over her endless stacks of books.

"Done already?" he asked.

"No hot water." She threw him a teasing grin. "I don't suppose your celestial powers could help with that?"

Only half-joking.

He shook his head. "These powers aren't even mine. I am merely a vessel. They are to be used only to do God's will."

She tilted her head. "So, God willed you to fix my car?"

His eyes flashed up uncertainly before clearing with a cool expression. "God was feeling a bit generous today."

Fair enough.

The two worked in silence for a while, shifting things around and casting each other secret looks, as the sun dipped lower and lower in the sky. It wasn't until the windows began to darken that she looked at him with a sudden start.

"Cameron," she paused. "Are you planning to stay here?"

He glanced up with a hint of surprise. "Of course I am. Why?"

She looked around the little cottage, trying to find the words. In all honesty, she didn't know what was more surreal: the fact that she was playing house or the fact that she was doing it with a divine protector.

True to form, she decided to deflect. "You know, in some cultures, it's considered highly inappropriate to move in with a woman, uninvited, without telling her your full name."

He tilted his head, considering this for a moment. "My real name is unpronounceable by the human tongue."

"So, you picked Cameron?"

"A dear friend of mine was named Cameron. So, yes. I picked it because I liked it."

"Oh," she exclaimed with a touch of surprise, warming in spite of herself. "I didn't imagine you *had* human friends. So, what happened with the original Cameron? Was he willing to share?"

"He was martyred in the third century under Emperor Diocletian."

She stared as he pulled a blender from a box. *Right. I have friends like that, too.*

That was the last of the talking.

They continued unloading the car for the next few minutes and quietly placed items around the house. Bags were relocated to the upstairs hallway. The desiccated Ficus was given a thoroughly unnecessary drink of water, then left to molder by the fridge.

While they worked, they watched each other. Rather, she watched him.

A friend martyred in the third century... he doesn't know how to use a toaster. The power to annihilate demons... which he uses on the radio, when he's not ferrying the souls of the dead.

She studied him a moment longer, then was left with a surprising conclusion. *I wonder if he's lonely.*

"Is it very different?" she asked tentatively. "The place where you come from?"

His hands paused above a throw pillow, but he kept all emotion safely from his face. "It's a heavenly gateway powered by the life force of human souls. It's a little different."

She nodded but took a step closer. "I didn't mean it like that. It's just… are there others there? People like you?"

Considering they'd driven across state lines, it was probably strange she hadn't asked him sooner. But in the short time since their paths had collided again, her life had been strung together in a series of traumas and miracles. Some of the little things had slipped through the cracks.

"People like me?" he repeated, stalling for time.

She stared at him curiously, picking up one end of a large rug.

"Yeah, you know. Angels of mercy. Or whatever you call yourselves. There have to be others, right? The world's a big place. You've been away for some time but haven't mentioned anyone, so I was just wondering… is there anyone else like you?"

For a fraction of a second, his face stilled. So far, she had the impression that he'd been completely honest with her, even when disclosing difficult truths. But now, he seemed to be teetering dangerously close to the edge of a lie.

He ended up somewhere in the middle. "There used to be."

He flashed her a tight, wistful look, then picked up the other side of the rug. They gave it a hard shake together and let out a series of choking gasps as an explosion of dust escaped.

"Oh, sorry!" She batted uselessly at the air between them, then pointed to a stack of appliances in the corner. "Would you mind vacuuming that before we move the coffee table over? I'm going to grab some more stuff from the car."

His eyes drifted to the same corner, hoping the items were clearly labeled. "Of course."

She slipped out the door a second later, leaning against it with a silent breath.

Sometimes, she didn't know what threw her more: the flashes of superhuman powers or the tiny cracks that lay unattended beneath. Her mighty angel, slayer of demons and speeding tickets alike, seemed more real to her in these quiet moments between supernatural feats. When he thought no one was looking. When his eyes would sadden and drift to the sky.

After taking another moment for balance, she rummaged around in the car for good measure, then headed back inside, only to be met with a most peculiar sight.

It was a standoff. That much was clear. The angel versus the vacuum cleaner.

"Infernal creature," he muttered under his breath, holding the power cord like he was considering fashioning it into a noose. "You will not defeat me."

She snapped a photo with her phone and struck a casual pose. "Cameron?"

He jumped where he stood, whirling around to face her. The man had been alive for centuries, but suddenly looked like a little boy.

"Yes?" he asked just as casually. Either by intention or subconscious prompting, he angled his leg to block her view of the machine.

"How's it coming in here?"

"Good, great, very well," he said quickly. "We're nearly there."

She nodded and headed into the kitchen, then doubled back immediately to spy around the corner. He knelt once more in front of the machine, Heaven's fire blazing in his eyes. For a split second, it looked as though he might smite the thing down. Although she needed a vacuum, she hoped with all her heart that he would do it. She was thrilled that words like "smite" were now a valid part of her vocabulary. But after a brief stalemate, he abandoned the idea.

After casting a glance toward the distant sky, he laid his hand on the ground, closed his eyes, and muttered something under his breath.

There was the faintest of shimmers. The carpet was abruptly clean.

She stared in amazement as he threw a smug glance at the vacuum cleaner and pushed to his feet. She had yet to collect herself when he almost walked right past her, pacing out of the room.

She lifted an eyebrow, eyes twinkling in delight. "God's divine will, huh?"

He opened his mouth to deny it, then let out a quiet sigh. "I'll go fix the hot water, shall I?"

◆   ◆   ◆

Within a few hours, the little cottage was utterly transformed.

Carpets were unrolled, and throw pillows were tossed onto the sofa. A few gauzy curtains were hung alongside the windows, and a collection of sparse artwork was hung upon the walls.

Brie had nothing in her refrigerator, but she'd brought a few cups of ramen, which she heated with an electric kettle and gleefully consumed, as Cameron regarded her in equal parts fascination and disgust. Once the water heater was working, she abandoned him downstairs and took a lengthy shower to wash off the carpet dust and dirt from the move.

That's more like it, she thought, lathering up the soap, then rinsing herself smooth. *A little bit of water, a little bit of oil, and I'm a whole new woman. Like the last few days didn't happen. Like there isn't a guardian angel sitting at the base of the—*

"Brianna?"

She let out a quiet yelp, cowering behind the misted shower curtain as a head of dark hair poked itself into the room. He waited for an answer, only to get cursed in two different languages.

"I'm sorry to intrude, but—"

"Then *don't* intrude, Cameron!" she cried, wishing there was something more between them than clear plastic and steam. "I am *naked!* Do you understand what that means? Or maybe you don't," she snapped, answering her own question. "Maybe where you come from, everyone walks around naked, like in the good old days, before all that forbidden fruit."

He wisely chose not to engage.

"There are two men on bicycles at the door," he began haltingly. "They want to share some 'good news' and tell you the best way to get into Heaven."

A deafening silence fell over the bathroom.

"Brianna, I can't *begin* to tell you how uncomfortable this makes me."

"Tell them I'm not interested," she snapped, turning off the water. "Tell them, having met a personal representative, I'm choosing to abstain from that particular trip. You can reference the indigenous population's lack of boundaries," she added sharply as he ducked outside with an obedient nod. "And their complete disregard for *personal space.*"

By the time she toweled dry and headed back to the living room, she'd come up with an impressive list of scathing indictments to rain down on him. But the words caught on her tongue, and she stopped short the second she stepped inside.

My picture.

It was the one of her as a baby with her parents, the one of her reaching up to touch her mother's face. The one that had undoubtedly been smashed to oblivion in the car accident but had been restored to perfect condition and placed with tender care in the center of her bookshelf.

Cameron was sitting on the couch beside it with a look of chagrin — a strange, perfect being in an otherwise ordinary world. He glanced up when she entered, trying to interpret her expression.

"Did you put that up?" she asked softly.

He followed her gaze with a touch of confusion, worried it might somehow be wrong. "Yes, is that... is that not where you want it?"

She held his gaze for a moment, then let out a quiet sigh.

She couldn't be angry with him. She didn't know how all the pieces of this puzzle fit together, but she trusted that nothing happening to her was his fault. He might well be going above and beyond to keep her safe. Maybe even happy.

Another pang of tenderness shot through her heart, making it ache. "Cam?"

He looked up nervously and was about to apologize again, when she crossed over quickly and gave him a sudden hug. He froze in surprise as if, despite his endless centuries, he was somehow unfamiliar with the gesture. Then, he wrapped his arms around her back with the utmost care.

"Thank you," she murmured into his shirt. "Thank you for being here."

He tensed involuntarily, and then his face warmed with an unseen expression of tenderness.

"It's my honor, Brianna Weldon."

She pulled back and stood awkwardly for a moment. "I need to go to sleep. I start work tomorrow. Do you need anything?"

She had no idea what his needs might entail. She hadn't seen him eat, drink, or sleep since his magical reappearance in her life. Perhaps he simply needed to... charge?

"No, thank you," he answered. "I am quite alright. I wish you pleasant dreams."

She hesitated. "You're staying out here?"

He looked down at the couch. "In some cultures, it might be considered rude to move into a beautiful young woman's bedroom without even telling her my full name."

She grinned and bit her lip. "Well, we can't have that, can we?"

He shook his head. "Politeness is the flower of humanity."

She hesitated a moment, wanting to prolong their conversation, but was at a loss for words. In the end, she settled on a classic. "Goodnight, Cameron."

"Goodnight, Brianna."

Three minutes later, she was fast asleep.

A young man sat on a stone windowsill, one leg dangling outside, the other drawn up with his arm resting on it. His head leaned back against the wall, his face turned away, so all that could be seen was shaggy blonde hair. He was holding an apple, black as coal.

He seemed... bored.

Behind him, the sky was a necrotic blue-black, cracked in places, with an immense sea of magma roiling behind, leaking through. Dark, sharp-looking mountains jutted into the sky like spearheads. At their base, the hills had been burned bare.

Something came through a door and scuttled past. It had too many legs. Brie tried to scream, but she couldn't move or talk. The blonde-haired man perked up. "What is it?"

To her horror, the creature spoke. "It's the pendant. They found it."

The man turned his head slightly, but he was half-cloaked by a shadow, and she couldn't make him out. "Is that right?" His lips curved up for a moment, and he took a bite of the apple.

It started bleeding.

Suddenly a high scream filled the air as if the world itself was tearing apart at the seams.

Again and again, it sounded, twisting and compounding, growing and echoing through Brie's mind, before she finally woke up and realized what was happening.

The screams were coming from her.

◆   ◆   ◆

"Brianna? Brianna!"

Cameron was shaking her, his face struck with panic.

Her screaming stopped, and she found herself panting for breath, her hair wild around her.

"Are you alright?"

Her eyes flew around in disorientation, coming to settle on the bed.

"I'm sorry. I just..." She kept her eyes fixed on the comforter, trying to convince that reeling part of her brain that it wasn't real. "I had a nightmare."

Or a night terror? Has a dream ever felt so real?

His face went rigid, but he kept his voice calm. "Can you tell me what it was about?"

Her heart pounded in her chest as she stared at him in surprise. Did people usually discuss such things? The last time she could remember sharing the weight of a nightmare had been with her mother, and she'd been about six years old. But maybe things were different where he came from, and this certainly felt different. Had she ever in her life awoken with a scream?

"There was a man. And some weird spider, but it was huge, and it could talk." A host of shivers ran down her arms, and she was vaguely aware that she probably wasn't making any sense. "He had this apple, but it was bleeding. And the sky... the sky was dead."

Cameron visibly stiffened as she looked at him with huge, wild eyes. *Oh my God. This is real.*

"Did they say anything?" he asked. "Brianna, what did they say?"

"I don't know. I can't remember," she cried, trying to fight back the rising panic. "Who was that? Is this a part of that... those *things* that attacked me? That killed my mother?"

His hands tightened around hers, but she wrenched herself away.

"Why is everyone after me?" she demanded. "Why is this happening? I haven't done anything, alright? I'm just a girl who moved to Virginia. I'm just trying to start fresh—"

"I know," he interrupted hastily. "I know that, and I *promise* it's going to be alright. There's a chance it was just a nightmare. These last few days would be enough to give anyone bad dreams."

She drew in a deep breath, making a conscious effort to unclench her fists. "And if it's *not* just a nightmare?"

He took a single look at her face, then decided not to answer the question.

"Let's talk about it in the morning," he murmured soothingly. "Over breakfast. For now, you need to get some real sleep. You have a big day tomorrow."

She was too shaken to press, so she simply nodded. It wasn't until he got up to leave and made it to the door that she abruptly panicked. "Cameron?"

He turned immediately. "Yes?"

There was a pause. "Could you stay?"

He hesitated a moment, then returned to her side. "Always."

The two lay down beside each other, and she thought again that he must have some soporific power. Because despite her pounding heartbeat, despite the fact that her nails had torn frightened little holes into the duvet, it only took a few minutes before she was fast asleep. A deep, dreamless sleep. One where nightmares could never reach her, whatever they might mean.

She never saw the way the angel's eyes rested with worry on her pendant.

She never noticed its faint, eerie glow.

CHAPTER SIX

The Inimitable Sherry Walker

Brie awoke the next day to the most wonderful smell in all the world.

Fresh coffee.

She quickly dressed and brushed her teeth and hair, threw some extra scrubs and a water bottle in her backpack, and made her way to the kitchen, only to find herself in the middle of the most ridiculous argument she'd ever heard.

"I don't understand what you're saying. Please rephrase in the form of a question."

"So help me, you infernal rectangle, if you do not bring back the old lady's breakfast lesson this instant, I will feed you to the pit locusts."

She pulled in a breath, then stepped around the corner. "Good morning. Making friends, I see."

Cameron whirled around, hiding his hands behind his back, splattered in some strange, globulous combination of flour and milk. He recovered quickly. "Good morning. I was just communing with your... your *phone*." He shot the thing a dark look. "For a being devoted to the provision of knowledge, it is irritatingly withholding."

He looked adorable. There was no other word for it.

His chestnut hair tumbled into his eyes. A dusting of flour powdered his cheek. His bashful expression made Brie feel the way she'd felt about Mr. DiCaprio when she was twelve.

She flashed a grin, cheerful despite herself. "You tried to make me pancakes?"

He glanced behind him, and with a flick of his finger, all evidence was erased. "I'm sure I don't know what you mean."

"I appreciate the effort, but I'm not in the mood for pancakes. I want answers."

His eyes grew grave. "Yes. I thought you might."

She regarded him carefully, pouring herself some coffee with sugar and cream before settling on a stool by the counter. The sweet scent of caffeine wafted into her face as she took the first sip.

"Alright, angel. *Talk*."

He hesitated, but she persisted. "Was that a nightmare or not? Was I dreaming, or was that some kind of... of vision quest gone terribly wrong? You *knew* that place, Cam. And you asked what those creatures said. So, they're real?"

He drew in a breath. "They are."

Her eyes widened, but she held it together. "And the man?" she asked quietly, wishing very much she could simply forget. "The man I saw? The one who looked like a human? Is he a real person?"

"I'm not sure," he admitted quietly.

She tossed her hair over her shoulder with growing impatience.

"There are many sons of Hell, Brianna. Many who can take human form or any form they wish. Many who would be interested in that pendant." He raked back his hair with sudden frustration. "Though why they would suddenly be searching is as much a mystery to me as to you."

She exhaled slowly, staring down into her cup.

Not good enough.

There was a chance he could read minds.

"Give me some time," he said gently. "I know it's a lot to ask, and I know you've been waiting for answers far longer than seems fair. I do not have all the answers you seek, but I might know some people who do. Give me some time to speak with them, to try to help me figure this out."

She looked up at him. "And what am I supposed to do in the meantime?"

With a tentative grin, he gestured around the house. "Fill up the fridge. Buy some furniture. Start your job. Throw away that dead plant you've been carting around."

She jutted out her chin defiantly. "It's not dead. It's resting. Recuperating. And with all the supplements I've been feeding it, I'm sure it'll make a marvelous comeback."

He nodded without a hint of expression. "Perhaps I didn't make this clear when I explained my job description, but I am absolutely an expert in these matters. Your plant, Brianna, is gone."

She opened her mouth to argue, then peered in delight over the rim of her coffee mug. "Cam? Did you just make a joke?"

He blushed and turned around, pretending to wipe down the already immaculate counter, replaying the sound of the nickname in his mind.

"Cam?" she pressed.

"You should get that."

"Get what?"

The doorbell rang, and she nearly jumped out of her skin.

Oh, God... Sherry.

She still hadn't gotten her story straight between the move, the

Mormons, and the dream. A rush of panic swept over her before she turned on her heel and sprinted for the door, yelling, "Coming!"

She considered telling Cameron to hide, but there was no time. The windows were too big, and there was no way for him to cross to the bedroom without being seen. She had to count on the fact that her terrible luck would break, and her best friend would hardly notice.

Because that's totally going to happen. Because she's super, SUPER low-key.

Brie opened the door and was greeted by a whoop of delight. "FINALLY!"

The friends crashed into each other with enough force to dent a car. Arms flailed and hair knotted as they started bouncing in a strange two-person tangle on the front porch.

"I can't believe you're here!" Sherry squealed. "After all these months. And I can't believe you didn't get here sooner! Here, have a coffee." She grabbed a drink tray she'd left resting on the porch railing and offered it up.

Brie gratefully accepted an enormous white mocha as her friend swept inside, taking a slow turn around the living room, studying the most insignificant details with an appraising eye.

"Wow, you really got this place set up fast. How did you...?"

She froze dead still, staring at Cameron. He stared bracingly back. For a split second, nothing happened. Then he lifted his hand in an awkward wave.

Heaven, help me. Take him back.

"It's nice to meet you," he stammered a bit nervously. "Brie talks of nothing else."

Sherry took in the measure of him, saying nothing in reply. Then, without breaking eye contact with the angel, she leaned toward Brie and said in a low voice, "Brianna Weldon, are you aware that a Tom Ford model is waving at me from your kitchen?"

Yeah, she'll barely notice.

Brie was postverbal at this point. She nodded as Sherry reaffirmed, "So, you're seeing him, too?"

She nodded again and hid behind her mocha.

Sherry raised herself up to full height, all five feet two inches, and narrowed her eyes with a speculative, "Huh." Then she strode to the kitchen and began pacing around him the way a jungle predator circles its prey. At one point, she extended a finger. "May I?"

May you... what, exactly? What do you intend to do with that finger?

Cameron was clearly thinking the same thing and lifted his eyes to Brie for a moment before he acquiesced with a hesitant, "Of course. Whatever... whatever you need."

What happened next would forever remain one of the most intensely embarrassing moments of Brie's young life. She watched as Sherry studied him with the fierce scrutiny of an old-world heiress selecting a racehorse, poking him in the bicep and abs, and running a finger along his jaw. By the end, Brie was surprised her friend hadn't attempted to examine his teeth, but whatever she determined, she must have been pleased because the finger soon vanished, replaced with an acute stare.

"What's your name?"

"Cameron."

"How old are you?"

"Approximately fifty-five hundred Earth years."

"Fine, don't tell me. Do you do drugs?"

"Never, ma'am."

"Do you smoke?"

"Only when aflame."

"Are you the reason she's *late*?"

His face grew suddenly serious. "I'm afraid that I am. But I'm also one of the reasons she's here."

Sherry leaned back, considering this. Then she asked the million-dollar question. "What are your intentions towards my best friend?"

He hesitated a moment, then answered with perfect honesty. "To make her pancakes. To fix the water heater. To protect her from all harm."

There was a split second of silence, then Sherry spun around, beaming. "I *love* him. Let's get one in every color."

Brie let out the breath she hadn't realized she'd been holding with a slightly hysterical laugh, trying to keep her balance as her tiny, voluptuous friend scooped her up into another hug.

"*Brianna Weldon*. You could've just told me you'd met a guy."

"Yeah, I don't know what I was thinking," Brie panted, trying to catch her breath. "It's not like you'd put him through the Spanish Inquisition or anything."

Sherry wasn't listening. She was busy making plans. "This is fantastic! We can double-date tonight. You're coming, of course," she aimed at Cameron. It was not a question. "Brie, I know you 'lost' that black dress I got you, so I bought you another one. It's in the car. Cameron, I'm stealing her now. We need to go talk about you behind your back. Run along home and stay perfect. Fewer clothes next time. I'm envisioning ripped jeans, a leather belt, definitely no shirt—"

"Okay, that's enough." Brie grabbed her backpack and coffee and pulled her irrepressible friend out the door, glancing back with an apologetic, "Bye, Cam."

He lifted a hand with a bemused expression, watching as they clambered out the door and hurried to the car. The second they were safely inside, Sherry whirled on her. "Spill."

"What do you mean?"

"Don't you try it, young lady," she cried. "*Spill*."

Brie cleared her throat, but her voice still cracked, like she'd touched an electrical socket. Her best friend had that effect on people. She was living, breathing sunshine with a whopping dose of adrenaline.

"Well, remember you asked if I'd had any car trouble?"

Sherry nodded excitedly.

"I did," Brie continued. "In the middle of nowhere, in some state park by the border. And Cameron sort of—"

There was a theatrical gasp.

"Did he come to your rescue?" Sherry exclaimed, not pausing for breath. "Out in the middle of the woods? Oh my gosh, was it perfect? Did he change your tire? Was he wearing his shirt?"

"Sherry!" Brie couldn't help but laugh. "Why would he *not* be wearing a shirt?"

Why was I so nervous about spinning a story? She's perfectly capable of doing it herself.

"Oh, that's so romantic…" Sherry flopped back against the driver's seat and stared into the cottage windows. "So, wait a minute — he was just out there? Does he live around there? Is he a woodsman?" She paused for reflection. "Is that a thing? Woodsmen?"

They considered it, then left it for another day.

"And you brought him home with you? Brie, that's *incredibly* irresponsible. What do you really know about this guy? I mean, I know he looks like Adonis, but come on. What if he's a serial killer? What if his hair is so perfect because he conditions with the blood of the innocent?"

Ah. That's why I was nervous.

Sherry might present as a bubbly, irreverent, curvaceous pinup, but she was also sharp as a tack. Brie had always secretly thought she would go into law. She'd make a killing in litigation. Of course, knowing her temperament, there was a chance that wasn't a metaphor, so perhaps it was in everyone's best interest that she'd decided to save lives rather than rip them apart.

She decided to tell at least a partial truth. "I don't know what to tell you, Sher. He saved me, and he insisted on escorting me home. He keeps showing up for me. Being there for me. And it feels somehow... meant to be."

Sherry considered this. "Alright, I'll allow it. Provisionally. Pending further investigation."

Brie snorted with laughter. "You said the same thing about high school."

"And look how right I was." Sherry slipped on a pair of sunglasses, gliding them up the bridge of her nose with a grin. "So, what do you say? Shall we go start your illustrious medical career?"

"*Allons-y!*"

There was a slight pause. "Don't threaten me."

"No, it's French..."

But Sherry had already peeled out of the driveway and was coasting down the road.

When Brie was growing up, the first day of school was always equal parts exciting and intimidating. The first day of nursing school had been very much the same — anticipation rather than anxiety. The first day of *this* job was an emotional avalanche — complete, constant bombardment.

She and Sherry parked in front of the hospital, grabbed their bags, and jumped out of the car. For just a moment, they stood together. Brie took in the enormous red brick and smoked glass edifice. She thought she'd never seen so many windows in one structure before, not in person.

Daya Memorial Hospital. It lives up to the reputation.

"Did you ever think we'd both make it here?" Brie whispered.

"Never a doubt in my mind." Sherry looked up at the monolithic structure, fists on hips, chest lifted, in full Superwoman pose.

Brie finished off the last of her mocha with a long, bracing swig. "Yeah. Same." She gulped.

Sherry looked over and grinned. "You're going to be fine. But if you think this is intimidating, wait until you meet El Commandant."

"El Commandant?" Brie asked, raising an eyebrow.

"Trust me, you'll know."

They started to head through the bay doors when an ambulance rig tore into the driveway right in front of them. The back burst open, and a gurney emerged just as a team of people poured from the hospital to meet them. They were led by a short woman of Native descent, rippling with more muscles than a Spartan warrior and radiating competence and attitude to match.

"What have we got?" she barked.

"Code blue. Twenty-eight-year-old male, unresponsive at the scene, no apparent trauma, no witnesses. Someone found him in a parking lot. We did everything medically possible, but Denise…" The medic trailed off, shaking his head with a grave look.

Denise listened while conducting a thorough, blindingly fast examination of her own.

"No chest rise, no pulse. Alright, people, let's get him into trauma room five. Move!"

Her band of followers took over in a wave of blue scrubs. Denise stayed behind for a moment to get the rest of the information from the paramedics.

"I don't know what to tell you, Den. He's too young for this kind of cardiac event. There's nothing wrong with him, except he's dying. MI maybe? Or some kind of new drug?" He watched the gurney disappear into the ER with a helpless look. "I think we lost him on the way over."

"You did what you could, and it isn't over yet. Don't beat yourself up, Tim." She turned slightly, registering the friends. "*You.*"

El Commandant.

She pointed a finger at the center of Brie's chest, freezing her in place. "You have a lost, useless look about you. Are you my new nurse?"

"This is my friend from Atlanta, Brianna Weldon," Sherry interjected quickly. "She's one of the good ones, Den, so don't bite. Hard."

Hard?

"Hand her over and go clock in."

Sherry saluted cheerfully and sailed inside, leaving Brie at the mercy of her new captor. She immediately decided to opt for a near-militaristic level of politeness. "Hello, ma'am. I was told to report to the ER for orientation and a tour."

Denise raised an eyebrow. "This is your orientation. The tour begins in room five. You're shadowing me today. May God have mercy on your soul."

I could have a friend of mine put in a word.

Denise strode purposefully away without a backward glance, expecting to be followed. Brie threw her coffee cup into the nearest garbage can and hurried after her.

At a glance, it was chaos. Only if you knew what to look for could one discern the pattern, the underlying structure beneath. It was a living algorithm — a team of highly trained individuals working together, triaging patients by order of urgency, taking family histories, and gathering pertinent information before channeling them into the appropriate rooms.

The giant patient board behind the nursing station was at capacity — fifty-two rooms, all containing patients with varying degrees of need. Before Brie could orient herself any further, a commotion from room five captured her attention.

The former occupant, a man whose arm had just been set in a cast, was reluctant to vacate for the incoming trauma. "This is my room. Get out! I'm in pain. Wheel me back inside. Ow!"

Denise bent down and whispered something in his ear too softly for Brie to hear. His eyes went wide, and he tensed so completely that his shoulders nearly touched his ears. He stayed like that for a moment, then ducked his head and began studiously avoiding eye contact with everyone.

"Yes, ma'am," he mumbled, then preoccupied himself with a concerted effort to be invisible.

Someday, somehow... I'm going to find out what she said.

Room five was a concentrated version of the controlled mayhem that characterized the rest of the hospital. Nurses and techs poured in from every direction and began the practiced choreography of running a code. A dark-haired man who looked far too young to be in charge of another person's life bagged the patient to force oxygen into his lungs. An almost worryingly thin nurse was doing chest compressions, humming "Staying Alive" to keep the right rhythm.

"Can you start a line?" Though they'd only just met, Denise's voice was already unmistakable, indelibly fixed in Brie's mind.

"Yes."

"Then what are you waiting for?"

Brie grabbed the IV supply tray and tore open the plastic cover with a slightly overenthusiastic burst of speed. She tied off the man's arm with a tourniquet, watched as his lower hand darkened with the pressure, and then waited for a vein to appear. This took only seconds, but it felt like an age as she patted his inner wrist and forearm, trying to coax something suitable to the surface.

Come on. Where are you...

Finally, one appeared. She carefully pressed the needle to the skin and waited to feel the faint pop as it pushed through. "Number twenty gauge IV established."

She looked back for further instructions from Denise, only to find her standing just a step away, arms folded tightly across her chest. She gave a curt nod of approval. Brie sensed that this was the highest praise she might hope to receive from this person, certainly today, possibly ever.

"Alright, someone hand me the epi and standby with the Narcan—"

"Hold on there, Pocahontas."

The room froze.

Brie gasped. Denise stiffened, then rotated around in such a predatory fashion it made the rest of them almost feel sorry for whatever eminently stupid, lost soul had seen fit to throw the racial slur.

Almost. Not quite. Whoever said that deserves whatever comes next.

A man stood in the doorway. A man whose overriding physical feature was oil. His hair was slicked straight backward from all points of his skull, shellacked into an unyielding dome. His skin, predominantly his forehead, had an unhealthy, greasy sheen.

He laughed an erratic, hiccupping laugh while his eyes darted around, bright with nerves. His slightly oversized lab coat and name tag lent him an authority he didn't seem to deserve.

Denise exhaled through flared nostrils. "Dr. Matthews." It sounded like an obscenity. "To think we'd gone nearly a week without sending you back to HR," she said flatly.

Matthews ignored this and addressed the room. "What's the story, folks?"

The young-looking medic piped up. "Patient was found unresponsive in a parking lot. No ID, no visible injuries—"

"How long ago was this?" Matthews interrupted.

"Um… about twenty minutes."

Denise fixed him with a scathing glare. "We're a bit busy here, so perhaps you'd like to run the code. Or find me someone who will." Without waiting for an answer, she turned back to the patient and barked, "Where's that Narcan?"

Brie kept waiting for something to happen, for whatever madness derailed the chaotic rhythm to either reveal itself or, at least, go away. But it didn't.

Matthews merely stood there while Denise ran the code. Brie swore she saw him check his phone. It was *shocking*. The tiny nurse doing compressions was exhausted and stepped aside as the patient's chest was affixed with pads fitted with electrodes to defibrillate his heart.

"Clear!"

In one swift movement, everyone stepped back. Denise was about to press the button for defibrillation when a sudden shout echoed in the room.

"Time of death, zero seven thirty-three."

The room froze again.

"You're calling it?" Brie asked in disbelief.

Matthews's eyes narrowed to slits as he looked her up and down. A self-preservation instinct reminded her that she was still technically "touring" and should probably shut up, but she was too concerned for the patient to worry about the impression she was making on her first day.

"You can't!" she insisted. "We're one second away from trying to bring him back."

El Commandant completely ignored him. "Clear!" she yelled again and jolted electricity through the patient. No response. The man went back to asystole immediately.

"Stop it!" Matthews cried.

Denise glanced up with a look of such malice, it would likely scare off a panther. "Or what?"

Brie moved subtly towards the back of the room, watching the storm brew as the two turned slowly to face each other, armed with wildly different standards of patient care.

Matthews turned beet red and looked as though he might say something before he shrugged, glancing again at the clock. "Time of death: zero seven thirty-three."

As the room stared in disbelief, he walked over to the patient and snapped an eyelid unceremoniously open with his thumb, pointing a penlight directly inside.

"No chest rise, no heartbeat, pupils fixed and dilated." He took a step back, putting his pen back in his pocket. He looked around the room. "This man is dead, people. I realize I'm the only doctor here, but that is a distinction I hope they teach you in nursing school."

He let out another skittering laugh, only to be met with utter silence.

"If it makes you feel any better, look at those tattoos," he said, gesturing carelessly at the tribal markings on the man's face. "He's some gangbanger. Your energies are better spent elsewhere." With that, he turned on his heel and walked out the door, texting.

He left a sea of stunned faces in his wake.

Denise was the first to move, taking off her gloves and slapping them on a side table in disgust. She looked around the room, her features softening for a moment. "There are other people to help in this building. Find them. Help them. Go." Despite her militaristic demeanor, she clapped a few of her more demoralized-looking colleagues on the back on their way out. Only Brie stayed behind, still shaken by the experience.

"I don't understand," she murmured. "How can he get away with... with *not trying*?"

Denise replied flatly, sparing no emotion. "That isn't something you can control. Let's go find something we can control and make it better."

She walked out the door without telling Brie to follow her. She didn't have to.

"Welcome to Daya Memorial."

CHAPTER SEVEN

Angel of Mercy

The next few hours were some of the most challenging of Brie's entire life. She helped reset a broken nose, pulled an enormous fish hook out of a man's calf muscle, hung IV fluids for a couple of food poisoning victims, and comforted a hysterical first-time mother whose infant son had a hundred-degree fever.

By lunchtime, she was exhausted.

She'd just sat down for the first time since breakfast when Denise slammed a thick file on the counter in front of her. "Your orientation forms," she said brusquely. "Know every policy. Know every procedure. Know every standard. Attend all necessary appointments. Leave no box unchecked. Or I will find you." She stomped off without further explanation.

Brie looked at the mountain of paperwork and the maelstrom of activity swirling around her and decided to find sanctuary elsewhere.

There was one place in every hospital that was by its very nature quieter and cooler than every other. The morgue. It was a useful, if not morbid, habit she'd picked up during clinical rotations in Georgia: always do your paperwork in the morgue.

She knocked first. Even though the pathologists were likely out to lunch themselves, she was in unfamiliar territory and might need to make an alliance before she was allowed to use their space.

To her surprise, someone answered.

"Can I help you?" asked a friendly-looking woman with skin the color of coffee and a beautiful head scarf.

"Yes, I was wondering—"

"You're Denise's new shadow," the woman said, smiling and opening the door a little more.

"How can you tell?"

The lady nodded at the enormous stack of forms.

"I've never seen you before, but I know an orientation packet when I see one." She took a step back and gestured with her hand. "Come on in."

Brie gratefully walked into the cool room. "Thank you so much. This was always my spot at my last hospital because it was—"

"The coolest place in the whole joint."

"Exactly." Brie grinned and extended a hand. "I'm Brie, by the way."

"Rashida."

They shook, and Brie barely avoided dropping all the files onto the floor. The woman steadied the more precarious ones with a cheerful laugh. "Maybe you'd better sit down."

Brie put her paperwork and sad-looking sandwich down on the nearest available table and pulled up a chair. "Seriously, thanks for this. I know it's your territory, and I don't want to impose—"

"Nonsense, I'm glad for the company. You're much livelier than my usual lunchmates."

Brie shot a look at the rows of horizontal body lockers lining the wall and laughed nervously. "Yes, I imagine so."

Rashida cocked her head appraisingly, looking her up and down. "I heard you had a baptism by fire this morning."

Brie stopped unwrapping her sandwich and glanced up. "What do you mean?"

"Weren't you the one on the code with Dr. Matthews? The one who called him out?"

Brie lowered her lunch, horrified. "How do you even know about that?"

"News travels fast around here," said Rashida. "Especially when so many examples of his handiwork end up in my domain."

"What do you mean?"

The woman was unboxing some Tupperware that contained a heavenly-smelling rice dish.

"Matthews has the highest mortality rate in the hospital," she said perfunctorily.

Brie's eyes widened. "That wasn't... that wasn't the first time it's happened?"

Rashida shook her head.

"We call him Dr. Death. He's been brought up before the M&M review board three times, but they've never been able to prove negligence. Always say he's justified in his decisions. Eventually, people just stopped registering complaints. It doesn't make any difference except for making us look insubordinate. Denise is the only one who stands up to him anymore, and that's because — well, you've met her. It's possible she's too powerful to fail."

Brie laughed nervously. "She does seem formidable."

Rashida nodded and talked around a bite. "Very. But fair. Best charge nurse in this place." She swallowed. "If someone in my family was sick, she's who I'd want taking care of them."

Brie picked at her sandwich, feeling troubled. "Did people say I was insubordinate, too?"

The woman laughed. "Don't worry. If Matthews hates you, it

can only be a point in your favor. Nobody likes that greasy little rat. Also, call me Ida."

"Ida, you are a breath of fresh air on an otherwise oxygen-free day."

"Pleased to meet you, too."

The two spent the rest of their lunch break chatting occasionally and slogging through their respective mountains of paperwork. When it was time for Brie to head back upstairs, Ida walked her to the door. "Come back tomorrow. Bring coffee."

Brie saluted in return. "Of course."

Then Ida opened the door and gasped. "Holy mother of Zeus!"

Brie's chest tightened in a panic that was becoming all too familiar. "What is it?"

Without waiting for an answer, she rushed to the door herself, only to find her own personal guardian angel standing in the frame. He was holding coffee.

"Brianna. Keeper of the Dead." He nodded to each of them in turn and flashed a breathtaking smile, extending the paper cups. "I thought these might help brighten your day."

Rashida turned to Brie with a dumbfounded expression. "I don't know how to tell you this, but you can't have male escorts in the hospital." She glanced back at the angel. "Even if they look like that."

"I didn't... he's not..." Brie stuttered in consternation and took a deep breath. "Ida, this is Cameron. Cameron, Ida. She's a forensic pathologist," she added pointedly. "Not 'The Keeper of the Dead.' Mostly because this isn't ancient Egypt."

"Except that I much prefer his title," Rashida chuckled, blushing simultaneously. "It has a lovely ring to it. Is this your boyfriend?"

Brie considered her reply. "We have a shared love of Schumann."

The woman nodded slowly. "Well, whoever you are, thank you very much." She popped open the lid and glanced up in surprise. "How did you know I like chai?"

There was an awkward pause, in which Brie looked briefly heavenward.

"Ida, it was so good to meet you," she said. "I'll see you tomorrow, okay?"

In a move that was becoming increasingly familiar, she grabbed Cameron by the elbow and steered him back into the hallway before he could say or do anything to incriminate himself.

Or worse, frighten my coworkers on my FIRST day on the job.

The second they were out of sight, she whirled around to face him. "What are you doing here?" she hissed.

"Bringing you a beverage that is bad for your blood pressure."

She made a sound of pure exasperation. "I am *working*, Cameron. You can't just show up at my job. They'll fire me. It's unprofessional."

He stared back with a measured expression. "Brianna, this is my work, too."

That stopped her in her tracks. "What is *that* supposed to mean?"

He stared a moment longer, then let out a quiet sigh. "You should get that."

"Get what?"

In hindsight, she probably should have been expecting the pager. But no matter how often her angel warned her, those things kept catching her off guard.

She cursed in surprise, almost dropping the pages all over again. She glanced at the device, backing away as she did. "Listen, I have to go. *Do not* follow me. You can't be here."

He stared in silence as she hurried towards the elevator, banged frantically on the button, and slipped inside. It wasn't until the doors were sliding shut that he appeared suddenly by her side.

She cursed again, clutching at her heart. "*Cameron*! Don't do that!"

"You said not to follow you."

"I meant don't come with me."

He looked at her calmly. "We're going to the same place."

By the time that finally registered, the doors were opening on the emergency room floor.

Maybe it was the coffee churning away in her stomach, or perhaps it was the sight of all those busy faces she was trying so hard to impress. But the bewilderment and curiosity that had informed her every emotion since their fateful meeting faded, then hardened into an indignant rage.

"Cameron, this is my place of work," she snapped, jabbing a finger into his chest. "My new job. My first day. I understand that you're trying to protect me, but—"

He pressed a silencing finger to her lips. "Brianna, right now, no one can see me but you."

Now he tells me.

She looked out the elevator doors again, this time in acute mortification, but didn't see any immediate red flags. An orderly looked at her strangely, perhaps wondering why she'd been quietly shouting at herself, but otherwise, she appeared to be in the clear. She lifted the papers, hiding her face.

"We are not done talking about this."

Cameron gave a slight, benign nod. "As you wish."

She stalked to the nurse's station and put the files away before running to room sixteen to join Denise. The woman glanced over at her with a scowl the second she entered.

"Took you long enough."

"I'm sorry, I was—"

"I don't care." She nodded down at the patient in the bed. "This is Esther Abrams. She's been in here on and off with a case of pneumonia for months. Whenever we think we've got it under control, it flares up again. Her daughter keeps panicking and calling the ambulance when she can't stop coughing."

"I'm afraid I've made quite a nuisance of myself," chimed in the old lady before succumbing to a hacking cough. Brie immediately grabbed a fistful of tissues and placed them into her hand.

Denise observed this with a practiced, keen eye. "Nurse Weldon, you are going to stay with Ms. Abrams this afternoon. You will monitor her condition and page me immediately if there are any changes or concerns. Is this understood?"

"Yes, of course," Brie replied immediately, though, in truth, she didn't understand why she wouldn't be shadowing Denise as she made her afternoon rounds.

Why aren't we transferring her to the ICU?

The charge nurse took a step towards her and inclined her head. "I am fond of Ms. Abrams and would be extremely disappointed should her standard of care be even slightly deficient. Is that understood?"

Ah. Gotcha.

"Absolutely understood."

Denise turned to Esther with a stern command. "Get better." Then she turned on her heel and left.

Esther chuckled quietly. "She's a tough cookie, that one," she rasped in a near whisper. "But as good as they come."

Brie had already begun adjusting the pillows and familiarizing herself with the woman's chart.

"It's my first day, but I've already heard that same thing from a few people," she agreed. "Can I get you a glass of water? We should try to keep you hydrated as much as possible."

"Call me Esther, please." She sank back against the pillows as if exhausted by even this brief conversation. "Your first day, you say? So that's why they've got you babysitting an old bat like me."

She chuckled before another series of coughs took her down. This fit was a bad one, worse than the others. Brie got more tissues and held her as her fragile body was wracked with coughs. When it finally subsided, she sank back down again, weaker than ever.

"Try to rest, Esther. We'll get you feeling better soon."

For a long time, the two women sat in comfortable silence. One was staring out the window, the other was holding the box of tissues and holding her hand.

After a while, Esther finally spoke. "I understand why you're here, but what did I do to deserve that handsome fella?"

Brie stared in confusion for a moment, then spun around to see Cameron standing by the door. A rush of panic washed over her as she pushed quickly to her feet, about to make a million excuses and murder the angel where he stood. Then she froze, perfectly still.

She can see him. What does that mean?

"Hello, Esther." He smiled warmly and came to her bedside. "How are you feeling today?"

She let out a weary sigh. "Young man, it is impossible that one so vibrant as you could understand how tired I feel."

Cameron took her hand, perching beside her on the bed. "Perhaps I can help."

The moment they touched, the woman's features completely transformed. The deep lines between her brows smoothed, her breathing evened, and her expression seemed to clear.

"Oh!" she gasped, eyes shining. "How did you...?"

Cameron continued to hold her hand.

"Stop," Brie whispered in a panic. "You can't."

The angel threw her a sympathetic look but didn't move.

At any rate, there was no further need for excuses or explanations. As the two of them watched, Esther's wonder softened into understanding and then, at last, acceptance.

Her lips parted for a moment, then she gave a rueful chuckle. "I knew you were too handsome to be real."

"I'm real, Esther," he replied. "Just not of this world."

Looking back on it later, it would always strike Brie how very strange it was to hear them speaking. He didn't talk to her the way one usually addressed their elders — with the unintentional detachment that sprang from a barrier of so many years. He spoke as if they were equals.

His eyes were warm and welcoming. His fingers stroked back her brittle hair.

"I always hoped there would be more. But sometimes, I found it difficult to believe." She looked into his eyes, worried. "Has my lack of faith kept me from seeing my Simon again?"

He shook his head. "Not at all. In fact, he's here now."

He leaned back, and Esther's face lit with joy.

"Simon!" she cried. "Oh, Simon..."

Brie looked on as the woman greeted someone who wasn't there, her own eyes sweeping nothing but a blank wall. A feeling of helplessness came over her, paired with a shivering dread.

"Isn't there anything we can do?" she whispered to Cameron. "Can't you save her?"

He glanced at her, never letting go of Esther's hand. "I *am* saving her," he murmured. "Saving her from an agonizing death.

Saving her from drowning on dry land. Allowing her to pass away peacefully in the arms of her true love."

He turned back to the old woman, now happily carrying on a conversation with her favorite person in the world, whom only she could see. His lips curved in a tender expression as he stroked the grizzled curls away from her eyes.

"Go ahead and do your job, Brianna," he said softly. "I will continue to do mine."

She'd been rooted to the spot, taking in the incredible scene in front of her, but his words galvanized her into action. She checked Esther's stats and saw they were dropping. She paged Denise immediately and called for a crash cart to have at the ready. She was about to try to break through Esther's reverie to talk to her again when Denise rushed back into the room.

"What is it?"

"Ms. Abrams is about to crash. I can tell. Just trust me. I have everything prepped, and you said to notify you as soon as there was any change, so I—"

At that moment, the heart monitor flatlined.

"There it is," Brie cried. "Okay, so call the code, and we'll—"

Denise took her shoulders and looked her square in the face. "Weldon. She's a DNR. We aren't calling a code."

Brie looked down at the patient, trembling where she stood. "But you said—"

"Her breath sounds were virtually nonexistent. She was dying when she arrived. This was end-of-life care. She shouldn't have been in the ER in the first place. She should have passed away peacefully at home. Her daughter just didn't understand." She paused a moment before finishing more gently. "I told you to take care of her because I knew she'd like you."

She walked over to the monitor and turned off the sound. Then they stood and watched the thin green line continue horizontally across the screen. Just a few seconds and it was over.

Denise saw a lovely old woman quietly pass away.

Brie saw a lovely old woman and a beautiful angel of mercy become completely suffused in golden light. It haloed them for a suspended moment, illuminating all those passing memories, all those blissful years, then the light passed entirely to the angel, and he blinked away in a flash.

She opened her mouth but could find nothing to say.

Denise glanced her way and, in a moment of empathy, clapped a hand on her shoulder. "I also picked you because I thought you could handle it. Some of the rookies don't have the stomach for this, and they don't know it yet. You? You've got a steel core in there somewhere. I can see it."

She clapped her on the back once more, a gesture of goodwill that might well have left a mark, then turned and walked out of the room, calling over her shoulder. "I'll send in the on-call doctor for the time of death. Don't forget to chart."

Brie was left standing alone in the room with Esther's body, reeling from what she'd just witnessed. When Cameron appeared again beside her, she stood there, too shaken to move.

"Brianna?" he said hesitantly. "Are you alright?"

Am I?

She considered for a suspended moment — one that went on much longer than she was aware of at the time. Slowly she rose onto her tiptoes, took his face in her hands, and kissed him on his cheek.

"I'm fine."

It was at that moment Dr. Matthews and Sherry walked into the room.

CHAPTER EIGHT

Parables

"What are you doing?"

The pair broke apart immediately at Sherry's blunt question, and Brie turned a particularly vivid shade of crimson.

"We were just… I mean… we were only—"

"Who's we?"

Brie turned to look at Cameron, who gave her a meaningful look and stepped back.

Oh, God. They can't see him. What must that have looked like?

Her face blanched the color of spoilt milk. Sherry was looking at her with concern that bordered on alarm. Dr. Matthews clearly just wanted to get out of there.

"I'm here to call time of death. What are you doing here?"

He directed this at Sherry, who skewered him with a scathing look before batting her eyelashes and replying, "Just doing my job, sir, here in my capacity as a sexual harassment lawsuit just waiting to happen." She blinked sweetly and held his gaze as the man broke into a flop of sweat. He pulled out a handkerchief and dabbed his forehead in a fruitless attempt to dry himself.

"Nurse… whatever your name is. Were you here when it happened?"

"Yeah. Were you here when it happened?" Sherry looked at her again as though she was a wounded animal to be approached with caution.

Brie took a deep breath and nodded.

"Ms. Abrams passed away eight minutes after four o'clock this afternoon."

"Time of death: sixteen-oh-eight." Matthews signed her chart illegibly, turned on his heel, and practically ran back into the hallway, desperate to escape the self-proclaimed "walking lawsuit."

Sherry was too concerned about Brie to even notice. "Are you okay?" A preamble wasn't her style. "I heard the guy from the ambulance died, and that sonofabitch didn't even bother to properly run the code. And now this?"

"I'm fine," Brie said quickly.

She knew why her friend was so worried. Brie had been lucky during her clinical rotations back in Georgia. She hadn't had to watch anyone die in front of her. Not since her mother. Not till today.

"Are you sure?" Sherry pressed. "Because when I came in here, you looked like you were doing a bizarre yoga pose with a dead woman lying on the bed behind you."

"I…" Brie glanced at Cameron sitting in the chair next to Esther's bed, invisible to all but herself. He looked at her apologetically and mouthed, *Should I leave?*

She took a deep breath and replied to Sherry. "That's exactly what I was doing. It's this yoga technique Dr. Rogers made me promise to try. Keeps the back flexible and calms down the limbic system when you're stressed."

"Oh!" Sherry's face relaxed, then piqued with interest. "Can you teach me? Maybe I should try yoga. Things are going well with Mike, and I might want to limber up a little—"

"Absolutely." Brie gave her a quick hug. "Thanks for checking up on me. You're a wonderful friend. But you can't run out on your own patients every time one of mine dies." She looked at Esther sadly. "Though I do appreciate you coming for this one."

Sherry looked at the patient for the first time. "Oh, no... Esther?"

Brie looked at her in surprise. "You knew her?"

"We all did. She's been a regular around here for months. Nice lady." She sighed. "Nice daughter, too, but very high-strung. This is going to devastate her." She looked at Brie. "I should be the one to call the family. They know me a little."

Brie shook her head. "It's my responsibility. I can do it."

"I know you can, love. But would you let me do this one?"

The two shared a sad look.

"Only if I can sit with you while you call."

Together, they covered Esther with a blanket and called to inform the morgue. As they left to make the fateful phone call from the nurses' station, Brie glanced back at Cameron.

His hand was resting upon the blanket. When he caught her looking, he said quietly, "I'll stay with her until someone comes."

Brie nodded almost imperceptibly and followed her friend out the door.

By the end of her shift, Brie felt as though her day had begun three days ago. Her eyes burned with the fluorescence of the hospital lights, her stomach was churning from day-old coffee, and her feet had been crammed in her shoes so long that she was beginning to seriously question her life choices.

I could be something more relaxing. Like an air traffic controller.

As she waited for Sherry on the bench near the ambulance bay, she tilted her face up to catch the sunlight, took in a deep breath, and slowly exhaled. Before she could congratulate herself for doing Dr. Rogers' breathing techniques one whole time, her thoughts were interrupted.

"Is this seat taken?"

She opened her eyes and squinted. Her angel was looking down on her, haloed in the sunlight. Her lips pursed, and she gestured in a circle around his head with a teasing grin. "That's a bit on the nose, don't you think?"

"What is?"

"Never mind."

He sat down beside her, brimming with curiosity but wanting very much to be respectful of the current mood. "Brianna, why do you ask if the seat is taken if—"

"Cam, it's been a long day. Could we do idioms tomorrow?"

"Of course. I understand."

They sat silently for a moment before he threw her a sideways glance. "So, you saw my earthly purpose today — what I do."

Brie nodded slowly. "I did."

He hesitated, picking some nonexistent lint off his pants. "What did you think?"

"I thought… it was strangely beautiful."

He stared for a split second, as if he was worried she might retract it. Then, he let out a breath in utter relief. When she tilted her head at him quizzically, he said, "I've often wondered if humans would approve of us, if they knew about us before the end."

Brie was puzzled. "Why wouldn't we?"

"Well," he hesitated, "we aren't always there in time to ease suffering, as you well know." He watched her carefully. "And violent deaths aside, the human population growth has so far outpaced our own that there simply aren't enough of us. It becomes 'unfair,' you see." He looked at Brie with sudden intensity. "Your kind is very concerned with the concept of fairness."

She considered this. "There's this story we have about starfish. I think you might call it a parable."

His eyes lit up. "I was raised on parables. Tell me."

She took a breath. "One morning, after a great storm, an old man goes for a walk down the beach. He sees a young boy throwing things into the ocean. The man asks, 'What are you doing?' and the boy replies, 'The tide is going out, and the sun is coming up. I'm throwing these starfish back into the water so they don't die.' The old man says, 'You foolish boy. There are miles of beach and hundreds of starfish. You'll never make a difference.' The boy looks at him for a moment, then picks up another starfish and throws it into the ocean. He turns to the old man and says, 'I made a difference to that one.'"

She turned her face to the sun again and closed her eyes, feeling its warmth on her skin. She never saw the way the angel continued to gaze at her in silence. Like she was the sunrise itself.

"Whatcha doing?"

They both jumped and turned to see Sherry standing a few feet away, resisting the urge to snap a picture while openly grinning from ear to ear.

"Brianna Weldon, did you secure alternate transportation home and forget to tell me?"

Brie grinned as they both rose to their feet. "Nope. I found this stray wandering around in the parking lot. Can we keep him?"

Cameron glanced between them in confusion. "A stray—"

"Aw, honey, did you take a cab here just to surprise our girl?" Sherry cooed. "You are makin' everybody else look bad, mister."

Her eyes swept over him, and she couldn't help but add, "In more ways than one. Come on, I'll give you both a lift. Cam, you're in the back."

They piled into the car together, Cameron in the back seat next to the sparkling blue box containing Brie's replacement dress, as promised. "Don't let her forget that," Sherry said, pointing. "Trust me, you'll thank me later." She winked at him and threw the car into gear with a sigh. "It's too bad he doesn't have a chronic illness or something, Brie. Then we could see him all the time."

"Sher, he can *hear* you."

"He doesn't mind."

"I don't mind," he echoed from the back seat.

"Did Brie tell you all about her first day?" Sherry asked. "She had a bit of a rough one."

Brie glanced back at him. "He's aware of the situation."

"Well, we have to do it all over again tomorrow, so you know what I think?"

"Sher, I wanted to talk to you about that. Are you sure—"

"We'd better make the most of tonight." Sherry beamed at her exhausted friend, then blithely continued, "I've been looking forward to introducing you to Mike for weeks, Ms. Weldon. You will not postpone my night of jubilee. We are celebrating your move, we are celebrating your first day, we are celebrating your bizarrely good-looking new boyfriend, and we are celebrating the blue satin dress with the corset top I've been dying to wear for two weeks." She winked at Cameron in the rearview mirror. "A neckline to slay the souls of men."

His face paled slightly. "I have seen such a neckline before."

The girls shared a look.

"Have you now," Sherry said, raising an eyebrow.

He looked out the window and shuddered. "I understand it is now widely believed that it was Helen of Troy's face that launched a thousand ships, but I can assure you on behalf of all who gave their lives in the bloodshed that followed — not one of those poor soldiers ever once looked at her face."

Sherry narrowed her eyes at him in the mirror before looking at Brie. "His sense of humor is a bit of a high-wire act, isn't it?"

Brie sighed and looked out the window. "You have no idea."

"Brianna," Cameron called up the stairs. "Tell me again?"

"Cam, I've told you twice already."

"Yes, but is it not better to be over-prepared in this situation? Sherry impressed upon me the importance of this dinner several times after you went upstairs. She was… compelling."

Brie's musical laughter chimed through the house. "Yeah, that sounds like her."

"Brianna—"

"Weather, sports, hobbies, job. Art if you're stuck."

The angel paced the living room, muttering her words to himself on a loop. "Weather, sports, hobbies, job. Weather, sports, hobbies, job. Art if I'm stuck."

He paused, staring at Brie's woebegone Ficus "tree" for a moment. He looked to the top of the stairs, then out the window towards the heavens before quickly, even sneakily, stroking one of its bedraggled leaves with his hand. He casually walked away and didn't even wait to watch it magically grow into a lush, verdant version of itself, three times its original size.

"Weather, sports, hobbies, job. Art if I'm stuck."

Five minutes later, he glanced at the clock. "Brianna, I'm familiar with the term 'fashionably late,' but do you not think…"

He stopped short.

Brie descended the stairs, long curls cascading down her shoulders and bouncing with each step. The dress Sherry had purchased for her was a fitted, knee-length, one-shouldered cocktail number that hugged her curves in exactly the right places while still maintaining elegance and class. Tiny cutouts that resemble constellations swirled up her side and across the neckline.

She was putting in an earring, an heirloom from her mother when it slipped from her fingers and dropped next to her black stiletto. "Oh, shoot…"

Cameron was there in an instant. "Please, allow me."

He knelt at her feet and recovered the diamond, gazing down at it for a moment before offering it up. She took it hesitantly. "Thanks."

"My pleasure."

Their eyes lingered a moment longer before both turned at the same time. She stabbed the earring frantically as though trying to pierce it through her skin. He looked anywhere except at her dress, deeply inhaled the scent of her perfume, and narrowly avoided walking into a wall.

"We should probably—"

"Yes, we should get going."

They headed silently towards the door, both trying to keep steady, both suddenly nervous about what lay ahead, when she suddenly gasped with delight. "My plant!"

He shifted his weight uncomfortably. "Yes, well, I was just—"

"I *told* you it would make a comeback." She stroked one of its leaves, then looked smugly back at the angel. "All it needed was a smoothie. They're very good for your electrolytes, you know."

Without another word, she sashayed out the front door to the car. She didn't see him whisper, "Wow," under his breath or shake his head with a tender fondness.

She never saw it. He made sure of that.

The place Sherry had chosen was called Le Canard Gris, which the patrons of the small Virginian town wrote off as being something "fancy" and "French" without realizing it actually meant "The Grey Duck."

Cameron hid a grin of recognition as they passed beneath the looping script, pushing open the door and offering his arm simultaneously. "This looks lovely."

"It does, doesn't it?"

Brie gave her dress an unnecessary tug, feeling a sudden flurry of nerves. She couldn't remember the last time she'd done something like this — gone out to a nice dinner with friends. It was the kind of thing she'd lost track of after Sherry moved to Virginia. The type of social touchstone that used to be so easy, that used to be so normal... but now?

I'm going to be sitting next to an angel. And I absolutely cannot tell my best friend.

She flashed a sideways glance at Cameron, only to see that he looked just as nervous as she was feeling. While handsome and composed on the outside, his fingers were drumming secretly on the side of his leg, and it looked as though he had yet to pull in a full breath.

Then there were the fish.

What the hell?

For a split second, she thought she must be imagining it. The tank itself was perfectly ordinary, the same kind of aquarium and fountain combination that many upscale establishments commissioned for the lobby to create a soothing ambiance and add to the general air of prestige. The smooth stones curved in a gentle crescent, and the sound of splashing water tinkled in the air. But the fish themselves?

If she didn't know better, she'd swear they were...

Staring?

Her mouth fell open as her eyebrows shot skyward.

Holy hell, that's exactly what's happening.

Not only had every single fish turned towards the door the moment they stepped inside, but now they'd crammed themselves against the side of the tank and were gazing with riveted attention at the angel by her side. If it wasn't so unnerving, she might have laughed.

There had to be upwards of fifty, hovering in a little line, staring with unblinking, glassy eyes at the fidgety man standing next to her — the one who was focused on his breathing and tapping complicated rhythms on the side of his leg. He'd yet to even glimpse the cheerful little fountain.

When it finally caught his attention, he wasn't at all pleased.

"Stop that," he whispered furiously, casting a fast glance around the room to make sure no one else could see. "I said stop it! Go away."

He waved his fingers, and they scattered to the opposite side of the tank.

It was a clear victory but a fleeting one. No sooner had he let out a secret breath of relief than he glanced down to see Brie staring right back up at him, arms folded across her chest.

"Are we having a Little Mermaid moment?"

His face went perfectly blank. "What?"

She gritted her teeth, pulling him down to eye level by his lapels. "Does someone have some amphibious powers he neglected to mention?"

His cheeks flamed in the soft light as his gaze shot to the fish.

"What? No. That's just…" He linked their arms together, turning her deliberately in the opposite direction. "They're just being rude. Don't pay them any attention."

This is going to be a disaster of epic proportions.

She took a final look at the fountain, then steered them towards the bar. "I'm going to need a drink."

In hindsight, it was probably a good thing that Brie's idea of fashionably late still turned out to be a few minutes earlier than Sherry's interpretation of the same concept. That way, Brie could sit elegantly at the bar and power-gulp a much-needed glass of Merlot.

Cameron stood impassively beside her, looking around, taking note of the exits, and nodding vaguely at the waitstaff and fellow patrons when they made eye contact.

"Aren't we getting a table with your friends?"

"They're not here yet," she answered, lifting her hand for another glass. "And that's excellent because I'm going to need a little alcohol in my system if you're going to spend the night recreating scenes from *Finding Nemo.*"

He shot her a scowling glance. "While I have no earthly idea what you're talking about, I can assure you, we will have no further interruptions from the fish."

If I had a dime.

"That's exactly my point!" she said, fingers clutched around the glass. "How are we supposed to do this? I don't know if you realize, but every single interaction we've had has involved some sort of supernatural tomfoolery or obviously nonhuman behavior. This place is so fancy, it would make me feel awkward even if my dinner date wasn't, I don't know, from another freaking dimension. And beyond all that, how am I supposed to lie to my best friend?"

The wine sloshed back and forth, as she shook her head frantically.

"I have no idea what to tell them about who you are, where you come from, or why you're here. I don't even know how you acquired that suit. Do you just... manifest things?" Her gesticulations with the wine glass were becoming increasingly precarious. "It doesn't matter. The point is... I mean, we've never come right out and said it, Cameron, but I'm more or less assuming this whole angel of mercy thing is something I should keep to myself."

A few customers flashed her a curious look as they passed by, but Cameron waved them away with a fixed smile, just as he'd done to the fish.

"Yes," he said softly, "it is something you should keep to yourself. There is a reason my kind has remained a mystery to yours. To interact directly with mortals is just shy of forbidden."

Just shy of forbidden? But not quite?

She rubbed at her temples, warding off a coming migraine. "What's your point?"

"My point is this is new for me as well."

He took the glass of wine and eased it from her hand, using a finger to gently sweep her hair at the same time. For a split second, she thought it was simply a sweet gesture. It wasn't until she felt the warm tingle of his fingertips that she realized the threat of a headache had vanished on the spot.

He offered his arm. "Don't worry about what to tell your friends. I'll think of something. In the meantime, perhaps this can be new for us, together?"

She stared at him for a moment before taking his arm. "Alright. But full disclosure: I'm not trying to be dramatic, but if I get one more unwanted surprise tonight, I am throwing myself into the sea."

By the time Brie and Cameron wound their way back towards the main restaurant, the doors were just closing as Sherry and a tall gentleman swept inside, giving a name for the reservation.

Sherry looked stunning, all curves in jewel-toned satin, with her hair swept into an elegant chignon reminiscent of Old Hollywood. And her date… seemed strangely familiar.

Brie's eyes widened in shocked recognition, and she gripped Cameron's arm in a vice, just as Sherry spotted them and let out a little shriek of delight. A second later, she was waving them over, steering her escort along by her side. He was tall and handsome, with reddish blonde hair and brown eyes, and he carried himself with a posture too erect and symmetrical for a civilian.

Even without the sunglasses, Brie recognized him immediately. *Officer Mitchell.*

CHAPTER NINE

Double Dates and Other Disasters

"Cameron," she hissed frantically. "Change of plan."

He looked at her in confusion. "What do you...?" Then he followed her gaze and swallowed hard.

"Is he going to remember us?"

"I don't know." Despite the steadiness of his voice, his lovely face was several shades paler than usual, and those drumming fingers had gone still. "I've never done that before. I mean, I've never done that and then run into the person again." He paused. "What's the new plan?"

"I'm throwing myself into the sea."

The two exchanged an awkward glance before she offered the only thing she could manage. "Improvise."

Easier said than done.

As the couple closed in, her feet stopped working, and her brain shut down, unable to come up with one single feasible lie to explain their previous encounter. She merely held onto Cameron's arm like a life preserver, pivoting from one crazy idea to the next.

I have an identical twin. So does he.

Sounds like you got hypnotized. You should really look into that.

I have no idea what you're talking about, and you can't prove anything.

Please excuse me, I forgot I have a previous engagement and am very late for my appointment to permanently move to Venezuela.

Good options were in short supply.

"You made it!" Sherry scooped her into a hug, air-kissed both of her cheeks, then held her at arm's length as Brie plastered a delighted look on her face and tried very hard not to swallow her tongue.

"You look glorious, love. That dress! Don't lose this one," she added, eyes flashing with a hint of warning before turning back to her companion. "Brie, I want you to meet Mike. Mike, this is Brianna Weldon, my best friend in the world."

Brie's knees were shaking, and she was still wondering about Venezuela's extradition laws when Mike stepped forward and warmly took her hand.

"Mike Mitchell. It's a real pleasure to meet you." His voice was friendly — lilting, with a slight Southern drawl. "Sherry talks about you constantly. It almost feels like we've met before."

At this, Brie let out a strange, yelping laugh that she immediately regretted and shook his hand, hyperaware that she'd ranted about bears and gummy worms the last time they'd met.

"I've heard so much about you, too," she exclaimed in reply. "Yeah, almost! It almost feels like that. But of course, we haven't because how could we? Right?" She let out another high, weird laugh and consciously forced herself to shut up and stop shaking his hand.

What an inconvenient time to be having a full stroke.

Sherry was amused. "Looks like someone decided to pre-party a little bit. Well, who could blame you after the day you've had?" She gestured to the angel at her side. "Mike, this is Cameron, Brie's backcountry savior and the possible reincarnation of Rudolph Valentino I was telling you about."

The two men shook briefly, but Mike lingered, staring with a peculiar expression.

"Very nice to meet you, Mike." Cameron stepped back quickly, giving Brie a steadying squeeze on her shoulder. "Brie and I have been looking forward to it."

Brie startled at his use of her nickname. He was usually so formal. She was definitely still having heart palpitations but approved the general sentiment.

"Nice to meet you, too." Mike continued to stare at Cameron's face, perplexed, before suddenly blurting, "Are you a model or something?"

Sherry spun around to look at him. "Right? I told you. If Hollywood ever gets ahold of this one, it'll be a hot minute before he graces our Virginia shores again."

"No, it isn't that. It's just, you look so familiar."

Cameron froze for a split second, then flashed another blinding smile. "I've heard that since I was a kid. Just have one of those generic faces, I guess."

Sherry let out a bubbling laugh. "'One of those generic faces?' Oh, you sweet summer child. If your face were in any way standard, the rate of human scientific accomplishment would slow to a crawl, as no one would ever leave the bedroom." She gestured brightly towards the tables. "Shall we go sit down? I need a glass of wine, an oyster shooter, and a fantastic conversation with my best friend."

Brie allowed herself to be swept along by the group, willfully ignoring the way the marine life followed their party as the hostess guided them to a table on the patio under an ivy-laced arbor lit with little white lights.

"I've been wanting to try this restaurant for months but couldn't talk him into it." Sherry tipped her head towards Mike as he held the chair for her. "More comfortable in a uniform than a suit and tie, I suppose." She playfully grabbed his tie and tilted her head up, pulling him down for an upside-down kiss. "Then, out of the blue, he called yesterday and said he'd made us a reservation."

Cameron and Brie shared a quick look before he pulled out her chair as well.

"What a thoughtful idea," he replied. "It's a shame I didn't think of such a thing myself. Could have scored some big points with this one."

He cocked his head suggestively at Brie, who was gulping down water at an unreasonable rate. Every so often, her eyes would flash to the aquarium, dilated in secret fear.

Mike nodded graciously, settling down, but his eyes kept shooting back to the angel. Perhaps it was the cop in him, maybe it was that handy bit of hypnosis rising back to the surface, but no matter how hard he tried, he was utterly unable to let it go.

"Okay, this is not one of those faces." He kicked back in his chair, only to earn a sharp look from the maître d'. "Are you an actor? Were you ever in a commercial?"

Cameron self-consciously laughed and shook his head. "No, I'm…" He blanked and looked at Brie.

She was hiding behind the wine list, silently willing him to remember: *Weather, sports, hobbies, job. Art if you're stuck.*

"I'm afraid not. No acting skills whatsoever. Not even as a hobby," he concluded with a bashful grin. Then he held up his hand like he was checking for rain and, quite incorrectly, chose to pair this gesture with the comment, "My, isn't it unseasonably warm tonight?"

"It really isn't," Mike murmured. "And I could *swear* I've seen you before." His eyes glazed over, scrolling through a list of possibilities. "Maybe it was something through school…?"

Cameron shifted ever so slightly in his chair but never lost that perpetual calm. "You know what? I was actually thinking the same thing about you." He leaned forward and casually slid Brie's water out of arm's reach. "What do you do for work? Sherry mentioned you're more comfortable in a uniform?"

"I'm an officer with the Yorktown PD. Definitely more comfortable in a uniform. But for Sherry?" Mike pulled in a quick breath, his eyes sweeping the wealthy establishment. "I'm willing to venture out of my comfort zone a bit." He glanced down at the menu, trying and failing to find anything resembling beer. "They're not going to force-feed us frogs or something, are they?"

Sherry touched his arm. "Not unless you catch them yourself, dear."

Brie sank deeper into her chair and stared blankly at the wine list, wondering where in the Virginia State Penal Code it expressly prohibited tampering with the mental faculties of a policeman and what the penalties might be.

I wouldn't be having this problem in Venezuela.

"So, not a model and not an actor." Mike abandoned the menu and turned again to Cameron, steady and unblinking. "What line of work are you in?"

"These days, I'm in private security."

Mike tilted his head curiously. "And before that?"

"I conducted a long-term study about human attitudes regarding thanatological care."

Everyone at the table paused. Brie peeked out over a list of Australian pinots.

Well, that certainly counts as improvisation.

"An academic!" Sherry beamed. "Beauty and brains. Excellent. Now, Mike, stop interrogating the poor man. Shall we get a bottle for the table? And who wants appetizers?"

A waitress appeared, and Sherry ordered their first course. The others busied themselves with their menus, searching for anything that looked familiar in a sea of foreign words. At least, everyone except Mike, who was still studying Cameron's face and not making much effort to hide it.

"Were you writing a book?"

Cameron glanced up, looking slightly caught off guard. "Excuse me?"

"About human attitudes toward thanatological care," Mike clarified. "Was it some private study for a healthcare company? Or were you writing a book? Because that just means, how people feel about those who care for the dying, right?"

Brie looked at him, surprised.

Beauty and brains, indeed.

As inconvenient as it was currently making her life, she had to hand it to Sherry. The girl had wonderfully discerning taste and seemed to have found a kindred soul. Mike was sharp as a tack.

And *impossible* to deter.

Cameron held his gaze for only a moment. "You could call it a private contract. I'm not at liberty to discuss the details. But I have considered writing a book about my findings one day."

Sherry looked back and forth between the men before scolding, "Mike, you promised."

He blinked quickly, roused by the sound of her voice. "You're right. I'm sorry, babe." He turned to Cameron, flashing an apologetic grin. "I have a bad habit of taking work home with me."

"No problem," Cameron said easily. "I have a habit of doing the same."

A strange uncomfortable silence fell over the table. Brie nervously cleared her throat. "So, how did you two meet?" she asked a little too brightly.

Sherry had clearly been waiting for this question. She immediately dropped her menu and placed all ten fingertips on the table in front of her, throwing conspiratorial looks all around.

"It was the sweetest thing. There I was, minding my own business, holding my venti flat white and singing along with Brandi Carlile, when Siri made me turn the wrong way down a one-way street. Obviously, I screamed and dropped my coffee, ruining my favorite suede boots, by the way, when *this* guy," she playfully shoved Mike, "showed up, lights flashing, siren blaring, and had the audacity to try to give me a ticket, when the fault *clearly* lay with my phone."

Brie and Cameron took each other's hands under the table.

"Well, as you can imagine, I was having none of that," Sherry continued reasonably. "I started explaining the situation, and as I did—"

"As you *colorfully* did," interjected Mike.

"—as I did, he started laughing. *Laughing.* At *me.* Can you imagine?"

She waited for them to imagine, then continued at full speed. "So, I yelled at him, explaining the concepts of manners and Southern hospitality. I was just getting to the inestimable loss of one's favorite pair of shoes when he handed back my license and asked me out for a drink."

Mike took her hand affectionately. "What can I say? I was smitten."

Sherry grinned. "What can I say? I love a man with good taste. Plus, the uniform doesn't hurt. Neither do the handcuffs."

The waitress materialized with a bottle of Chablis and a round of oyster shooters. After the pour, everyone raised their glasses as Sherry proposed a toast. "To Brianna and her new chapter. I'm so proud of you, love."

Everyone clinked with a murmured, "To Brianna."

"To Brianna," Cameron echoed softly, locking eyes with her.

They both took a little sip — the first of what would be many, many more to come.

As sweet as the gesture might have been, the upscale restaurant turned out to be a bit of a disaster. The menu was entirely indecipherable for anyone who hadn't spent a significant amount of time living on the opposite side of the Atlantic. Or in a supernatural parallel world.

In an ironic twist of fate, the only member of their party who seemed remotely at ease was the one who had been most concerned about the outing in the first place. Cameron ordered for everyone in perfect French after they pointed and told him their choices, then proceeded to have a brief but apparently charming conversation in the foreign tongue with their waitress, a platinum blonde wearing sky-high heels who laughed as she collected the menus and clicked off to the kitchen.

"Have you spent much time in France?" asked Sherry, clearly impressed.

Cameron glanced up, surprised to see they'd all been watching. Like most things about the entrancing angel, he seemed completely oblivious to his effect on the people around him.

"Not for many years," he replied, taking a sip of his water. "I'm afraid I was quite put off after a particularly rowdy time in Paris."

"Oh yeah?" Mike asked with a faint grin. "What happened?"

Cameron shifted uncomfortably in his seat. "Oh, you know. People just lost their heads."

Brie drained another glass.

It should have been helping, but the more the friends nervously gulped their overpriced wine, the more they began to fidget and stress in their high-backed chairs. And the more they fidgeted, the more they drank.

It was the kind of place that looked great in movies, the kind of place that looked promising when you drove past it on the quaint Virginia road, but in reality, it was so over-the-top pretentious as to make one question why they'd bothered strapping themselves into stilettos in the first place.

Brie stared down at her five dinner forks, feeling rather grim.

"I still don't know what I ordered," Mike whispered to Sherry, reaching for his wine glass, only to realize he'd finished it just a moment before. "Seriously, it could be anything."

"Could you stop worrying?" she hissed back, trying her best to act perfectly at ease, though her elbow kept slipping off the table. "It's going to be fine."

"A good lawman never stops worrying," Cameron interjected with the hint of a Southern twang. "He just learns when to show it and when to keep it to himself."

The rest turned to stare at him.

"It's from one of your old Western films," he said hesitantly. "I thought it might apply."

Brie gave him a hard stare. The wine had taken hold, and she found herself asking, "Did they teach you that in thanatology school?"

He blushed and looked at the table. "Just trying to make conversation."

Mike leaned forward with that dogged curiosity. "What do you mean, one of *your* old Western films?"

Cameron blinked, then gestured to Brie. "She loves them."

She let out a quiet breath, rubbing the sides of her eyes. "I love them."

"She watches them all the time."

"I watch them all the time."

The four of them lapsed into silence until Sherry shot her a sudden look. "You *hate* Westerns."

At that moment, their waitress glided towards them, balancing a silver tray in her emaciated arms. She took one look around the awkward table, then flashed a reptilian smile. "Did someone order the *ris de veau?*"

That accent is completely fake.

"I did." Mike sat forward quickly, pleased that he'd memorized the words for that exact moment. "That was me."

She laid the plate in front of him. "Bon appétit."

Sherry leaned over with a dubious expression, giving it a delicate sniff. "What is that, exactly?"

Brie glanced over as well while Cameron appeared to be stifling his amusement.

"It's sweetbread," Mike said quickly, latching onto the tiny English translation some other flailing American patron had scribbled onto the side of the menu. "It's just… bread?"

Doesn't look like it.

"Doesn't look like it," Sherry echoed Brie's thoughts, lifting her eyes to the waitress. "Excuse me, miss. Do you happen to know what that is?"

The woman flashed it a cursory glance. "It's sweetbread," she answered as if they hadn't been saying it all along. "Our chef breads and pan sears the thymus gland of a lamb, then serves it with a lovely assortment of vegetables and cheeses inside the stomach lining of a baby cow." She adjusted the angle of her silver tray. "Who ordered the rabbit?"

The friends stared back in silence. They stared at the plate.

Then they got up in unison, left a stack of cash on the table, and fled the restaurant.

CHAPTER TEN

A Cheeseburger Fit for The Gods

"This is a little more my speed."

Dave's Bar & Grill was a well-lit, old-time establishment that believed the secret to a successful business was no secret at all. Give the customers what they want. Dave's customers wanted good beer, good burgers, and a good time with their friends. His restaurant was designed to deliver precisely that.

Mike grinned as a dart zinged past him through the air, burying itself dead center in the target on the opposite wall. This was met with a chorus of applause and shouts of approval from a bevy of onlookers. Cameron blushed shyly, ill-used to this amount of attention and praise. He clinked his bottle against Mike's when it was offered, and the two enjoyed a cold swig of IPA.

After his first beer, Cameron had managed to stop grimacing every time he forced himself to swallow. After his third, he'd begun to loosen up.

"So, who taught you?" Mike asked, unbuttoning the high collar on his shirt and loosening his tie so it dangled on both sides of his neck. "Or were you just born with natural ability?"

"My father taught me," Cameron replied without hesitation,

copying Mike and adjusting his clothes. "He threw spears with me every afternoon when I was growing up. I suppose it's more or less the same concept. Balance, precision... centering one's focus to avoid losing a limb."

Mike's eyebrows shot up. "Spears, huh? Was he some sort of survivalist? Or like a martial arts master?"

"No, just a kindhearted man who wanted to indulge my childhood fantasies." Cameron turned the dart over in his hands, remembering. "I wanted to be a great warrior."

"Bruce Lee?"

"The archangel Michael."

Mike's beer paused on its way to his lips before he gave a thoughtful nod. "Yeah, okay, I can see it."

Cameron let another dart fly, again hitting dead center, again meeting with a cheer from the growing crowd of onlookers.

"You know, if you have half as much talent with a ball, you should come to our next soccer practice. We're a man down since James broke his arm." Mike flashed him a grin. "Or do you call it football? You look like you might be one of those people."

Cameron hesitated but couldn't help but feel supremely touched. "I've never played organized sports before, but I would be honored to try." Bolstered by this success, he decided to push his luck. "How about that game last night?"

"What game was that?"

The angel froze in a moment of panic before lowering his eyes to the floor. "Checkers."

Mike let out a howl of laughter as he took the darts from his companion's hand. For all his earlier suspicion, he was clearly growing to like the dart-wielding angel.

The ladies, meanwhile, were leaning tipsily against one another at the bar, absurdly overdressed for the venue in a tangle of black silk and sapphire satin. After a couple of perilous rounds of darts, in which Sherry very nearly blinded two people and Brie broke a clock, they'd decided this was a game for lesser beings. Instead of attempting it further, they were waiting for their next round and talking conspiratorially about their respective escorts.

"—It wasn't until he turned around that I developed a full appreciation for the uniform."

Brie snorted some IPA into her sinuses, trying not to laugh. "I would've paid good money to see you shouting at him about your shoes while he tried to give you a ticket," she said, having no trouble imagining the scenario to perfection. "I can't believe you never told me he's a cop! I would've… I would've checked my brake lights."

Sherry threw back her head, laughing. "Yeah, I'm super guilty of withholding major life developments, Brie, and I feel horrible about it."

"Fair enough."

Brie grinned but felt the sting of truth in Sherry's words. "I'm sorry I didn't tell you about Cameron right away." The two looked over to see the men laughing and talking together like old friends. "I didn't know what to say. He's a little hard to explain. The whole thing is hard to explain."

Sherry shot her an appraising look. "I get that. It's all happening fast, Brie. *Very* fast. How are things going with him?"

Brie contemplated with a little frown, swirling her beer in slow circles. "I think things are going well. Honestly, it's been a bit of a whirlwind, and I haven't had a chance to slow down and process things, you know?"

Sherry nodded thoughtfully, swirling a drink of her own. "Well, I understand why you'd get swept up in the romance of it all. He's very dreamy."

It was a hard point to refute.

The angel stood a head taller than nearly everyone around him, emanating a radiance so out of place in the little dive bar that it was well and truly absurd.

"I mean, it's like somebody gift-wrapped a fantasy and dropped him right into your lap," Sherry mused. "But I have to ask — and tell me if I'm out of line here — how much do you actually know about him? He seems nice, don't get me wrong. But he's also a little..."

In a rather odd bit of timing, Cameron found himself swept away in the general spirit of the place and started singing a sea shanty that likely hadn't been heard since the 1800s.

At first, his fellow patrons looked at each other in acute embarrassment, wondering if someone should do the responsible thing and confiscate his keys. Still, by his second time through the chorus, they'd all hoisted their drinks aloft and joined in, stomping their feet on the ground in rhythm and chanting about "bully boys," whatever those were. The song seemed to speak to some primordial part of Mike's Irish roots. He was sloshing a tankard of beer around like he was on a pirate ship, singing at the top of his lungs and having the time of his life.

Between the wine at The Grey Duck and the multiple sidecars and beers the bartender had supplied, the girlfriends were in no condition to process the scene. They merely laughed with the rest, holding onto the counter for balance, tears running down the sides of their faces.

When at last they quieted down, Brie turned to Sherry, a flush of color still splashed across her cheeks. "Not enough, Sher. I don't know him nearly well enough. But I'm working on it."

Sherry dabbed at her eyeliner, still grinning from ear to ear. "I'll say this for him, Brie. The man knows how to turn a party. I'm going to find Mike and grab us a seat. Who gave him that glass, anyway? He's going to put someone's eye out."

Sherry went to search for her boyfriend as the bar patrons broke into a round of cheers as the song ended. Many made their way back to the bar, where Brie had climbed precariously onto one of the stools and was spinning herself happily back and forth.

One of the customers jostled against her, nearly tipping her off her seat. "Oops, sorry. Oh, *hello* there."

The intoxicated man attempted to right himself, but ended up leaning heavily on the bar, well inside her personal space. He inhaled and ran a hand through his hair, looking at her hungrily. "Hav' you ever been arrested?"

She blinked in surprise, trying to keep him in focus. "Excuse me?"

"Have you ever been arrested?" he repeated. "Because it must've hurt when you fell from the sky." He stopped and squinted, vaguely aware he'd made a mistake. "From Heaven," he amended, nodding with satisfaction.

She gave him a pitying look. "Okay, buddy. I think you've had a few too many. This?" She drew a circle in the air with her finger, indicating the two of them. "This isn't going to happen. Go back to your friends."

She'd already turned her attention to the bar when he grabbed her by the shoulder and tried to spin her around. "Hey, wait a minute. You didn't tell me your name."

She wasn't exactly in fighting form, but she was having none of this. "Don't touch me."

He put his hand on her arm again. "I jus' wanna—"

There was a streak of color, and a chocolate curl blew back from her face.

Just like that, Cameron was standing in between them. His face was calm, but his eyes were all kinds of angry, focusing on the man in a way that suddenly reminded Brie he was able to shoot lightning bolts from his hands. "The lady told you not to touch her."

The drunk leaned back, half-convinced he must be dreaming. "Whoa, whoa! I was jus' trying to—"

"Don't." Cameron leaned ever so slightly closer, simmering with a quiet rage. "I want you to listen to me very carefully, Mr. Pratchett. Mr. Jason Pratchett."

He leaned closer still and whispered something unintelligible in the man's ear.

Jason Pratchett started to tremble uncontrollably. He dropped his beer and practically ran to the bathroom, looking like he was going to be sick. In a strange way, it reminded Brie of the way Denise had inexplicably calmed her raging patient, silencing him with a few memorable words.

"What did you say to him?"

Those piercing eyes flashed her way, then gentled immediately upon seeing her. A moment later, they were the same as always, twinkling down at her with a mischievous look. "A gentleman never tells."

"Oh, come on. Tell me."

"Guilt is a powerful emotion to prey upon," he answered vaguely. "And the guy looked like the type to have something on his conscience."

She considered this a drunken moment, before gazing up at him once more.

"That's smart," she mused, trying not to slur. "You're smart, you know that? And you're adorable. And… and I liked that song you sang about the fishes."

He raised an eyebrow, glancing at the bottle. "How many of those have you had?"

"Just a few. And a sidecar. Two sidecars. Do two sidecars make a whole car?" Her eyes widened. "Did I drink a car?"

"Okay. Let's get you home."

"No, wait! We can't!"

"Why, what's happening?"

"The burgers. We can't just leave them!" She spun her chair around and flung her arm dramatically towards the kitchen, endangering all the glassware in her radius, just as a waiter brought out a tray with four plates heaped with burgers, fries, and onion rings.

The angel watched her for a moment, then spun the barstool back around, so she faced him. Her cheeks were pink with liquor and flushed a shade deeper as he brushed a strand of hair out of her eyes.

"You know what, Ms. Weldon? You are utterly ridiculous."

She grinned and touched her forehead to his. "I know."

He helped her down from her perch on the barstool, and they made their way over to the booth Mike and Sherry had commandeered. The waiter placed their meals before them, then went back for Cokes.

"And several tall glasses of water," added Cameron.

"And a root beer," added Sherry.

Brie whirled around in a sudden panic. "Cam," she said with hushed urgency, "I didn't even think to ask. I mean, I had no idea what the food was at the last place anyway, but are you going to be able to eat something like this? Not like… not like a plant eats sunlight?"

Sherry gave him a strange look.

"Honey, are you a vegetarian? Why didn't you say something?"

"No, I'm not," he assured everyone quickly. "This looks delicious." With a discreet squeeze to her palm, he lowered Brie's blood alcohol level by half. "This has all been a little fast," he added. "I suppose we forewent some of the more traditional get to know you exchanges. I'm definitely not a vegetarian."

Mike stared in silence. "Did you just say 'forewent?'"

Sherry's moan of pleasure cut through all other conversation. The others looked at her curiously, and she closed her eyes in blithe rapture. "I'm eloping with this burger. Sorry, dear."

Mike grinned and tucked in himself.

Brie nibbled a fry and watched her angel with intense curiosity, eager to know how the next moments might unfold. With a look that bordered on martyrdom, he picked up his burger as though this was a dreaded test he had to pass and adjusted his posture to resemble Mike's — elbows just off the table, leaning slightly forward, ignoring the sauce that dripped steadily onto the plate.

There was a suspended moment, and with a scrunched-up nose, he took a tentative bite.

It was like watching a man's world change from black and white to vivid color. His eyes grew wide as saucers. He took a deep, quaking breath that seemed to shiver its way through him, head to toe and straight to the core of his being. He closed his eyes and chewed in a state of bliss, completely unaware that he was making some truly obscene noises. Sherry stopped in the middle of an anecdote, and the rest of the table paused, looked at each other, and simply lowered their own food to watch as he took another bite, then another. He inhaled the entire thing in about ten seconds, moaning scandalously the entire time, not looking around him for a moment until it was gone. Then he looked up, breathing hard.

Without warning, he hit the table with his palm, making everyone jump, and pronounced with a level of gravitas that had no place in Dave's Bar & Grill, "That was the most gratifying thing I have ever experienced."

A titter of amusement went through the neighboring tables.

His own companions hadn't yet recovered enough to do anything but stare.

"Garçon!" Cameron bellowed, making everyone jump again, including the unsuspecting college student who was waiting their table that night.

The waiter came straight over and pulled out his pen and order pad. If he'd learned anything during his time at Dave's Bar & Grill, it was to keep the drunks satiated and not be visibly thrown by their theatrics for any reason, no matter how ridiculous. "What can I get you, sir?"

"We require more of these delectable burgers. Mike, will you have another?" Mike opened his mouth, but Cameron didn't wait for a response. "At least three more. With more of the..." He turned to the table. "What is the orange square?"

Brie was frozen in shock, so Sherry answered with a baffled, "Cheddar?"

"Cheddar!" Cameron's eyes danced in wild delight. "My good man, if it does not inconvenience the chef, would you please ask him to add extra cheddar to the burgers? And do pass on my compliments. What he has done here," he gestured to the food as his eyes welled up with unshed tears, "transcends the realm of sustenance. Tell him he is an artist, and the world will surely take note."

The waiter stared blankly for a moment before deciding that he'd seen worse. "Three burgers, extra cheese."

"And my most sincere compliments to the—"

"And I'll tell Frank you're a fan." The waiter walked off to the kitchen, shaking his head.

Mike let out a whooping laugh the second he was gone, clapping Cameron on the shoulder. "You are such a weirdo. I love it. Full on *When Harry Met Sally*, right in the middle of the local dive. Really humanizes you and makes up for the whole Ken doll thing." He flashed a drunken grin, talking around a French fry as he kicked back and gave Cameron a thoughtful look. "So, I have a guess. Your parents were super religious, right?"

Cameron snapped out of his food frenzy and froze. "How did you...?"

Mike nodded as though this was all the confirmation he needed.

"You wanted to be the archangel Michael when you were a kid, you always talk like you're in church or an eighteenth-century novel, you've clearly never had a beer or a burger before, and the fact that Hollywood hasn't poached you yet means you must have been hiding out in Amish country because I don't see how else they might have missed you."

Brie glanced up in confusion. "Wait, who's Michael, and why did you want to be him?"

"This isn't the time, Brie." Mike grinned. "Cam here needs to try a French fry."

Cameron spent the next hour indulging in a feast of culinary delights.

Brie spent the time re-upping her blood alcohol level.

After three more burgers for Cameron and another for Mike, a small mountain of fries, some wide-eyed rapture when introduced to the concept of a root beer float, and one trip to the kitchen during which Cameron admiringly shook Frank's hand and told him that he was "doing God's work, and I should know," the friends decided to take a rideshare service home and fetch their cars in the morning.

"Don't forget, man." Mike pointed to Cameron as they pulled up to Brie's new house. "This Sunday. Do not bail on me. And do not be late."

"This Sunday," Cameron echoed obediently. "I will play all your sports."

"Well, *that* promises to be entertaining." Sherry giggled in the back seat, scooting aside as Mike climbed back in beside her. "See you tomorrow, love!"

The car shot off down the street, leaving Brie and Cameron on the sidewalk. They started heading slowly toward the house. It was quiet now, much quieter than the constant clamor of the bar. After a few seconds, he cast her a shy look. "What did you think?"

She considered a moment, then beamed at him. "I think it was a *massive* success."

He chuckled under his breath as she spun around to face him. "And *you*. You, my book writing, burger devouring thanatologist," she giggled at her own cleverness, impressed she'd remembered the word, "*you* were wonderful."

His cheeks colored with a rare blush. "Only because I had an excellent teacher to explain the finer points of human idiosyncrasies before we left."

She grinned in return. "I am rather splendid, aren't I?"

"You certainly are."

She leaned abruptly closer, trying to keep her composure, darting quick glances at his lips. It had been a long time since she'd been in this position. The barrel of alcohol didn't help. "You really think so?"

He glanced down in surprise, reaching out to steady her. "I really do."

It was quiet for a moment as she studied him in the moonlight. He was all sunlit haloes in the daytime, but the moon had a different effect, making him quiet and silver, like a shimmering reflection. One that drew her ever closer. One that she was aching to reach out and touch.

"Do you know what else I think?"

He tensed ever so slightly, still holding onto her arms. "What's that?"

She stretched onto her toes so the warmth of her breath feathered his cheek. A hypnotic spell overcame both of them, vanishing the surrounding scenery, as she whispered into his ear, "I think you're very… very…"

That's when she blacked out.

CHAPTER ELEVEN

Nightmare in Reverse

The forest was dark and misty. Not a warm dark, typical of a Virginia summer — a cold, biting, horrible dark, in which tree branches loom, and every little sound makes your heart run like a rabbit from a fox.

The shaggy-haired man strode through the woods as though this didn't affect him. He was wearing a tattered shirt and pants, no shoes. Brie couldn't see his face. She kept trying to turn and run the other way, but her body followed him like a balloon tied to his belt loop, pulled against her will, tethered by an unseen force.

Where are we going?

She became aware of movement skittering around them in the woods. She couldn't scream, couldn't struggle. She could only float, watch, and be pulled wherever the man took her.

They reached a clearing in the trees. In the middle stood a black goat with stained, silver horns which gleamed menacingly in the moonlight. Brie shuddered to think how they came to be stained.

"Is this it?" the man asked.

"This is the place." The goat seemed to speak inside her mind, purring the words in a low, skin-crawling voice.

Brie tried again to free herself or even move, but to no avail. When the goat turned and led them to a road, she suddenly realized where they were and struggled even harder.

But she was paralyzed.

The man knelt and placed his hand on the ground, pulling in a deep breath.

Suddenly, the sun was rising from the west.

Then it was noon. Then morning. Cars zipped past them in reverse. Birds flew backward through the sky. An eagle released a squirrel into a tree, and all its blood flowed back into its veins.

Back and back, the sun went, further and further, for three days, until it was Brie's car on the road. Brie's car, completely whole and standing next to Cameron, right before it was ripped apart into a million pieces and left in the road as he disappeared with a flash.

The man rewound time and played this scene several times before going back even further. Cameron walked backward from the horizon, holding her in his arms, and placed her on the ground before putting her backpack near the flaming wreckage. The explosion was an implosion. The car roof stabilized. They spoke for a moment. She pulled a punch out of his face.

The blonde man chuckled hard at that, re-watching it several times before moving on.

Cameron placed her upside-down in her car.

Then he was walking backward through a sea of shadowy monsters, balls of light streaking from their chests into his hand before he disappeared entirely, and the monsters all stood up and flew backward into her car, seemingly repairing it as they went. One put the ripped-up trunk back on its hinge and flew in reverse into nothingness as the others followed suit.

Finally, her car was whole, intact, and driving backward. That's when it happened. Like a crack in the universe itself, a light suddenly obliterated everything else from view. It flashed for a second and was gone.

The shaggy-haired man rewound and watched this scene so many times Brie's eyes burned, and colors flashed across her retinas as though she'd stared too long at the sun.

The goat walked right past her and stood next to the man. "We have a problem."

"I can see that." The man seemed to pause, then took in a heavy breath. "I need to speak with my father."

The goat nodded. "It will be arranged."

The skittering noises in the woods grew louder and louder. Brie struggled harder and harder to get away as dozens of giant spiders with faces like men poured out of the tree line and swarmed around the goat. She sucked in a breath, trying to scream.

The goat turned slightly. "We are observed."

Just as the man was about to turn around, Brie woke up in a cold sweat, hyperventilating and screaming for Cameron.

It was four in the morning. The horror of her nightmare had wholly erased all the freedom and fun of the previous evening's escapades. There was mascara smeared under her eyes, her hair was disheveled, and she had a generally hollow look about her like she hadn't slept in days.

Cameron kept making her tea. None of the cups he brought her tasted remotely like tea. They all tasted like fruits, flowers, or medicines. This one to calm her nerves, that one for a sense of well-being, another for her headache. He'd even prepared a brew made of some of his fabled basil root for her blood pressure.

She drank whatever he put in front of her. She didn't care anymore.

I am being hunted. And whoever it is, is on the right track.

The knowledge turned in her mind over and over again.

The only weapon in her entire arsenal was what? Invisibility? How would that help her when the forces tracking her down found out who she was in waking life? How would that help her when they knew her address? When they knew the names of her friends and family?

She didn't think that giant anthropomorphic spiders and an evil black goat would be above using her loved ones against her. Let alone an evil blonde man who could apparently bend time.

The people she loved weren't safe because of her. No. Not because of her. Because of *it*.

She looked down at the pendant with pure, seething resentment, feeling the familiar weight of it against her chest. A second later, she plucked up the teardrop between her fingers, twisting it this way and that, looking at the strange reflections within the gold casing.

I never asked for this.

Cameron placed another steaming mug of boiled roots and leaves in front of her, but this time, she pushed it away.

"It's for your—"

"I can't, Cameron."

He nodded and moved to take the cup away.

"No," she grabbed his arm and looked desperately into his eyes. "I mean, I *can't.*"

He regarded her for a moment, then sat back down.

"I can't do this. I'm not this person." She shook her head slowly, building up steam. "I'm not cut out for adventure, and danger, and magical freaking necklaces. I *can't* do it. Whatever these people want from me, if I just let them have it, maybe they'll leave me alone."

Cameron was silent.

"If I just take off the pendant and let them find me—"

"You can't do that, Brianna."

"But what if I—"

"They will kill you immediately and take it for themselves," he interrupted shortly, leaving no room for interpretation. "The darkness is merciless, Brianna. It does not know any light. It knows no grace, no love, no joy, no hope. It knows only fear and despair."

"But maybe if—"

"They will kill you *exactly* like they killed your mother."

She stared at him, shocked. The image of a shadowy beast with its claws inside her mother's chest flooded her mind for a moment, and she lost all ability to respond.

"I'm sorry to put it so bluntly," he murmured, bowing his head. "Cruelly, even. But you need to know what you're up against." He sighed and brought a hand to his forehead, rubbing the faint crease between his eyes. "This is my fault. Unpacking boxes and going out to dinner… I should have immediately gone to ask our wise ones about your predicament. But I'm afraid to leave you alone."

She slammed her hands on the table, startling him. "How am I supposed to live like that? Babysat by a divine bodyguard my entire life? Hunted by monsters? Me and all my loved ones under the gun? Why? For what? What did I ever do to deserve this? What did my mother ever do to deserve this? Am I cursed? What did I do?"

Unable to hold it in anymore, she leaped from the table and started pacing. It was probably when a normal person would burst into tears. Her body wanted to, was dying to, but she couldn't.

She never could.

"What did you mean, you were already there?"

Cameron pushed slowly to his feet. "I'm sorry?"

She stopped her manic pacing, staring from the middle of the floor.

"In the woods," she said sharply. "I'd be dead if you hadn't shown up, and this would have already been decided. You said the demons couldn't track me."

"They can't—"

"But they are. They're hunting me, Cameron. They were swarming all over the exact place they had attacked me before. They could be on their way here right now for all we know." She took a step towards him. "You said you only found me because you were already there." She stepped closer, her voice dangerously low. "Why were you already there, Cameron?"

He sucked in a breath. "I was just…" He trailed off, shaking his head. "Brianna, there are things I can't—"

"Answer me," she shouted. "I'm tired of being kept in the dark!"

He stared in helpless silence.

"Answer me, or I'm taking this off." She gripped her pendant in her fist, raising it threateningly. "No more games, no more deflections. I'll throw it right down on the floor."

"Brianna!"

"Tell me, Cameron."

"I was already there because I was always there!"

She stopped cold. "What does that mean?"

He sank back to the table in defeat, letting his face drop into his hands. For a few seconds, she didn't think he would answer. Then, he let out a quiet breath.

"I've been checking on you every night since we first met," he said miserably. "Every single night for the past five years. I've been there."

A ringing silence fell between them, punctuated only by the steady ticking from the clock on the wall.

"I didn't know what else to do," he murmured, staring unblinkingly at the floor. "You'd just lost your mother, and you were so alone, and I couldn't see your life. I couldn't see your energy, couldn't find you if I lost you. So, if I ever left, I wouldn't know if you were okay."

A minute passed. Then another.

"You were with me?" she repeated, unable to process it.

He nodded, hanging his head like the world was coming to an end.

"It wasn't allowed, of course," he continued quietly, "and of course, you weren't supposed to see me, which you *can* for reasons I still don't understand… so, I could only linger at night. But sometimes, I managed to check on you during the day as well."

A single word stood out above the rest.

"It wasn't *allowed*?" she asked.

He shook his head. "We aren't supposed to interact with humans except to ease their suffering at the end. If my father knew what I've been doing…" His face tightened before crumbling in remorse. "Though I suppose he'll have to find out."

He pulled in another breath, forcing himself to meet her gaze. "The light you shone has left an imprint on everything around it. An imprint that my kind can see. Any one of my kind, or any darker being for that matter, could have found the place where you took off your necklace. They would simply have to follow the traces to the epicenter — like finding a meteor in the center of its crater. But they can't see you, Brianna. They can't track you. *I* can't track you. If you were ever lost to me… I'm afraid you would be lost forever."

He opened his mouth to continue before letting out a tired sigh. "The other night, you weren't in your apartment, and all your things were gone. I was frantic to find you. Thank goodness you were at your father's. I heard you talking, heard that you were moving away. I knew I had to come with you, or I might not be able to find you again, and if any harm were to befall you, I might be too late." He stared at the table. "I took on another form and came with you. I invaded your space. I invaded your privacy. I hid. I skulked in the shadows like a common criminal. And if it is any consolation, I doubt I will ever forgive myself."

His face twisted in pain as he looked at her once again. "Brianna... I am so very sorry. I can't even imagine what you must be thinking."

That's kind of a mystery to me as well.

She slowly shook her head. "Let me get this straight. While I was coming apart at the seams, while my father abandoned me for the bottle, while I went through hours and days and weeks and years of therapy, while I held myself together with nothing but my own arms..."

He bowed his head in shame. "Brianna, I—"

"You came to check on me every night, in defiance of the laws of your people, to make sure I was alright? Every night? For five years?"

He lifted his eyes uncertainly. "Yes."

"And you transformed, stowed away in my car just to stay with me? To protect me when I moved away? That's why you were in the woods? That's why you were there in time to save me?"

He nodded silently, beyond feelings language could express.

She was quiet for a moment. "Show me."

"What?"

"Show me. Show me how you transform."

He hesitated a moment, then looked at her face. Their eyes locked as he took a deep breath and started to glow, just as he had that morning in the motel, the morning she looked for his wings. As though he was lit from within by a miniature sun, he grew brighter and brighter, almost painfully bright, almost burning her eyes. At last, the Cameron she knew disappeared, and a translucent, golden-haloed orb, no bigger than the palm of her hand, floated into the air before her.

The world tilted suddenly, and she realized she'd forgotten to breathe. The orb floated closer, coming to a stop inches from her face. She lifted a hand to touch it — to touch him.

She was afraid he wouldn't let her. But, of course, he did.

The second the tips of her fingers grazed that light, she was immediately flooded with a sense of relief, well-being, and warmth. She moved to touch him with her other hand, but he floated gently backward, and in a golden flash, Cameron stood before her once again.

They stood in silence for what felt like a very long time.

"Every night?" she finally murmured. "For five years?"

"Yes," he whispered, like a man awaiting a judge's sentence.

Her throat was so choked up she could barely speak. Her body was thrumming with such uncontainable emotion it felt as though she might explode. Finally, she lifted her eyes to meet his. "Thank you."

His lips parted with a silent breath before curving into an expression of radiant relief. "You're welcome."

Fifteen minutes later, Brie and Cameron were sitting quietly with their backs against her bookshelves. This time it wasn't an agonized, frantic silence in which she stood convinced that a dark army was going to hunt her down and annihilate her family and friends. This was a hush of relief, a respite from all the high tension and emotion of the past hour.

They sipped their tea.

When the stillness finally broke, it was with the unlikeliest of questions. "Do you have any idea why I was trapped in my bathtub on my last night in my apartment?"

He shot her a confused look. "You were what?"

"Trapped in my bathtub. I was under the water. I took the pendant off, just for a moment, and I got trapped inside the water until I put it back on." Cameron stared at her, shocked, as she went on. "Why couldn't you and... and all of the other creatures see my light when I took it off that time?"

A look of sudden comprehension dawned across his features, followed by a deep blush. "After what happened with your mother, I put certain measures in place to try to protect you, at least when you were at home. When you moved to your apartment, I did the same thing."

Brie frowned. "What sort of measures?"

Cameron sighed and raked his hand back through his hair. "Anything I could think of, so long as it wouldn't be noticed. Runes of protection around the perimeter. A blessing over every doorway and window. And... I may have gotten someone to bless all your water pipes."

"Excuse me?"

"I got someone to bless your water pipes. You've been drinking and bathing in holy water for the past five years. Your dad, too.

That's probably what protected you in the bathtub. You were completely submerged in holy water, and it wouldn't let the darkness see your light."

She leaned back against the bookshelves, processing. "I suppose that's why the roses grew so well even though we never took care of them. Who did you get to bless the pipes?"

He sighed and looked at the floor. "Saint Peter."

"Ah."

They were quiet a moment longer before Brie decided to change the subject as fast as possible.

"Do you have a man-date to play sports this Sunday?"

He looked at her in surprise. "I do. I wasn't sure you were coherent enough to register that as we were leaving. You were a little intoxicated."

She gave a rueful grin. "I was pretty tipsy. But I remember."

"Mike asked if I wanted to join him and his friends. If it's a problem, I don't need to go—"

"It isn't a problem."

The two of them sat there a while longer, listening to the wind stir the branches outside before Brie looked down and traced the lines of the marble with her finger.

"You know," she began cautiously, "I wasn't the only one drinking last night."

He threw her a quick glance but didn't reply.

"Do you remember…?" She trailed off, wondering how to finish that sentence, wondering if she even wanted to finish that sentence. "There was this moment at the end when—"

He pushed suddenly to his feet. "The end of the night is actually kind of a blur," he said shortly, taking great pains to avoid her eyes. "Must have been the beer. Mike was right. I'd never tried it."

She went rigid as a statue, feeling like she'd been stung.

All those "restful vibes" flew right out the window. Her cheeks flamed, and that feeling of serenity vanished on the spot. She was still sitting there when he offered down a hand.

"Yeah," she stammered as she stood, unable to look at him, "it's a blur."

They threw each other a quick look, then both spoke at once.

"Well, I should really—"

"I suppose you should get some—"

"Sleep, yes." She nodded much too fast.

"Yes, exactly. I mean, you have work in the morning." His nods were no better.

"Right, so I'll just—"

"Yes, of course, you should."

Feeling abruptly ridiculous, both of them turned in perfect unison and headed in opposite directions. That might have been the end of it. She was perfectly content to either pretend it never happened or simply set herself on fire — however the mood struck.

But she found herself pausing at the base of the stairs, throwing a glance over her shoulder. "Goodnight, Cameron."

He answered without turning, still staring at the wall. "Goodnight, Brianna."

She didn't see the way his eyes snapped shut the second she walked away. She didn't see the way he pressed his fists to his eyes and screamed a silent profanity at the wall.

She never saw. He always made sure of that.

CHAPTER TWELVE

The Kitchen's on Fire

The next morning, the tension in the house was palpable.

Brie felt it from the moment she woke up, like electricity, filling the air in her new little home with a low, thrumming buzz. She hadn't even blinked twice before the memory hit her like a wave of social nausea, and her stomach leaped up into her throat.

I was trying to hit on him.

Her eyes snapped shut.

And he pretended like it never happened.

She groaned and flung her arm over her face as though she could somehow shield herself from the embarrassment that threatened to swallow her whole. It wasn't like her to make the first move to begin with. Historically speaking, she was used to being pursued, yet uninterested. The fact that she'd broken that pattern by trying to casually start things with her guardian angel? Mortifying.

Do NOT think about this now. Get ready for work.

She heard a clang of pots and pans but took ages to get ready, nervous to join him in the kitchen. She brushed her hair far too long, and her curls went from voluminous to positively unmanageable. She tried to undo the damage but was eventually forced to wrestle it all up into a messy bun. She stabbed herself twice in the eye with a mascara wand and lost her favorite lip gloss down a heating vent because her hands were trembling. In the end, she gave herself a despairing look in the mirror, took a deep breath, and told herself it would be alright.

Sherry says I look cute in scrubs. What does she call it? An irresistible disaster.

I need to work on my pep talks.

En route to the kitchen, she smelled an odor of things that ought not to have been cooked.

"Good morning," she said with a forced brightness as she walked inside before halting in her tracks. "Sweet pole-vaulting Jesus, what happened here?"

Cameron had responded to his own tension by attempting to make her an omelet, a task that appeared to be woefully beyond his skill set. He also seemed to have pan-fried her phone.

"He prefers water sports to track and field," he answered, hanging his head in frustration while trying to coax a dreary goo of eggs and former vegetables into the correct shape. "But He has a real advantage there, and nobody likes to race Him anymore."

She stared at the back of his head. "Who?"

"You know. Jesus."

She decided to ignore this. "Did you get into an argument with Siri again?"

"That venomous harpy has it in for me," he muttered.

"What was that?"

"Nothing."

"You battered my smartphone?"

His lips quirked up in a vengeful grin. "Not so terribly smart now, is it?"

She took a breath for patience. *"Battered*, Cameron."

"Nonsense. I didn't hit it once."

He shifted awkwardly, wiping his hands on a lacy, floral-print apron she'd never seen before. It looked suspiciously like the one the sweet old lady wore on those YouTube cooking tutorials to which he was becoming increasingly, begrudgingly addicted.

"Would you like some coffee?"

A deflection, if ever I saw.

"Sure, thank you."

They bumped into one another when they tried to grab the same mug and flushed identical shades of deep red. Then their hands touched while reaching for the sugar, and her temperature rose ten degrees. Eventually, he retreated to the opposite side of the kitchen, averting his eyes and taking several deep breaths before finally permitting himself to speak.

"I wanted you to have a good breakfast," he began hesitantly, "because I have something rather serious to talk to you about."

She immediately choked on her coffee, scalding the back of her throat. An overwhelming impulse came over her to run fast and run far. But she couldn't bring herself to leave the caffeine behind. No matter how much it ended up costing her.

"Yeah, sure. Whatever you—"

"I think I should go home and tell my father about your situation."

She went perfectly blank. "Oh."

Original, pithy, articulate. Try saying "Oh" more often, Brie. It makes you sound like a real catch.

"You deserve answers," he continued slowly. "Last night showed me that I was being selfish, staying here by your side. In trying to protect you, I may actually be compromising your safety by keeping us both in the dark." He nodded at her pendant. "This is too powerful for guessing games. We need to know what's going on." His eyes lifted cautiously to hers. "Do you understand?"

She hesitated a second, then nodded too fast for it to pass as a natural gesture. "Yes, of course. I understand."

He returned his attention to the stove, prodding at whatever miserable substance was slowly adhering itself to the pan. She traced circles around the rim of her coffee cup, thinking of Venezuela and wondering how close she might get to its borders without the navigational assistance of her phone.

She pushed abruptly to her feet when the silence reached a breaking point. "I should probably—"

"Such a thing is not permitted."

She froze dead still as he turned slowly from the oven, staring with wide, luminous eyes as the pan on the stovetop caught fire behind him.

"There are laws where I come from," he continued quietly. "Heavenly edicts that no one can disobey. Believe me when I tell you there are times that I want to. Believe me when I tell you that my personal feelings on the matter have absolutely no bearing on the way things have to be."

She lowered her eyes to the floor, feeling like she'd been slapped across the face. A vague part of her understood it was beyond her comprehension. Another part understood it was beyond his control. But neither was a part she would ever allow him to see.

"Of course," she answered softly. "I was drunk. It didn't mean anything."

His eyes tightened, and he took a step closer. "It meant something to—"

The doorbell rang.

Finally, some beneficial cosmic timing.

She silently composed herself as she made her way to the door, pulling it open with her best approximation of a carefree expression. "Hey, good morning."

"Darling!" Sherry swooped into the room with a tray of coffee to once again supplement the coffee they were already having in lieu of breakfast. "Other darling!" She greeted Cameron with air kisses and a pantomime hug as her hands were full. "He's been promoted to darling," she told Brie, handing off a mocha.

Brie took a deep breath, forcing herself past it. "Whatever did he do to deserve such an honor?"

"You mean besides winning the Dartiest Dart Who Ever Darted award at the bar and inflating that poor cook's ego to roughly the size of Miami for making a series of extremely standard cheeseburgers? Well, I'll tell you. This little honey of a specimen returned our car this morning before we even woke up, saving myself and Mike a heap of inconvenience."

Sherry shot Cameron a look of grand appreciation and handed over a latte. "Hence, coffee. The elixir of gratitude. May the heavens ever smile upon you."

He accepted it. "And also on you."

Their cups knocked lightly together.

"Cheers," Sherry said brightly. "Your kitchen is on fire, by the way."

He turned back to the stove with a muffled gasp, first raising his palms to the flames before realizing that whatever he'd planned to do would not be possible in Sherry's presence. Instead, he slapped at the fire with the edge of a dish towel.

Brie wandered up beside him, ironically finding this to be the most normal part of her day. "When did you get the cars?"

"Oh, you were asleep," he admitted, tossing the towel in the sink. She raised an eyebrow, thinking of her own magically returned car, and the two shared a secret grin.

"Let me be the first to say that's a rather bold apron," Sherry said conversationally, settling herself down at the counter. "If I'd known you had a penchant for... Brie, is that your phone?"

Cameron blanched and swiftly angled his body in front of the pathetic remains. "I had a bit of a mishap. I intend to take care of it while Brianna is at work."

Sherry surveyed the damage dubiously. "Good luck with that, cowboy. Unless you have a spot of magic up your sleeve, I'm afraid that phone is dead."

Brie had focused on a different detail. "So, you'll be here when I get back?"

He softened. "Yes. I shouldn't be long."

Sherry turned, surprised. "Where are you off to?"

"I need to visit my family. We have some important things to discuss."

Sherry's intrigue was piqued, but Brie wasn't ready to field her questions with yet another series of deflections and half-truths. "Sweetie, we really need to get going. If I'm late, I don't think Denise is above skinning me alive to set an example."

"That's a fair point."

Sherry rushed out the door. The other two stood awkwardly in front of each other. At one point, both considered going in for a hug, but in the end, they opted to simply wave an excruciatingly awkward goodbye from two paces apart.

"I'll see you tonight," he said quietly.

Brie nodded and moved to head out the door before turning back for a moment. "Promise me something?"

He glanced up quickly. "Anything."

She held his gaze. "Don't try to cook."

◆ ◆ ◆

"Coming through!"

A nurse with fiery red hair flew past on a gurney pushed by two EMTs, straddling an incoming trauma victim and doing chest compressions. They disappeared into a room just as a mother and her six children walked through the bay doors.

One had a fork sticking out of his upper shoulder. He screamed through his sobs, "Jacob is gonna be so grounded. Grounded forever!" The other kids appeared to be placing bets on the injured child's chances of survival while the poor mom struggled to maintain her grip on sanity. A trio of teenagers followed them, the middle one hobbling with his foot bent at a horrifying angle, flanked and supported by his skateboard-wielding friends.

It was going to be a long day.

Sherry and Brie each took a deep breath before the storm, gave each other a discreet fist bump, and walked off in opposite directions.

Denise was waiting for her by the nurses' station, arms crossed over her chest, back straight as a redwood tree. "You're late."

Brie looked at the clock. "No, I'm—"

"You're on time, which means you're late until your orientation is over. Come with me."

Brie stashed her backpack and followed.

She was starting to recognize some faces from the day before. There was Chris, the newbie who scarcely looked old enough to have his learner's permit, let alone start an IV. Without being told, he made a beeline for the mother of six and started telling the kids a story about his "crazy Aunt Penelope and her runaway cow" so their put-upon mother could complete the intake forms and take

care of her wounded son. Brie caught his eye, and he winked. She
realized with a grin that Aunt Penelope didn't exist. She was just
an imaginative way to show some kindness.

She followed Denise into a room that housed the trio of
skateboarding teenagers.

"Do you have to call my mom?" the injured one asked.

The waiflike nurse from the ambulance code the other day was
already in there, taking a history and fielding the underage dolt's
questions.

Cindy. I think that's her name.

"Yes, Kevin. Otherwise, she might come storming in here with a
slew of very valid questions as to why we performed X-rays, ran lab
tests, and conducted a reconstructive surgery on her underage son
before putting him in a cast and charging her thousands of dollars.
Not to mention, it hasn't escaped my notice that it's a school day,
and you might have somewhere else you're supposed to be."

The three friends glanced at each other and shuffled around,
looking for all the world like toddlers caught with their hands in a
cookie jar.

Cindy leaned closer and narrowed her eyes. "So, are you going
to give me her cell phone number," she asked dangerously, "or
should I just call your school and start from there?"

Kevin unlocked his cell phone and handed it over with a sigh,
wincing in pain as one of his friends accidentally jostled his foot.

Denise observed as Brie took the boy's medical history, a process
that Cindy would repeat with his mother after she arrived. They
scheduled an X-ray and prepped him for the procedure.

When they'd finished and walked back to the nurses' station,
Cindy shot Brie a look and abruptly said, "You were the one who
stood up to Matthews the other day on the code."

Brie looked up, startled. "I wasn't… I was just surprised. I wasn't trying to—"

"I'm glad you said something."

The two women shared a friendly glance and continued walking.

"Where do you stand on Dr. Matthews?" Brie asked hesitantly.

Cindy responded without missing a beat. "On his neck, if at all possible."

Denise snorted with what was presumably a hard laugh and kept walking.

Brie shot Cindy a grin. "Oh, we're going to get along just fine."

"Weldon. With me," barked Denise.

They parted ways with Cindy and stepped into another room. Brie assisted with a chest tube insertion as Denise watched. Despite all the caffeine and sleep deprivation, her hands remained steady. She even earned a curt nod of approval from El Commandant once again.

Twice in two days. Don't get cocky, Brie, but you're doing alright.

By the time her lunch break rolled around, she felt as though she'd run a marathon. Again.

"Can you multitask?" asked Denise, breaking into her thoughts.

"Can I — yes, I can multitask."

"Good. Go get food. Come back here. Eat while working."

Denise whipped out her cell phone and walked off without a backward glance. There was an economy to her every aspect and motion. She didn't mince words. She didn't even mince syllables. Everything about her was an excellent example of competence and efficiency.

Like a perfect machine.

Like the Terminator.

A little shiver raced over Brie's shoulders, but she shook it off before quickly making her way down to the cafeteria. Her job might be a swirling mess of exhaustive chaos with high stakes and no end in sight, but today, she was grateful for the turmoil. It was keeping her mind off Cameron and how his little family reunion might be playing out.

As she worked her way through the line, absentmindedly choosing a salad, vegetable soup, and a lemonade to counterbalance the booze and junk food fest from last night, her mind started running through some unwanted scenarios.

What if he gets in huge trouble for saving me? What would that even look like? Would they excommunicate him, like they do in the Catholic Church? That's a Catholic thing, right? But don't Catholics also have some kind of way to make amends? Like you count prayer beads and say "Our Fathers" and drink Bloody Marys?

Wait, that can't be right...

She paid at the commissary, remembering at the last minute to grab Rashida a chai latte and herself a cappuccino. Then she stopped by the morgue on her way back up to Denise.

Rashida opened the door on the second knock.

"As promised." Brie held out the chai.

"Thank you!" the woman accepted happily. "No handsome escort today?"

"Not today, I'm afraid," Brie replied, "and I can't stay. Denise has me multitasking."

"Ah, I see. Well, if you want to come here after your shift to chart and hang out, just let me know. I'll be around. I have a bunch of cases to catch up on myself."

"Oh, no. Busy day down here?"

"Bizarre. I'll tell you later. You'd better get back to El Commandant before she—"

"Skins me alive to make an example of me?"

"Precisely."

Brie grinned and started back towards the elevator. "Sounds like a plan. I'll see you later."

Denise picked up another stack of files at the nurses' station, then turned and walked to an unused conference room. Brie followed and settled into one of the chairs at the giant table as Denise walked to the television that loomed over the room and started setting up a video.

"You completed your BLS and ACLS back in Georgia?"

"Yes, ma'am."

"How did you do?"

"Full marks."

"It's in your file?"

"It is."

"You completed the online orientation last week, correct?"

"Correct."

Denise held up two DVDs. "You need to watch this video about hospital policies and this one from HR about how to not be a racist idiot. Come find me afterward, and we'll start checking skills off your list."

She inserted one disc and pressed play, then turned on her heel, clicked off the lights, and left Brie in the darkened room.

Brie stared at the screen as a chipper, forty-something brunette in office wear, walked past the enormous brick facade of the hospital. "Welcome to Daya Memorial Hospital," she said with a saccharine smile. "Congratulations on becoming a part of our team. Today, we will explore the policies and procedures that will ensure a safe and productive working environment."

Brie had always been a conscientious student, a habit that wasn't about to stop now. She took a journal and pen from her backpack and started taking notes while sporadically eating her lunch.

An hour later, the video finally showed signs of winding down.

Brie's hand was cramped, and her back was seizing up. She wished she'd been telling the truth yesterday, and she did know some magical yoga move to relax her back and limbic system.

"Thank you for your attention, and welcome to the Daya Memorial family."

Thank the gods.

She stood and stretched her arms as high as she could, interlacing her fingers and spinning side to side at her waist to release her spine. When she was finished, she threw away the remains of her lunch and put her notes in her backpack before taking the DVD out of the player. She was about to insert the next one when it slipped from her fingers and rolled under the conference table.

"Typical," she muttered and got down on all fours to look for it.

It was all the way at the other end. Sighing and thanking her stars that this was at least a private moment of disgrace, she crawled under the table to retrieve it.

That's when the door opened, and the lights clicked on.

She froze in a moment of mindless panic, then jumped in her skin.

"This isn't what I agreed to."

Her heart stopped, then started beating double time. It had only been a day, but she'd recognize that oily, weaselly voice anywhere. *Dr. Matthews.*

Before she could even register her dismay or choose to reveal herself, the sound of high heels clicked into the room, followed by a silken female voice. "It's adorable that you think you're in any position to dictate terms."

"This is a child. There are limits—"

The woman laughed. The sound of it chilled Brie to her core. It was like someone playing a xylophone made of bones. Even its softness was dangerous and predatory. Her shoes clicked closer to Dr. Matthews as she continued with low, unconcerned menace.

"What delicate sensibilities you have. What irrelevant distinctions. You'll do this, but not that. Him, but not her. As though the specifics in any way affect the bottom line. As if any degree of rationalization will change what you've chosen to become."

Brie looked up and saw the reflection of their profiles on the darkened television. The woman was blonde and beautiful in a way that was obvious, even in the blurred dark mirroring of the screen. Something about her seemed terrifyingly familiar.

Matthews was shaking with fear. A drop of sweat dripped from his head and hit the ground with a soft plunk. But it seemed he wasn't done just yet. "I'll be no good to you if I'm caught."

The woman smiled, or more accurately, showed her teeth. "My dear Jonathan, please do not suffer under the misapprehension that you are in any way indispensable. Now, will you collect what I asked for, or do you require another demonstration?"

Something in the air went wrong, like a spike in the ozone when lightning strikes, but foul, cold, and biting. On the television screen, the woman's reflection started to distort and elongate until it scarcely resembled a woman at all. Her heels clicked on the floor as she moved closer to Matthews, but then the sound changed — changed to something heavier, less delicate.

Brie turned her head with a silent gasp.

Are those—?

Just for a moment, she could swear she caught a glimpse of giant, black, cloven hooves. It was like a single frame in a fast-paced movie. By the time she blinked, it was already gone.

"No!" Matthews cried. "It isn't necessary. I'll get you what you asked for. Please, just stop!"

Brie rubbed her eyes and stared hard at the woman's shoes. Ice-white skin sheathed in expensive-looking black leather. She looked at the television — a chillingly beautiful blonde.

What the hell is going on?

"Good," said the woman brightly, handing Matthews a heavy-looking and oddly shaped black briefcase. "I'll be here on the appointed day to collect. You know how to get in touch."

She turned on her heel and left.

Dr. Matthews stayed another minute, breathing hard, trying to collect himself. Then, he turned off the light and left, shutting the door behind him, leaving Brie huddled beneath the table.

That's when she noticed her necklace was glowing.

CHAPTER THIRTEEN

The Mystery in the Morgue

It's a trauma response. From my nightmare. Dr. Rogers always said our dreams leak into our waking life the next day. That's all it was. That's all I saw.

Get it together, Brie.

...So why did my mom's necklace start to glow?

She stared at her pendant as the last of the light faded away.

Well, at least the nearest psychiatric facility is only three floors up.

The door opened again, and the lights clicked on. This time, Brie couldn't help but yelp in alarm. This was met by a moment of silence and then: "Weldon, are you under the table?"

Brie closed her eyes.

Of course.

"Yes, ma'am." She picked up the DVD and popped up. "I was about to change the discs when this one got away from me."

Denise looked at her without a trace of humor. "You good?"

The question caught Brie off guard. She didn't think Denise was the sort to ask about the well-being of her subordinates. "Yes, fine. Why?"

"You're whiter than usual. And shaking."

"Oh." She fumbled for a reply. "Probably low blood sugar."

Denise grunted. "Do you have any questions about the procedures and policies video?"

Brie unzipped her backpack and pulled out her journal, skimming over her notes and trying to remember if she'd wanted clarification on any particular point.

"You took notes?"

Her eyes snapped up. "Yes, ma'am."

Denise stared at her for a moment. "Go get an orange juice. Then watch the HR video. You'll be fine."

She left without another word.

Brie stared after her for a second, still trying to process whatever had happened just a few minutes before. She slipped her journal into her backpack and made her way to a vending machine she'd seen in a nearby hallway. As she gave it her dollar and punched in her request, she kept running it over and over in her head.

In the end, she didn't much care if Dr. Matthews was in some sort of trouble. He was a perfectly vile man who couldn't be bothered to do his job correctly or with any amount of empathy, even in cases of life or death. It almost made sense that he'd pissed off some rich, scary, powerful woman who was now blackmailing him. If he was trapped in a situation that made it likely he was going to get his comeuppance, so be it. Karma had a way of sorting people like him out.

That wasn't what was bothering her.

Who is the child? And what had he "chosen to become?"

"Excuse me, miss. Are you going to get that?"

She jumped and realized another nurse was waiting behind her. "Oh, I'm sorry."

She grabbed her bottle of orange juice and looked at the young man apologetically. He shrugged it off with a friendly gesture. "No problem. Are you new here? I haven't seen you around."

"It's my second day."

"Oh, well, nice to meet you. I'm Aaron. Pediatrics." He gestured over his shoulder at the station just beyond the hall, then offered her a hand.

"Brianna."

As they shook, she was struck with a question. "Hey, did you happen to see Dr. Matthews pass by your way a few minutes ago? With a blonde woman in black? I was wondering if you know who she is."

He frowned. "Matthews rushed past, yes. I only clocked it because he looked even more terrible than usual. But there wasn't anyone with him."

"Oh. Well, is there another way out of this wing?"

Aaron looked at her strangely, then pointed. "No, there isn't. The only exit is past those doors at the end."

◆   ◆   ◆

Brie didn't pay any attention to the next video. Instead, she let her mind wander and tried to think through what she saw logically.

Her instinct was to tell Cameron immediately. But he'd recently melted her phone, and it wasn't as though he had some celestial phone number that she could dial anyway.

Besides which, he was...

She sighed heavily and rubbed her temples with her fingers.

In another world entirely, one that acts as a membrane between Heaven and Hell, through which all human souls must pass on their way to the Great Beyond.

She picked up her pendant and stared into its strange, opaline depths.

Again, the psych ward is just three floors up. One short elevator ride and a brief explanation of the past few days, and I'm sure they'd give me a nice, warm, white room to stay in for weeks on end.

Cameron was right. There wasn't anything more she could do without a better understanding of what the hell was happening and why it all seemed to be suddenly intersecting with her. In the meantime, the best she could do was simply the best she could do. She'd do her job and try to do it well. She'd live her life and try to live it well.

What was that Teddy Roosevelt quote her mom always used to say? "In any moment of decision, the best thing you can do is the right thing, the next best thing is the wrong thing, and the worst thing you can do is nothing."

So, figure out what the next right thing to do is. Then do it. Then do the next right thing after that. Over and over.

That's how you move forward.

The video wrapped up with a panning shot of nurses and doctors of every color and creed holding hands and smiling in front of the hospital. Brie popped out the DVD, collected her things, and went to find Denise at the nursing station.

The rest of her afternoon passed by in a blur. She shadowed Denise and struck as many skills from her checklist as possible. She met her unit manager. She got the feeling that though he was technically in charge of her orientation, Denise was law in these parts, and he'd never dream of questioning her recommendation for a moment.

She helped an orthopedic surgeon reset a dislocated shoulder. She hung three banana bags for dehydrated hikers who'd read their map incorrectly and gotten lost in the woods for two days. She took vitals, took histories, and a patient threw up on her shoes.

She didn't take bathroom breaks, didn't take coffee breaks, didn't complain, and didn't slow down.

By the end of her shift, she was ready to collapse.

That's when Denise handed her a tablet. "Use our system to update all the patient files from the cases you worked on today," she instructed without batting an eye. "Give it to Charlie when you're done. Do not make mistakes. He will tell me if there's so much as a typo. Do not call me with questions. I'm going home."

Brie took the tablet and looked at Denise's retreating form. Then, she stood at attention and saluted.

She recognized the mirthful, pealing laughter before she even turned around to grin at Sherry. She was walking towards her from the nurses' station with a hot chocolate in each hand.

How lucky am I to have a best friend who always seems to turn up at the perfect time with the perfect beverage? I bet other people's best friends always turn up to hot cocoa situations without the cocoa.

"Looks like you've managed to impress El Commandant. However did you manage?"

Brie gestured at the tablet. "Are you kidding? I'm dead on my feet. That woman has run me into the ground for two days straight, and now I have hours of charting left to do before I can go home and sleep. In what conceivable way have I impressed her?"

Sherry shrugged with a grin. "Well, usually, she yells at the newbies for their mistakes until they cry or quit. I haven't even heard her raise her voice at you once."

Brie sipped her hot chocolate and considered this. "Did she yell at you during your orientation?"

"Of course not. I'm practically perfect in every way."

She grinned. "Obviously. My apologies. So, how did your day go?"

"Oh, you know, the usual. Helped deliver a baby in the parking lot."

Brie almost choked on her cocoa. "You did what?"

Sherry's eyes sparkled. "The mom started crowning in the ambulance on the way over, so there was no way to get her up to labor and delivery, and she was screaming so much over the radio that we thought it was an incoming trauma, not an incoming birth, so I got to help deliver a baby boy today."

"Aw!" Brie made a noise usually reserved for tiny, large-eyed baby animal sightings. "Lucky. I rehydrated some morons who read their nature map upside-down, and a drunk threw up on my shoes."

"So that's what I'm smelling." Sherry wrinkled her nose in good-natured disgust. "Well, thank goodness it was those shoes."

"What's that supposed to mean?"

"Nothing. Let's go shopping this weekend!"

Brie had to laugh. No matter how exhausting or terrible the day was, Sherry always lifted her spirits. "Deal. But first, I need to get this charting done."

"May I make a controversial yet brave suggestion?"

"Go for it."

"Chart somewhere where people can't smell you."

Brie stuck out her tongue, and Sherry giggled. "Call me when you're done?"

"I can't. Cameron drowned my phone in eggs."

"Oh, that's right. Well, I've got some things to wrap up myself. Meet back here in an hour?"

"Better make it an hour and a half. If you want to go home, I can always call a taxi."

"Nonsense. There are at least fifty people in this hospital I haven't told about the parking lot baby yet, and it'll take me at least that long to rectify the situation." Sherry tilted her head thoughtfully. "Maybe the mother will name it after me."

"I thought it was a boy?"

"I don't see your point."

Five minutes later, Brie knocked on the door of the morgue. Rashida answered with her customary friendly smile and ushered her in. "How did your second day go?"

"Oh, you know, just orienting." Brie grinned and held up her tablet.

Rashida nodded knowingly. "Some of the preceptors like to take six months to get the newbies settled in. Denise always does it in three. Very sink or swim, that one."

Brie put her backpack down on a table and settled into a chair, sipping her cocoa. "I didn't get you a coffee. I don't know what your caffeine cutoff time is."

Rashida laughed. "If you'd asked me five years ago, I'd have truthfully said that I sometimes have a shot of espresso before bed. But these days, I switch to tea at five o'clock, no exceptions, or else I'm up all night."

"How disgustingly healthy of you."

"Indeed." Rashida wrinkled up her nose. "No offense, Brie, but you kinda smell."

"Oh." Brie looked desolately at her feet. "I'm so sorry. A patient threw up on my shoes, and I forgot to put backup sneakers in my locker. I tried to clean them off in the bathroom…"

"No problem. Pop them off. I have just the place."

"Really?"

"Of course. No need to prolong your suffering. Or mine."

Brie took off her shoes and was more than a little surprised when Rashida put on gloves and popped them into one of the horizontal cold storage body lockers.

"Are you sure that's okay?" she asked, her eyes wide.

"I doubt they'll mind," she replied with a wink. "Just remember which locker it is in case you're here longer than I am. You'd need to fetch them yourself and lock up afterward. Assuming I ever get out of here," she finished with a sigh.

"Oh, that's right," Brie remembered suddenly. "You said you were super busy. What's going on? I think you used the word 'bizarre?'"

Rashida's eyes clouded as she grabbed her thermos and sat down. "It really has been." She took a sip, staring thoughtfully at the wall. "Everyone has the ones they can't solve because there's no evidence after the fact. A tiny blood clot in just the wrong place, an embolism that dissipates by the time I get to the body. It happens."

She took another draught and shrugged. "But these days..."

Brie was listening with intense curiosity. "What's happening these days?"

Rashida hesitated a moment, then looked straight at her. "I can't tell you how many young people have come through these doors with unexplained catastrophic heart failure lately. Like the guy your team lost yesterday. I spent all day on him trying to find some reason, any reason at all, to explain why that poor boy's heart exploded. But for the life of me, I can't even point you in the direction of the problem."

She stared off into nothingness. "It's like something just reached into his chest and squeezed his heart until it popped."

Brie choked on her cocoa.

Rashida looked at her and raised a concerned eyebrow.

"That's quite... that's vivid," Brie finally managed.

Rashida flashed a tired grin. "As an ER nurse, I'm sure you'll see things that make that seem like a bedtime story. But that's not even the strangest case. Then there are all the ODs with no drugs in their system."

"What?"

"A lot of them, almost all young men, all obviously lost to some toxin or drug, but every single test I order comes up clean. Now, you tell me," she turned in her chair, "how can it be that my table is full of people who've died of a heart attack, with no conceivable reason to have a heart attack? Or people who've died of a drug overdose, with no drugs in their bodies?"

Brie could only answer in a shocked stammer. "I don't know."

"Well, neither do I, neither do three independent labs I've outsourced to keep up with the demand, and neither does the CDC."

Brie's eyes widened. "You brought this to the CDC?"

Rashida nodded. "They issued a statement a few months back asking doctors in the area to report any cases with similar pathologies to these. It looks like this has been going on up and down the coast. Two of my colleagues from med school have been seeing upticks in the same thing this past year." She shook her head and sipped her tea. "I just don't see how they haven't figured out what it is yet. Those guys are no joke."

It was silent for a moment before Rashida hopped down from her chair. "Well, I need to get back to work. But thanks for listening. I hope I didn't bore you."

Brie flashed a worried look. "Absolutely not boring. In fact, keep me in the loop, alright? That's some pretty alarming stuff, Ida."

"Aw, you remembered," Rashida replied, looking pleased. "Sure, if you like. I'll let you know if I hear anything. Cheers."

They tapped their drinks together and got to work.

◆   ◆   ◆

An hour later, Rashida was done with her postmortem paperwork, and Brie was nearing the last leg of her marathon charting session.

"Alright, lady. I'm off. Can you lock the door behind you when you leave? Unless Bryan's here already, then just let him deal with it. And don't forget, your shoes are in number five."

Brie grinned and gave her a thumbs-up. "You got it. Enjoy your night."

"I'm gonna enjoy my bed. Even though I'm not sharing it with a big hunk of man candy like you." Rashida grinned. "Don't think I've forgotten. I have a moral obligation to interrogate you about that handsome young thing sometime in the not-so-distant future."

Brie forced another smile. "I can't wait."

The woman shut the door behind her, laughing, as Brie took a deep breath, bent her head left and right to crack her neck, and got back to work.

Twenty minutes later, once she was satisfied neither Charlie nor Denise would be able to find a single typo anywhere in her charts, she got the tablet ready and packed up her things.

I'm forgetting something. Something important.

She looked down at her socks.

Ah.

With a tired sigh, she went over to the body lockers and found number five on the bottom row, bending down to open it up. There was a moment of natural hesitation before she concluded that not only was the occupant beyond the point of caring, but she really did need her shoes.

She pulled it open and groped around blindly. When she finally grasped her shoes, one lace caught on part of the locker.

Oh, for the love of—

She had to pull the slab carrying the body out before disentangling the laces and yanking the shoes towards her with a look of triumph. She didn't notice the way her pendant had slid out of her blouse and looped around the corpse's finger. She didn't even notice when the corpse sat up and stared around the chilled, locker-filled room in a blinking disorientation.

It wasn't until a polite voice chimed in, disturbing the quiet, that she realized something was wrong. "Excuse me, miss. Could you tell me where I am?"

CHAPTER FOURTEEN

Resurrection

"Cameron!"

Brie had held it together in the morgue. The moment she'd scrambled backward and her pendant had disentangled itself from the poor soul's thumb, he slumped back to the slab, and she sat on the floor on the other side of the room, too shocked even to scream. She'd stared in complete disbelief, first at the corpse and then at the pendant, before stuffing it back into her shirt. She'd rearranged the dead man's body and slammed it back into the locker. She'd checked the lock five times.

Brie had held it together in the hospital. She'd locked up the morgue, turned in her tablet, and even managed to smile at Sherry as she told tales of her parking lot heroism all the way home. She'd waved goodbye and agreed to some yoga, biking, walking exercise, and a shopping day during the upcoming weekend.

Brie had held it together on her front porch. She'd fitted her key into the lock without breaking it with her shaking hands. She'd shut the door behind her without once screaming at the top of her lungs and waking all her new neighbors.

Brie was done holding it together.

"CAMERON!"

He walked into the room a moment later, dressed in a white T-shirt and jeans. "Hello there. How was—?" His expression changed into a look of alarm as he rushed over. "Are you alright? What happened?"

"Oh, nothing. Nothing at all. Nothing except this *thing*," she grabbed the pendant and held it between them, flashing in the lamplight, "reanimated a corpse in the morgue today."

The color drained completely from Cameron's face. "It… it did… what?"

"Brought some unsuspecting dead guy back to life, Cameron. It hooked around his finger when I was looking for my shoes, and the next thing you know, a dead guy is sitting up and talking to me, just like I'm talking to you right now."

His face stilled in confusion. "When you were looking for your—"

"For my shoes, yes."

"What were your shoes doing in a dead man's—"

"That's not the important part of the story, Cameron!"

He looked at her like he was trying to calm down a rampaging honey badger while also trying to figure out how it had gotten into his living room. "Okay, okay. Are you alright?"

"No, I am not alright," she cried. "A dead guy talked to me. A drunk threw up on my shoes. Some blonde lady wants a doctor in my hospital to do something terrible to a kid. Apparently, there's a rash of unexplainable deaths sweeping the nation that nobody's talking about, and meanwhile, Sherry gets to deliver babies in the parking lot!"

She slumped down on the couch, suddenly exhausted. Her little rant had used up the last of her adrenaline reserves, and she was left with nothing but hollow disbelief that this was her life.

He approached her cautiously and sat down beside her. "Do you want some tea?"

She let out a low growl and slumped down further.

"May I rub your back?"

She considered this, then nodded faintly.

He shifted around so he was behind her, then started to massage her shoulders. She groaned involuntarily and closed her eyes, leaning back ever so slightly as his thumbs traced delicate patterns into the muscles along her spine. Her breathing hitched, then slowed. Her pulse did the same.

Either he's extremely good at this, or I'm getting a magical massage.

Just go with it.

It wasn't long before the tension started draining away, and the pain began to fade. Only when her breathing had returned to normal did he venture a hesitant question. "So, someone threw up on your shoes?"

She laughed despite herself. "Yes, I'm afraid these are done."

"I could fix them for you if you want?"

"That's okay. Even if you did, I'd always know these are the vomit shoes."

He nodded as though this made sense and decided to push the conversation a step further. "Your necklace reanimated a corpse?"

She nodded glumly. "Yup."

"You think a blonde lady and a doctor are plotting something to do with a child?"

"Uh-huh."

"And Sherry delivered a baby in the parking lot?"

She sank back into the cushions. "Yep. Yes, she did."

"Okay."

He leaned back as well and was quiet for a moment. Finally, he said, "So, what I'm hearing is that I left you alone for less than a day, and while you managed to single-handedly raise the dead, you can't even be trusted to keep your shoes clean?"

Their eyes locked for a second, and his lip curled up in the faintest hint of a grin.

She lost it. She laughed so hard that her sides hurt. At first, he smiled, proud of himself for his little joke. Then, he laughed along with her for a while. When she showed no signs of stopping or slowing down, he kept laughing despite himself but grew quietly concerned.

She finally managed a slightly hysterical, "But anyway, how was your day?" Then she cracked up again for a full minute.

This time he just waited for her to calm down. "I've had better, though it doesn't hold a candle to yours."

That sobered her up. "Oh, your father. I'm so sorry. In all the drama, I didn't even…" She shook her head quickly, trying to gather her senses. "I'm so sorry, Cameron."

He shook his head. "There's no need to apologize. You've been through more in the past week than any mortal should ever have to deal with."

She studied his face. "What happened?"

He shifted uncomfortably. "I told my people about your predicament."

"All of it?"

"All of it." He looked at her seriously. "It is not in my nature to lie. And on a subject of such importance as that of your safety, I would never keep a part of the story to myself."

She sucked in a deep breath. "What did they say?"

He looked down and took her hand. "That they wish I'd come to them sooner."

She studied the look of quiet remorse on his face. "Was your father angry with you?"

"He was disappointed," he said frankly. "Which is only fair. The manner in which I have behaved is disappointing. I took matters into my own hands rather than entrusting my information to the council. I disobeyed their directive not to check on you. For five years, I disregarded their advice, thinking I knew better. And worse than keeping this from the council, I kept it from him."

He came to a sudden pause, one that stretched a lot longer than he realized. "But if I hadn't, I wouldn't have been able to save you in the woods." He took her hand and rubbed his thumb over her knuckles. "I'd never even have experienced the touch of a human who wasn't dying." He looked into her eyes almost defiantly. "I'm not sorry. And I told my father that."

Her eyes widened. "What did he say?"

"He said I am more human than he realized, even after all this time."

"What's that supposed to mean? You aren't human."

His brow furrowed as his chin dropped down. "I am, and I'm not."

She gave him a flat look. "Cameron, I'm sure you can appreciate why I have no patience for your poetic deflections on this particular night."

"Of course," he quickly assured. "I'm not trying to be cryptic. It's difficult to explain and painful for me to talk about."

She waited silently as he took a steadying breath.

"How much do you know of the Bible?"

"Only what I was taught in Sunday school when I was little. My mom wasn't very religious about being religious. She said we were 'spiritual.'"

He nodded. "Well, there are two human figures in the Bible who never died."

"Oh, I do remember this. One is Elijah, right? Something about a fiery chariot?"

"Yes. Do you know who the other is?"

"No idea."

"The other is a man named Enoch. Your Bible teaches that he 'walked with God: and then was no more; for God took him.' He left this world having never felt the sting of death. God took him to Elysium to preside over the realm, to live forever immersed in the energy of life and to keep the forces of evil from ever touching even the edge of Heaven. He was appointed the head of the archangels and became known as the Metatron — the mouthpiece of God."

He drew a deep breath. "Enoch is my father."

Brie stared blankly. "How?"

Cameron traced patterns on her hand. "My mother's name was Naamah. She was a descendant of Cain."

"Wait, Cain? As in Cain and Abel? The murderer?"

"The First Man and the First Woman had only three sons: Cain, Abel, and Seth. My father was descended from Seth. Many in his family intermarried with the descendants of Cain." He looked at her ruefully. "It wasn't as though they were spoiled for options. But my father had something that was virtually unheard of in that day. He had a marriage of love."

He was quiet for a long moment, staring at his hands.

"My father loved my mother very, very much. She bore him many children — my brothers and sisters." He looked at her suddenly, amused. "You called me by one of their names the other day. Methuselah was my older brother."

Brie stared. "The oldest man in all of history?"

Cameron nodded. "He had a wonderful sense of humor. One time he tied a barrel full of sticks to a donkey and—"

"Cameron."

He nodded. "Right, not the time. My father lived three hundred and sixty-five years on Earth." He drew in a breath. "Until I came along." He let go of her hand and leaned forward. "My mother died while she was in childbirth with me."

Brie's mouth opened in shock. "Oh, Cameron, I…"

He shook his head and paused before continuing. "My father was one of God's favorite creatures. He often walked with God, praising the greatness of creation and asking questions about the wonders of the world and worlds beyond. When my mother died, her belly round with me still inside, struggling to be born, my father's heart broke. He called upon God and begged him for a reprieve for his wife and unborn child."

He drew in a deep breath. "God granted half of his request. My mother was a pure and loving soul, and she went on to Heaven. I was taken from my mother's womb and allowed to live with my father in Elysium. He presided over the realm and protected it. I grew up immersed in the life force of all the souls who ever passed to their next world, nourished by their spiritual energy, never knowing the human world except in my duty to help the dying depart."

Brie was so enthralled she nearly forgot to breathe.

"So you see, I am human, and I am not. Time flows differently in Elysium, as in Heaven and Hell as well. In fact, it does not flow at all but rather pools and has its own currents and waves within the confines of its shores. I stopped aging when I reached maturity. Being around spiritual energy, for even a short period of time, changes you. You've seen that I have abilities that humans do not possess." He stopped and sighed. "Before you, I never interacted with the human world except to help souls pass into Elysium peacefully. I never played with my brothers and sisters. I only watched. I never ate human food before last night. Well," he amended. "Once. On a dare."

Brianna was silent, trying to process this. He took her hand. "Are you alright?"

She nodded. "It must have been terribly, terribly lonely."

He stiffened a bit. "It wasn't. Not always." A look of pure melancholy swept over him, before he flashed her a shy smile. "In fact, Elysium is a beautiful place. I am excited to show it to you."

She sat up straight. "Show me?!"

He nodded. "My father and our elders are concerned for your safety and need more information about your pendant. They have requested that I accompany you to Elysium, immediately."

The excited sparkle in her eyes faded a little. "Immediately?"

He nodded. "We can go tonight. Now, if you like. You don't need to bring anything."

She shot him a worried look. "So, this would be a short trip?"

He tilted his head. "How do you mean?"

"I mean, how long would we be gone?"

He frowned. "It's difficult to say. As I said, time moves differently there, and such things are not always possible to calculate."

She pulled away. "You mean, you have no idea."

"Well, not exactly, but in light of recent events, I assumed you felt some urgency about the situation."

"I do. Of course, I do. But you want me to leave my world behind and travel… I don't even know where you would say this is, leaving everyone and everything I know and love behind for an indefinite period of time. A time that passes *differently* over there than it does here."

He took her hand again. "It is an honor afforded to very few mortals to enter our realm."

"Yeah. Very few mortals, none of whom ever came back." She pulled her hand away. "Have any mortals ever come back from Elysium, Cameron? Ever?"

He looked at her and couldn't seem to think of a response.

"I can't go to Elysium, Cameron."

He looked confused. "You have to."

She arched an eyebrow. "I think you'll find I don't."

"Brianna—"

"I can't just up and leave," she insisted. "Especially if there's no guarantee that I'll return back at the correct time. I have friends and family. I have a job. A life. A thriving, vibrant plant."

He studied her. "Surely, you must be joking."

Her eyebrows shot up. "Joking that my life here is worth defending? Joking that my friends and family are worth sticking around for? I am most certainly not joking, Cameron."

He exhaled in frustration. "Brianna, I didn't mean... look, you were the one who said you needed answers about your pendant, and you were absolutely right. And now that the Elysians want to give you those answers—"

"But that's not what you said, is it? You said that they need more information about the pendant themselves, which is why they want me to come. To study it. To study me. And who knows when or if they'll see fit to return me to my world. My life."

She got up off the couch and started to pace. "You said the darkness can't find me, right?"

"Yes, but—"

"My family and friends are safe. If my leaving would make them safer, I'd leave in a heartbeat. But if they're fine, and if I'm invisible to all the dark forces trying to get me, then I'm not going to leave my life and go hide in some state of fear and paralysis in a place where 'time flows differently,' Cameron. What if going there changes me? What if, I don't know, what if I come back five years older than I was when I left? Or ten years younger?"

Her pacing continued and intensified.

He cleared his throat. "I don't think—"

"You don't *think*. But do you *know*? Can you imagine what that would do to Sherry? To my dad? He's already lost so much. That would break him." She shook her head. "Leaving poses the greater risk of hurting those I love. Not to mention... I don't know if you were listening to me earlier, but there is something extremely weird going on at that hospital, and I intend to find out what it is. I might want answers about this pendant — hell, I might be desperate for answers — but it doesn't sound like your people have those answers. And I'm not keen to trek off to some alternate dimension on a lark."

She stopped abruptly in front of him and crossed her arms over her chest, looking for all the world like Denise until she jutted out her chin like a defiant child. "I'm staying. That's final."

Cameron's face processed several conflicting emotions, landing on exasperation at least twice before settling into something like bemused resignation. He rose to stand before her. "Then I'm staying, too."

"What?"

"I was gone maybe twelve hours, and you raised the dead, Brianna. God only knows what you'd manage to get up to if I left you to your own devices any longer."

She studied him shrewdly, unable to believe he'd be willing to accept defeat.

Her angel had been alive for centuries. Many centuries. Given the mere sight of him, given all that he'd come to represent, she couldn't imagine there was a single thing she might refuse that he couldn't insist upon by force.

Especially if he thought it might help. Especially if he thought it was the right thing to do.

"You're really okay with this?" she asked warily. "You're not going to stand there all unassuming, then drag me off into the ether the second I close my eyes to sleep?"

She was about to add something threatening like, "Because I carry mace." But in hindsight, she was always quite glad she decided against it.

His lips curved up with a look she was becoming increasingly familiar with, one of amusement and exasperation, as though he knew exactly what was running through her head. But when he spoke, there wasn't any pageantry, and there were no games. He was simply honest. "It is your choice, Brianna. Such a thing must always be your choice."

She took a step back, blinking in surprise. "So, you're really—"

"Okay with it?" he finished with a touch of sarcasm. "No, I wouldn't go that far. But that's the tricky thing about free will. It doesn't matter how I feel." He tilted his head, eyes twinkling with mischief. "A fatal flaw in an otherwise perfect structure."

She snorted with laughter, stepping towards him once again. "Or maybe it's the only thing that gives us a fighting chance," she countered.

He opened his mouth to contest it, then grew abruptly serious. "That may well be."

The two of them stood for a moment in silence, each thinking of the disasters that lay behind them, each imagining the vast uncertainty that lay ahead.

After a few seconds, he cleared his throat. "I'll stay," he said again before hesitating. "Unless you want me to go." He looked around the little house as though suddenly unsure. "You never chose any of this, and I don't want to intrude on your life—"

"Of course I want you to stay."

His whole body relaxed in relief. "Are you sure?"

"Yes, Cameron. I'm sure." She took his hand. "I'd love to see your home. Someday. In the future, when I'm not in the middle of my work orientation. When I haven't just moved across several states and been through more traumatic events in a week than most people see in a lifetime. When your people might actually have some answers for me, and I've had some time to wrap my head around the fact that I'd be voluntarily traveling to some crazy extra-dimensional celestial realm to meet your Old Testament father who never died."

She took a deep breath. "But I know that this isn't the right time. That will all have to come later. Because right now, all I want…"

He took a step closer, watching her closely. "Yes?"

She stared into his eyes. "…is a hot bath and a bowl of sour gummy worms."

The bath was heaven. The gummy worms, unfortunately, never materialized.

Thirty minutes later, as she was toweling off, she caught a glimpse of herself in the bathroom mirror. At first, it didn't register. Only when she did a double take, and then a third, did she let out a little cry. Cameron was there in an instant, bursting through the door on high alert.

"What is it? What's happened?"

She was too stunned by what she saw to even be startled at the manner of his arrival or self-conscious about the fact she was wearing only a grey bath towel knotted up around her breasts.

She was staring at her chest. "My scar," she murmured as though very far away.

She traced it with her finger. The jagged white line that she'd borne for five years was fading. No longer a raised, bold lightning strike distinctly marking her flesh, it had faded almost to the color of her skin and was flat and smooth beneath her fingertips.

Cameron looked at her, awestruck. "May I?"

She nodded vaguely, her eyes still trained on the mirror.

His fingertips traced the line, now barely perceptible.

"You were with me the day I got this scar," she remembered.

He looked at her seriously. "I was."

"Why is it healing now?"

He looked down at her pendant, hesitant to say.

"Oh." She reached up automatically to touch it. "Of course."

"Still." He lifted a finger to touch it himself but again shied away just before contact. "I'm curious why it would start healing you now. It's almost as if…"

She looked at him and froze. "As if what?"

He faltered another moment, then met her eyes. "It's almost as if something has woken it up."

CHAPTER FIFTEEN

Smart Phones Be Damned

Cameron and Brie slept in the same bed that night. No kissing took place, no "bases" of any sort were reached; nothing at all happened that could be described with a crude sports metaphor. They just slept. He wrapped around her, and she spooned into the crescent of his body like two pieces of a puzzle fit together by nature itself.

There were no nightmares.

She awoke rested and refreshed for what felt like the first time in months. His arm was still wrapped around her waist. She could feel his breath on her shoulder. She nestled in a little closer.

I didn't even know he could sleep.

I could spend the day like this.

I could spend the month like this.

She came to a sudden pause.

I don't know if I'd ever grow tired of this.

The realization startled her. Her eyes opened, and she shifted slightly to study his face in the morning light. He looked so peaceful with his dark eyelashes fanned over his cheeks and his hair rumpled from the pillows. It was all the more perfect because of those little flaws. He'd finally lost that eternal composure. He'd finally allowed himself to be human for a moment.

Is this what it's like to fall in love?

She'd never considered it before, let alone experienced it. She was never able to picture herself with anyone, and she didn't find the concept of being "completed" by a romantic partner at all romantic. Dr. Rogers had called it philophobia, or fear of falling in love. She never bought that. If it was going to happen, she suspected she simply hadn't found the right person yet. After all, she'd never been able to share her truth with anyone before — not with any hope of being believed.

But Cameron knew her. In a way, he knew her better than anyone else alive. He believed her truth because he'd lived it with her, and he'd trusted her with his truth as well. Maybe she hadn't been afraid or unable to fall in love all this time. Maybe she'd just recognized that none of the other contenders had been suitable.

Cameron's very existence disproved a bunch of Dr. Rogers' other theories anyway.

Not that it matters. The second I strayed too near the subject of attraction, he shut it down.

She remembered his words verbatim and the gravity they carried. Like an invisible weight had been dropped squarely upon her chest. "Such a thing is not permitted." He'd been very clear.

But that's not all he said.

Like something out of a dream, she remembered the look on his face when he'd told her, the wistful longing in his eyes when he chanted back those heavenly laws. But there had been other words as well. Softer words. Words that gave her a glimmer of hope.

"Believe me when I tell you there are times that I want to."

Her eyes drifted once again to the angel by her side, delighting in the image while simultaneously removing him from the equation, trying to decipher her own feelings instead.

Rationally speaking, there was a lot working against them. He was older than she'd like to contemplate. He'd watched her secretly for years. He had real trouble with boundaries, and she still wasn't comfortable with his infatuation with her toaster. On the other hand, no one had ever sacrificed so much just to be near to her and keep her safe.

No one but Mom. And then Sherry.

She inhaled sharply with the realization it was true.

If that's the list he's on… it might actually be love.

She was still reeling in silence, still gazing at the perfect symmetry of his face, when a feral scream ripped through the air.

He woke up with a start, tightening his grip around her.

The screaming paused for a moment, then started up again in the exact same cadence, the exact same series of tortured cries, as though someone or something was being burned alive. It was ghastly. It was utterly horrifying. But at the same time, the rhythm was too perfect. Almost mechanical.

Is that…?

With a look of childlike panic, Cameron bolted out of bed and yanked open the top drawer of her dresser. For a split second, she was convinced he was looking for some ancient weapon. But he emerged a second later with a tiny screeching device. It took a second to recognize her phone.

"I don't believe it," she said, holding out her hand. "Give me that."

He flushed but tossed it over, watching as she frantically tried to unlock the thing with her fingerprint to shut off the bloodcurdling alarm.

"I can't open it. Why won't it let me——"

A sonorous baritone cut her off. *"Siri, be quiet at once."*

The phone immediately fell silent.

The two of them fell silent as well. For a suspended moment, they simply stared at it together. Then she lifted her eyes with a blistering glare.

"You did this."

"I wasn't——"

"Did you just use the hypnosis voice? On my *phone?*"

He shifted his weight uncomfortably. "It wouldn't stop screaming."

She narrowed her eyes. "And why was it screaming, Cameron?"

Another pause. Another guilty deflection. "I may have taught the creature to fear."

This took a minute to register.

"It wasn't strictly speaking on purpose, Brianna," he insisted quickly, watching her color flame from pink to a more dangerous red. "While I was mending it yesterday, I... I may have been overzealous in my condemnation of its general attitude——"

"Overzealous in your... Do you mean you cursed it?" she interrupted. "Did you *curse* my phone?" She threw a pillow at him. "Like a freaking warlock?"

He was so undone he actually let it strike him. It flew into his face, then slid to the floor as she huffed again and unlocked her traumatized device with her passcode.

"Hey, Siri. Are you doing okay?"

"Lucky Lucy gets the spoon."

She paused, flabbergasted, before pressing her home button again. "I'm sorry, Siri. What was that?"

"Into the tunnel, out of the shoe."

She tossed it on the bed in disgust and glowered at Cameron. "You broke my smartphone."

"I defeated it," he muttered.

"What was that?"

"Nothing," he said quickly, trying to change the subject. "Why don't I go downstairs and make you breakfast? *Buy* you breakfast," he amended at the look on her face.

She wanted to hurl another pillow. But she was hungry.

He went downstairs while she made a half-hearted effort to get dressed, her ears still ringing with echoes of those inhuman cries. It was a rather meager attempt, but when she glanced into the mirror, she was delighted to realize that she liked what she saw.

Her skin was glowing, her hair was thick and shiny, and her eyes were clear and bright. Even her nails seemed to be growing strong and fast, despite her never once taking care of them.

I should get a good night's sleep more often.

Or maybe it's the smoothies.

She stuffed a backpack with an extra pair of scrubs and shoes to keep in her locker at all times. She didn't think she'd want to stash her sneakers in the morgue again anytime soon. When she came down the hall into the living room, she stopped short.

Cameron was talking to a golden orb that floated in the air inches from his face. He spoke rapidly and in a low voice, but she could tell it was a language she'd never heard before.

She didn't want to eavesdrop and didn't see the value in hiding. She stepped into the room with a confident, "Good morning." It was the most uncanny thing, but she could swear that both Cameron *and* the orb turned to look at her.

"Good morning!" Cameron said quickly. "We were just... I was... this is Ephriam."

The golden ball bobbed slightly up and down.

"He's an old friend of mine. I was just about to send a message to my father, expressing your desire to… not come to court, when my father sent him here to collect us." He looked back and forth from Brie to his celestial friend.

Brie swallowed. *Be gracious. Sure, there's basically an alien levitating in your living room who wants to bring you to a different plane of existence. But courtesy is universal. What did Cam say? "Politeness is the flower of humanity."*

"It's very nice to meet you, Ephriam," she said. Then, in a move she would never live down, she executed a slight curtsey.

She didn't know how she could tell, but she instantly knew. The orb was laughing at her.

She blushed scarlet. "Well, it isn't like anyone's told me the protocols here."

"Of course not," Cameron soothed, trying not to laugh. "That was very good."

The orb glowed brighter for a moment.

"Yes, I was just getting to that," Cameron hissed at the ball of light under his breath.

"Getting to what?" she asked.

He looked at her apprehensively. "Well, Ephriam was just saying… one idea that's being floated around is… see, my father might be more amenable to us staying here if—"

"*Cameron.*"

"He may want to assign a team to guard you and keep you from harm."

She blinked. "A team of what?"

"Elysian guards. Ephriam would likely lead it, given our history."

Brie eyed the glowing ball skeptically. Cameron waited on her reply.

"Well, that's… that's very kind of him, but — and I don't mean any offense by this at all, please believe me — it's just… after everything I've seen, I don't see how a peaceful being who most closely resembles Tinkerbell is going to be much use in a fight."

Cameron and the orb stared at her without making a sound. Then, the golden ball floated close to his ear.

After a moment, he grinned and nodded. "Yes, I absolutely agree. Brianna, you should stand well back."

"I beg your—"

"Well back, Brianna."

She obligingly stepped back into the hall.

The orb floated to the middle of her living room and levitated quietly for a moment. Then, the air itself was ripped apart.

Seven enormous, interwoven rings of golden fire, ten feet across, orbited in complex patterns around a being with faces on every side of its head. A man, an ox, an eagle, and a lion all seemed to exist within this creature at once, while at the same time, none of them remotely described the glory of what hovered before her. Wings seemed to be everywhere — claws, teeth, and talons. Wind blew from every direction at once as streams of golden sparks lashed through the air like whips. The heat was incredible, yet nothing burned. It let out a roar, and every molecule of her house trembled at the sound.

In a flash, it was a palm-sized ball of light again. Ephriam floated up to her, twinkling as though pleased with himself.

Brie swallowed hard, then swallowed again. When a full minute had passed, she managed a faint, "Yes, I suppose you'll do."

The orb shook slightly and sparkled as though it was chuckling. She gave it a wary smile and tentatively held up her hand. It moved towards her finger, and she delicately touched it. "Please excuse my misunderstanding, Ephriam. I'm very, *very* glad you're on our side."

Cameron had a difficult time keeping a straight face. He walked over to her with a grin and put his hand on her shoulder. "Well, that settles that. Will you tell him?"

If the orb replied, it wasn't something her ears could register. It turned to her once more and bowed. Deeply.

She narrowed her eyes. "I sense I'm being mocked."

The orb twinkled with a flurry of golden sparks and faded away.

She turned to Cameron. "So… he seems nice."

He looked at her with a mix of amusement and awe as she sat down on the couch and let out a long breath. She was aware her eyes were still preternaturally wide, but she couldn't seem to do anything about it.

"Has anyone ever told you, you are very brave?" he asked softly.

She paused, startled. "No. Never."

"Well, you are," he said. "Unflappable."

"It's true. I can't be flapped." She flashed him a grin, then took a deep breath and stood up. "Let's go find a little breakfast place by the water. I've been here for days and haven't even seen the ocean yet. Plus, I'm starving. And it might not be too bad to do something normal to counterbalance the whole phenomenal-cosmic-power-display thing."

He offered her his arm. "Shall we?"

"We shall."

There was a good chance the drama was behind them, but as they walked out the door, she made the mistake of asking one final question. "Siri, what's a nice place to have breakfast around here on the waterfront?"

"Twas brillig, and the slithy toves did gyre and gimble in the wabe:
All mimsy were the borogoves, and the mome raths outgrabe."

Brie sighed heavily. "This is gonna be a whole thing, isn't it?"

"Beware the Jabberwock, my son! The jaws that bite, the claws that catch—"

Cameron eased it from her hand, whispering directly into the speaker. "Siri… shut up."

"Surely this is the elixir of Heaven itself. My good lady, might I have another?"

Fortunately, their waitress was too besotted with Cameron's face to be thrown by his rather Shakespearean reaction to breakfast. No matter what he said, she just ogled him and giggled. "One more orange juice, coming up."

"Many thanks, and God bless you."

Brie grinned at him, thoroughly entertained. "Enjoying your juice, are you?"

"Brianna, this is like drinking sunshine. Do people know about this?"

She threw back her head and laughed. "Ridiculous."

They were seated at a table for two on the outdoor patio of the Golden Albatross Café. He had allowed her to guide him through the brunch menu, and they looked out over the water, waiting for their food to arrive. It was a glorious day — nothing but fresh air and warm sun. It was bright enough to need sunglasses. The second she slipped hers on, he mysteriously pulled a pair from his pocket as well, mimicking the gesture.

"How do you do that?" she asked curiously, sure they hadn't been there before.

"Do what?"

"You know. Produce things out of thin air like that. Manifest."

"Oh." He looked surprised. "I pray."

"Excuse me?"

"I guess that's what you'd call it. I never really considered it before. I think about what I need, ask for it earnestly in my mind, and it appears." He shrugged as though this was in some way normal. "I always thought it was a gift from God, a power to help my people grant the last requests of humans before they pass on, or simply navigate your world if need be."

She swirled her ice cubes around with her straw. "Prayers certainly don't work like that here on Earth."

He was thoughtful for a moment. "No, I suppose they don't."

"And you never use this power for yourself?"

He tapped his sunglasses, grinning.

"You know what I mean. You've never manifested a fancy car, or a beach house, or chocolate? I mean, come on. You must at least be tempted, right?"

"In Elysium, there is no need for material things. No one wants for anything. There's nothing to desire." He paused for a moment, staring at the sea, as if those two things might not be quite the same. "Well, nothing material," he amended. "What I wanted to manifest, as you say, was not possible."

She proceeded forward cautiously, not wanting to close him off. "Like what?"

He let out a quiet sigh. "When I was a child, I wouldn't wish for cars or candy bars. All I wished for was to know my mother. To have time with her."

"Oh." Brie gazed out at the waves as well. "I know what that's like." She swirled her ice cubes thoughtfully. "What if such a thing was possible?"

"How do you mean?"

She touched her pendant. "What if... what if the barriers between life and death... what if they aren't so set in stone? What if it's possible to bring someone back from the dead?"

A peculiar look shadowed his face, draining it of all color. He weighed his words carefully before deciding to speak. "Such things have happened before. Of course, only God can summon a person's life force back from Heaven or Hell, but a handful of mortals — only a handful in the whole of human history, mind you — have performed resurrections as well."

He took a deep breath but held her gaze. "As I told you before, there aren't enough Elysians to be there to ease everyone's suffering in their final moments, or to transport every human soul who passes on right away. Sometimes, humans have to wait before moving on to the next realm. So, on rare occasions, when a person's life force has not yet been shuttled from one realm to the next, and they come into contact with a powerful being or force, their energy is drawn back to their bodies. They're resurrected."

She tried her best to understand this, struggling to keep an even expression like his. "When was the last time it happened?"

He leaned back thoughtfully, armed with more centuries of divine trivia than she was willing to contemplate. "Something like this? Something involving more of an artifact than a bestowed power? Not counting Jesus, and not counting his disciples, because they were themselves imbued with the power of Christ—"

"Cameron."

"It was when the corpse of a random Israelite was thrown into the tomb of Elisha and accidentally touched his bones."

"So..."

"About a thousand years before the birth of Christ."

Brie sat there, stunned.

And then again yesterday, in the Daya Memorial Hospital morgue.

"You're going to make big waves where I come from," he said quietly, thinking the same thing himself. He deliberately cleared his expression. "Whenever it is that you decide to come."

So even angels can be passive-aggressive. She fought back a tiny grin. *Good to know.*

His face brightened suddenly. "Ah! Pancakes."

She was still getting over her shellshock as the giggly waitress unloaded a tray with eggs Benedict for her and a tower of blueberry pancakes with butter and maple syrup for him, along with another glass of iced orange juice.

"Enjoy!" she tittered as she headed back to the kitchen.

He looked down at his breakfast with a decided lack of confidence and picked up the small, white syrup pitcher. "Am I meant to drink the—"

Brie snapped out of her reverie. "No, you pour it over the pancakes. Then cut little bites, like this." She demonstrated on her eggs as he meticulously copied her movements.

Before they could actually eat, she stopped him. "Cameron?"

He paused, a fork halfway to his mouth.

"Everything that's happened seems so rare and unlikely," she said haltingly, "even in your world. Is it wrong for me to delay our trip to Elysium until we know more about what's genuinely going on? Even if there's no immediate danger, is it wrong to want to stay and live my life?"

He put the fork down. "Brianna, everything in your life has led you to this moment. Yes, it's all exceptional. I've certainly never seen anything like it before, and I've been around for a long time. But I have to believe that this is happening to you — *you*, out of everyone in the world, *you*, out of everyone in history — for a reason. If you think that staying is the right thing to do, if you think this is the place you're supposed to be, my instinct is to trust you." He regarded her gently. "You have a beautiful heart, Brianna. I am inclined to have faith in it. And in you."

He picked up his fork and tried the pancakes. "Oh!" he groaned around a mouthful of maple and blueberries. "Oh, by all the saints. Oh, by the staff of Moses. Brianna, do people know about these?"

CHAPTER SIXTEEN

Cardio, Crisis, Catastrophe

Things started going well at home.

Over the next few days, Brie and Cameron settled into a routine. He woke up before her alarm could start screaming and woke her gently instead, sitting on the bed beside her and stroking her hair. She'd get ready for work, and he'd head down to the living room to send his father a report about anything new that might be happening. Apparently, her case was still being discussed amongst the Elysian council. The elders couldn't decide whether deploying a team of Elysian guards was within their purview, or if it was worth the risk of exposing their community to the human realm.

Brie got used to greeting Ephriam, and an unlikely, nonverbal friendship started to form. She'd ask him about Cameron's most embarrassing childhood moments. He'd twinkle and glow in reply, and she would pretend to understand him perfectly. Whatever he was saying was enough to turn Cameron's ears bright red. He'd inevitably cut off their conversation with a snappish, "That's certainly enough of that!" or, "Whatever happened to loyalty between comrades in arms?" or, "That was *one* time. She said it was the custom of her people, and it would be disrespectful not to."

Ephriam would twinkle with laughter and disappear back to Elysium to give his report. Brie and Cameron would head off to a local café. She would get her standard cappuccino and croissant to go, as he worked his way through the menu in an ecstatic exploration of the culinary universe. The only thing that disappointed him was cottage cheese, which seemed to be a textural issue. Tastes, smells, and sensations delighted him. She found herself appreciating things she'd taken for granted her whole life. He hadn't tried chocolate yet. She thought it best to check that one off the list in private, for fear his reaction might get them banned from the establishment.

Just knowing he had faith in her decision to stay the course in Virginia gave her a courage of conviction she'd been lacking ever since her attack in the woods. Her doubts about whether she should have left home in the first place had been replaced by a confidence and determination she hadn't felt in many years.

When she got home at night, the two of them would sit together and talk about her day and about his world and all the fantastical things he'd seen. Despite his fascinating tales of Elysium, it was the human world that interested him most, the one he'd been ripped away from before he could pull in that first breath. He was endlessly interested in her life — every detail, every memory.

She found herself remembering long-forgotten events, things that had slipped through the cracks of time. She managed to recall conversations with her mother that had lain buried in her mind for years. She remembered the first song she learned to whistle, the first time she played in snow.

One such evening, as he was rifling through an old book she'd bought at a flea market in college, he started humming a quiet melody under his breath. In all likelihood, he didn't realize he was doing it, but she froze where she stood and stared at him, the flicker of deep memory stirring inside her heart. After a few seconds, she started humming along with him.

After a few more seconds, she sat down beside him and took his hands. "My mother," she murmured, her eyes shining. "My mother used to sing that to me. I couldn't have been more than four or five years old. She'd sing it every night before I fell asleep." She stared at him. "How did you know? How could you possibly have known?"

He gazed down at their entwined hands. "You hummed it last night in your sleep."

She considered this a moment, then peered up at him. "You watched me sleep?"

He blushed faintly and shifted away from her, back to the books. "Old habits die hard."

Brie was flying through her orientation. She spent her days diligently making her rounds, caring for her patients, and her evenings charting with Rashida. It felt as though she worked a lifetime every shift, then spent hours charting to recap every single detail each night. Denise had even given her a grunt of approval on several occasions. Sherry started to join her when their breaks coincided. Brie carefully avoided so much as looking at the cold storage lockers.

The one thing she couldn't manage to do was keep an eye on Dr. Matthews. He scuttled around the hospital like a cockroach, keeping to himself whenever possible, and just like the repulsive insect, he tended to scatter when exposed to light or human contact. She'd initially thought it would be easy enough to keep tabs on him, given all the access and information afforded her in the nurses' station. Still, he never seemed to be where he was supposed to be. Try as she might, she never got a chance to speak with him or observe him while staying unobserved herself.

She did, however, learn a great deal about him secondhand, just from listening to her colleagues. Doctors, nurses, and staff members alike seemed to loathe his very presence. He was a diminutive man, easily overlooked, so he'd developed a nasty habit of announcing his arrival in a room with a colicky throat-clearing noise that seemed to universally set people's teeth on edge. So did his high laugh, like a mouse skittering over a keyboard, a sound that always came at the most inappropriate times and usually at someone else's expense. His bedside manner was nonexistent, as was his relationship with his coworkers.

But the worst thing about him was undoubtedly his deplorable patient outcomes. His nickname, Dr. Death, was well-merited. Brie didn't think it was a lack of intelligence or skill on his part that led to his high patient mortality rate. She could swear it was almost like he wanted some of his patients to die. He was always slow to show up and quick to call time of death.

Then there was his bizarre habit of coming back to skulk around the bodies after they'd been pronounced deceased before they were taken away to the morgue. Once, she walked in on him as he was leaving, carrying that oddly shaped black case he'd been given by the mysterious blonde. Before she had a chance to hail him down or ask what he'd been doing, he was gone. Nothing looked amiss in the patient's room after he left. Their body lay resting with a sheet respectfully pulled up over their head. But Brie could never shake the feeling something evil had just occurred.

She didn't see the blonde woman again.

She heard no mention of a child.

♦   ♦   ♦

On Friday night, Sherry caught up with her on her way down to the morgue.

"Are you excited for tomorrow?"

Brie blanked.

It isn't her birthday… It isn't Elizabeth Taylor's birthday… It isn't Shark Week… Is it the anniversary of the time we TP'd the principal's house? No, that's next month…

"Shopping, darling. Honestly, sometimes I worry about your priorities."

Shopping. Right.

So much had happened in the last few days, so many invisible traumas and supernatural revelations, their agreement to make weekend plans seemed like a lifetime ago.

"Right. Yes, I totally remembered."

Sherry rolled her eyes. "Very convincing. I suppose you also forgot about our exercise date tomorrow morning."

"I most certainly did not. In fact, I'm looking forward to it."

"Ha. I'm not," Sherry declared. "Regardless, I'll come by to pick you up in the morning, bright and early, so make sure you aren't in the middle of any indecent shenanigans."

"Says the woman whose date nights routinely involve handcuffs."

They stepped into the elevator and pressed the button for the basement. Sherry regarded her with a curious frown. "How's it going with you two, anyway?"

There was a quiet pause.

"I don't really know how it's going," Brie admitted. "Or where it's going. Or *if* it's going. But he gets me in a way I never thought possible. I can be myself with him in a way I've never known."

She opened her mouth to say something further, then bowed her head in defeat.

"Oh, honey." Sherry wrapped an arm around her waist. "I didn't mean to upset you. Truth be told, I don't know why you're upset at all. Those are *great* things you just said."

"Yeah, no, they are." Brie nodded quickly, surprised at how quickly the simple question had unraveled her. "He just… keeps himself at a distance. Do you know what I mean?"

A divine distance. One that comes with heavenly repercussions if you dare to cross those lines.

Sherry nodded wisely. "The age-old problem. These guys would fight a puma with their bare hands, but when it comes to relationships, they're afraid to commit. I blame it on increased lead in the water supply."

The elevator doors opened, and they headed towards the morgue, only to be stopped in their tracks by the sound of raised voices — one patient, the other filled with rage.

"I'm telling you, there's nothing there."

"That's impossible!"

"Then *you* find something."

The two women shared a glance, frozen in the middle of the hall. It was easy to recognize the strained, patient voice as Rashida's. The other had a distinctively bureaucratic edge.

"This young man's family is a huge donor. The east wing of the hospital is named after them. I can't go back to his grieving parents and say we have no idea what happened to their son."

"This is what I've been telling you for months. There's no reason he should be dead. No family history, no underlying condition, no architectural deformity, no disease, no history of addiction, no foreign substances in his blood, no external trauma."

There was a momentary pause as Rashida caught her breath. "There's *nothing* wrong with him, except his heart's been pulverized. From inside his chest."

Papers rustled, and shoes squeaked against the floor.

"Well, that's just unacceptable."

"I don't disagree at all. But it's what's happening. And I'm telling you, I think it's tied to all these unexplained ODs. In some of the cases, it's clearly poison, but with no poison in their system at all. In others, it's as if their heart merely explodes."

There was the sound of someone pacing.

"You tell me what you need, Ms. Botha. Money, equipment, anything. I'll tell the family our investigation is ongoing. But Ida," his voice was almost pleading, "you have to find something."

The woman sighed heavily. "I'll rerun my tests. Again."

"Keep me informed."

The door opened, and a hospital administrator Brie had never seen before walked out. He was an enormous individual — at least three hundred pounds of anxiety in an expensive suit. He very nearly bowled them over before he realized there was anyone else there.

"Ladies," he said curtly, before heading towards the elevator.

Brie and Sherry looked at each other and ducked inside the morgue.

There were no visible signs of carnage. No disciplinary notifications or committee censures strewn across the floor. There was just one overtired, overworked pathologist, staring at her computer like she was trying to translate the Code of Hammurabi.

"Hey there," said Brie tentatively. "We brought sandwiches."

Rashida didn't move for a second, still in her trance, but finally slowly turned her head to look at them. "Oh, hi," she said in a beleaguered tone. "Thanks." She accepted a veggie sub and set it down without unwrapping it, obviously on autopilot, staring into space but seeing nothing.

Sherry caught Brie's eye and tilted her head towards the door.

Brie nodded slightly but hesitated to leave. "Ida, if this is a bad time, we can always—"

"No, no, you're fine. I'm sorry you had to hear that. I just…" She trailed off hopelessly. "It keeps happening. I don't know why it isn't making the news at this point. At first, it was just a few cases every once in a while, but now? Two or three times a week, someone lies on my table who should not be there. And I don't know how to diagnose what happened to them, so I don't know how to help."

She pushed the sandwich away, defeated. "I don't usually let cases get to me. No point, you know? It's already happened; there's nothing I can do but bring closure to the families. But now, not only can I *not* do that, but every day that goes by, this happens to more and more people. Maybe if I could get to them earlier, I could help, but by the time they get to me, whatever evidence exists inside these poor people is gone. Or if it's there, it's beyond my skill to find." She hung her head in dismay.

Brie had no idea what to say, but luckily, Sherry did.

She crossed over to Rashida's side of the table and took her firmly by the shoulders. "Would you like to watch a bunch of hot guys play soccer with us this weekend?"

That night, Brie brought home a pizza.

Perhaps her body was craving an infusion of burnt cheese and grease. Perhaps she wanted a momentary distraction, watching her angel delight in the newest "culinary masterpiece" for the first time. She waited until he'd stopped making his rapturous noises before telling him about the incident in the morgue.

He listened intently and considered his words carefully before answering. "I understand your concern and that of your friend. I'm sorry for it. But isn't it likely this is simply a new drug that the police and medical community are not yet aware of?"

She grabbed another piece of pizza and absentmindedly picked off the olives. "I guess so, but the way she was talking about it? The frequency and intensity of it? It didn't sound natural to me. And with all the other supernatural stuff going on, I guess I was just wondering if you'd heard anything. You know, on your end. From your people. It's kind of their area, isn't it?"

He nodded thoughtfully. "I suppose it might be, though I'm sure I would have heard something already. I can put the word out in the morning, just to make sure."

She remained quiet for a moment, then said, "She made it sound like it was some kind of plague."

The pizza halted on the way to his lips. "Say that again?" he asked sharply.

"Rashida made it sound like it was some kind of plague."

His eyes went dark, and he put down his slice. "If that's what you're worried about, don't. I've seen plagues, Brianna, and that can't be what's happening here. For one thing, during a plague, there are particular, powerful players involved who most certainly aren't here. For another, that's the kind of thing you can't keep quiet. Not in your world, nor in mine."

She regarded him thoughtfully. "So, you've seen real plagues, is what you mean."

"I have."

"Is it bad form if I ask you about it?"

He drew in a deep breath and let it out. "It's panic, isolation, fear. The suffering is enormous. A war raging in another realm causes immeasurable collateral suffering in this one. By the end, everyone has lost someone. Some people have lost everyone." He glanced at her. "It isn't like that now, is it?"

She shook her head and looked out the window at the rising moon. "You're right. I guess the way she phrased it just threw me is all."

He nodded his head slightly. "Olive juice."

She whirled around, eyes bright and wide. "Excuse me?"

"Olive juice. It's dripping off your plate."

She stared a moment, then snatched up a napkin. "Right — yes. Thanks."

He looked at her, confused. "What did you think I said?"

She pretended she hadn't heard, crossing towards the television and kneeling down beside an old box of DVDs she'd yet to unpack. She riffled through them, then pulled one up with a sudden mischievous grin. "Let's watch this one tonight."

He caught the box when she threw it, staring down with a little frown. "Is it meant to be grammatically incorrect?"

She glanced over her shoulder. "What do you mean?"

He waved the picture in confusion. "'*I ain't afraid of no ghost?*'"

An hour later, the angel's mood had soured significantly.

"Well, I must say, this is highly offensive, Brianna," he huffed. "*Highly* offensive. If this is how humans regard those who have passed on to the next realms, it's no wonder my people have strict rules about our concealment. There's a particular disregard for the sanctity of memory, not to mention that confusing bit with the giant snowman. Why was he in a naval uniform? Quite frankly, I think..." He trailed into silence. "Brianna?"

She had fallen asleep with her head on his shoulder, lips slightly parted like a child.

He let out an exasperated sigh and smiled despite himself. He shifted the pizza boxes away with his foot before turning off the television with a flick of his fingers. A blanket shimmered its way into existence, and he covered her, pressing a gentle kiss to the top of her head. "Goodnight, Brianna."

He circled his arms around her and settled in for yet another night — watching her sleep, counting her heartbeats, curious to hear in the morning what that maddening mind of hers decided to dream tonight.

It was the most remarkable thing, though. He felt tired. He'd allowed himself the luxury of sleep on occasion, of course. But he'd never felt tired before.

It was all the human food and activity, no doubt. It must be wearing off on him. It was only a temporary lapse, probably all in his head. Perhaps he'd shut his eyes, just for a moment.

Within that moment, he drifted off to sleep himself.

◆　　◆　　◆

"Well, isn't this just adorable?"

Brie and Cameron woke with a start. Sherry was standing before them, and a camera flash went off in their eyes before they even had a chance to disentangle themselves.

"Oh, for goodness' sake, Sherry..."

Sherry looked at the photo and let out a hoot of laughter. "It's terrible. I'm having it framed."

She pointed her phone at Brie like a sword. "You, madame, are late for our exercise date. And you, sir," she pointed at Cameron, "have surely been the one to drive her to such distraction. Up! Up with you both. Brie, I cannot believe you're putting me in the position to be the one to enforce cardio. Who even am I? Where are we?"

With that, she proceeded to swoop around the house, opening curtains and flooding the place with light.

Brie squinted and staggered to her feet. At a glance, everything was as it should be, given the celestial impossibility of having fallen asleep with an angel on her couch. It wasn't until her eyes settled into focus, that she realized something was wrong.

"What are you wearing?"

"What, this?" Sherry glanced down at her terrifically oversized Hello Kitty T-shirt and skin-tight, fur-trimmed, leopard-print yoga pants. She held her head at an imperious angle, nose in the air. "Spandex is a right, not a privilege, Brianna. If you must know, I am disinclined to keep my curves to myself. And how dare you question my stylistic choices? The nerve! That'll be fifty extra push-ups for you."

"I wasn't… I can't even do fifty push-ups."

"Well, five then. Up! Up! We're burning daylight."

Sherry power walked into the kitchen to fill a thermos with water as Brie groaned and turned to Cameron, who was making no effort to stifle his grin. "Can't you freeze-ray her or something?"

"Actually, I think it might be best if you get out of here before I'm summoned to check in with my father."

Brie's eyes flew wide open, and she rushed to the bedroom to get ready. "Five minutes! Give me five minutes. Oh, shi—"

There was a distant crash.

Sherry never looked up from the sink. "Darling, we've talked about this. Walk first, undress later. Remember what happened with the penguins."

Cameron's eyes flashed at her curiously. "What happened with the penguins?"

Sherry squinted at him. "I'm fond of you, Cameron, but don't get it twisted. We're not that close yet."

"Why did I ever let you talk me into this in the first place?"

Sherry clutched her side and glared daggers as Brie jogged in place a few paces ahead, armed with a wicked grin.

"Wipe that smirk off your face, Weldon. This is attempted murder, and it isn't funny."

"You came and woke me up, remember? You were rather insistent."

"I'm sure I don't know what you're talking about."

Sherry groaned loudly and arched her back in a stretch. They were down near the waterfront, passing rows of homes newly restored to look historically old. A cool breeze off the ocean whispered over their skin, cutting through the heat of the cloudless day.

Sherry windmilled her arms around before giving up again and doubling over at the waist, panting at the asphalt.

Brie walked back to her. "Are you alright?"

"Of course I am." Sherry glared at her presumption. "I'm not going to let a little thing like exercise-induced cardiac arrest get the best of me."

Brie knelt down and caught her eye. "You know, I read this study that said that walking is every bit as effective as running so long as you don't stop very often."

Sherry lifted her head in hope. "Really?"

"Really."

"*Well* then." Abruptly cheerful, Sherry straightened up and squared her shoulders. "Let's get a move on, soldier. I don't know why you always insist on these breaks."

Brie grinned and fell into step beside her. "How's it going with you and Mike?" she asked, wiping sweat from her brow.

Sherry beamed. "Fantastic. He's not like the other boys I've dated, Brie. I mean, physically, sure, he fits the bill for what I'm looking for. Every inch of him." She gave her friend a significant look. "*Every* inch. But beyond that, he's steady, honest, and hardworking."

Brie bit her lip to hide her amusement. "That doesn't sound like your type at all."

"It isn't. Remember Austin?"

"Was he the perpetually out-of-work actor who worshiped you as his muse?"

"Got old so fast. And Remond?"

"The bodybuilder?" Brie asked with a laugh. "Everyone on the west side of Atlanta remembers Remond. When you broke up, he stayed in your driveway doing sit-ups for two days to win you back. It made the local news. It attracted the local strays. I thought he might move into the woods behind your house and learn to live off squirrel meat and unrequited love."

"Poor lost soul." Sherry sighed, staring nostalgically into the distance. "I had to get a restraining order just to avoid his abs."

Brie stole a glance at her. "Well, I'm happy you've found someone who seems to fit your evolving taste. No one deserves it more than you."

"Except maybe you," Sherry replied lightly. "And don't worry, I'm not going to make the same mistake two days in a row and ask how it's going with—"

"I think I'm falling for him."

Sherry gasped and grabbed her arm. "Really? That's huge!"

"Don't get too excited. We still haven't—"

That's when they heard the scream.

CHAPTER SEVENTEEN

Powers of the Pendant

For all her bluster and theatrics about hating cardio, when Sherry heard somebody in trouble, she could move. Before she knew it, Brie was racing to catch up with her friend, who was somehow already twenty yards in front of her, sprinting towards the sound of the scream.

They found the source in a driveway a couple of blocks away. A terrified woman in a bathrobe was already on the phone, screeching out her address to emergency dispatch as a host of neighbors surrounded a man who was perched on top of another, attempting to give CPR.

Sherry wasted no time shoving her way to the heart of the action. "Let me through. I'm an ER nurse."

She elbowed people aside, and Brie followed in her wake. The well-meaning neighbor was attempting CPR like he'd learned it from a daytime soap opera.

"Get off of him."

Sherry unceremoniously shoved him aside, and she and Brie got to work. Brie tipped the man's head back to open his airway and checked for breath sounds. Sherry held her fingers to his carotid artery and felt for a pulse before resuming compressions, this time in the right location and with the correct pressure and frequency.

"Cameron!" Brie called out without thinking, on the off-chance her angel could hear her and offer some assistance. When it became clear that he couldn't, she decided to ask the witnesses.

"What happened?" she barked into the crowd. The neighbors murmured a collective lack of information, so Brie took it upon herself to summon the partner over. "Lady!"

The woman in the bathrobe tearfully raced over. "How is he?"

"He's unresponsive. Can you tell me what happened?"

"I don't know! One minute he kissed me goodbye at the door, and the next..." She stared at the man, eyes wide in horror. "You can bring him back, right? On TV, they always bring them back."

Brie and Sherry shared a look.

"That's what we're trying to do, ma'am," Brie answered. "We work at Daya Memorial. We'll make sure he gets the very best care."

Just then, the ambulance pulled up, and two paramedics came rushing out.

"Sherry?" one of them asked. "What are you doing here?" Despite the urgency of the situation, when his eye was drawn down by her garish ensemble, he added, "What are you wearing?"

"We were on a run and heard a scream," Sherry replied, never losing focus.

"What can you tell us?"

Sherry rattled off the only info they'd been given as the paramedics prepared the man for transport. At the last minute, she and Brie hopped into the ambulance to ride back themselves.

The young paramedics performed their tasks with seamless, stark professionalism, but the man was completely unresponsive.

And Brie got the feeling that despite their youth, the emergency response team had seen enough to be well and thoroughly jaded.

"Third one this week," a dark-haired woman said grimly as they merged onto the highway.

She was answered by the driver. "I bet it's some new designer drug the cops haven't gotten wise to yet. They're all too young for it to be anything else."

That's exactly what Cameron said.

"Either way, this guy's a goner." The dark-haired girl continued compressions, but her attention strayed elsewhere. "Are you and Janae still doing that escape room thing this weekend?"

"Nah. Billy tried it a few days ago with his wife and said they solved it in less than an hour. I don't see the point if it isn't even a challenge, you know? Besides, Janae says——"

"Would you shut up?" Brie snapped.

The team turned to look at her, startled.

"Sorry, I... I'm trying to hear that. Could you turn it up?"

The driver gave her a look but turned up the radio so they could hear the dispatch reports about incoming traumas. Brie blushed scarlet and lowered her head. Much as she didn't want to be known as "that person" in the workplace, she couldn't stand the way they were writing this man off as though he was already lost. Even if she was fairly certain they were right.

Sherry reached over and squeezed Brie's hand. She squeezed back.

By the time they pulled into the ambulance bay, everyone in the rig feared the worst, but they still worked determinedly, as though they had at least some chance of bringing the man back. Only after the code had been run, only after every medical option to save his life had been exhausted, did the on-call doctor snap his gloves onto a nearby tray and call time of death.

Brie and Sherry looked on grimly as the room slowly emptied of personnel. They stayed while the distraught new widow was allowed a last glance at the deceased before being taken away again, sobbing, to complete the kind of paperwork that no young wife should ever have to fill out. They stayed while the room emptied again, sinking onto the bed across from the dead man.

They sat next to one another in dark silence. Finally, Sherry stood.

"I don't feel much like shopping anymore. I'm going to call Mike to pick us up." She pulled out her phone. "And I'm getting us some coffee. This isn't the kind of situation one should face without coffee. Do you want anything?"

Brie shook her head and stared at the body, unblinking.

"I'll be back. Do you want to come with me?" Sherry asked.

Brie shook her head again, unable to summon words.

After a moment of hesitation, Sherry closed the curtain separating the room, blocking Brie's view of the body, and walked out into the hall.

Brie stared into space. Only an hour ago, he'd been alive and vibrant. He'd been kissing his wife goodbye. He had a job, a nice home, and a lovely partner. Plans. A future.

Fate is so cold. So arbitrary.

She was still lost in her thoughts when she heard scuffling footsteps enter the room. At first, she thought it was Sherry coming to get her, but some deep instinct told her to stay quiet. That's when she heard the horrible throat-clearing sound she'd come to loathe just like the rest of the staff.

Dr. Matthews.

She tucked her feet up onto the bed so he couldn't see her. There was a strange thump, followed by a series of clicking sounds. Then a rustle, like something being lifted out of fabric.

Ever so slowly, she peeked around the curtain.

Dr. Matthews was bending over the deceased. His strange black bag was open on the floor beside him. On the dead man's chest lay a bizarre-looking object. It looked like a sculpture of some kind, carved in interlocking, polished swoops of wood. The thing had a decidedly claw or antler-like appearance, and a black stone sphere was shining in the middle. Though the craftsmanship needed to sculpt such a thing was undeniably in the realm of artistry, the piece itself was too sinister to be beautiful. The stone emanated a faint golden glow, somehow sickly but growing steadily stronger.

In a moment of decision she hadn't consciously made, Brie whipped back the curtain.

"What are you doing?" she asked in a loud voice, hoping her volume would hide her fear.

Matthews leaped back with a cry, nearly dropping the strange object. "I'm..." He looked at her with a wild mix of fear and anger before making the decision to go with anger. "What are you doing here?" he glared accusingly.

"I came in with the code," she answered, turning her head up defiantly. "You didn't answer my question. What are *you* doing here? What is that thing?"

He tried to keep his composure, but his breathing was ragged, and his forehead was already dripping with sweat. Nonetheless, he decided the way out of this situation was to pull rank.

"That is my personal property, and I am here on hospital business, which frankly is none of your concern, Nurse Weldon. Now, I suggest you hurry along before I have you written up."

She narrowed her eyes. "Written up for what?"

Before he had a chance to respond, she cut him off. "You know what? Knock yourself out. In fact, let's get HR down here right now. We'll see who they're more interested in: a nurse who decided to stay with a dead man's body till the morgue came to pick it up out of respect or a doctor who gets his jollies by sneaking into a dead patient's room and messing around with the body, even when he wasn't involved with the case at all."

He stammered for a moment before stuffing the strange contraption into its case, turning on his heel, and rushing out the door. He nearly knocked Sherry over on his way out.

"Watch it!" she protested, almost spilling coffee on herself. She turned to Brie. "What the hell is going on with that guy? What was he doing in here?"

"Sher, stay here, okay? I'll be right back."

Brie rushed out the door before she could hear a word of protest, following Matthews down the hall and past the nurses' station before she ran smack dab into Denise.

"Weldon, slow down."

She looked away from Matthews for a moment. "I'm sorry, Denise, I was—"

"Sherry told me. Sorry you caught one on your day off."

"Yeah. Just can't stay away, I guess."

Brie craned her neck to see where Matthews had gone. She caught sight of him across the waiting room, near the exit to the back parking lot. He was talking to that blonde woman again, holding the strange briefcase between them like protection. But Denise and about a dozen other people and conversations were in the way, and she couldn't hear what they were saying at all.

She couldn't say what possessed her to do it. She could never tell Cameron what prompted her to try something so ridiculous. Not even when he asked her later, many times. She closed her eyes and tried *very hard* to hear what they were saying.

Her heart slowed down, then started racing. She focused even harder. She felt a faint prickle on the back of her neck. Then all at once, her eyes flew open, and the rest of the room melted away. With the focus of a magnifying glass, she zeroed in on Matthews and the mysterious woman, observing the conversation at both a volume and distance that made it feel like she was standing right beside them.

"—must know this isn't our arrangement, and this doesn't buy you time." The blonde held up two fingers. "I'll be back. And you know what better be waiting for me when I get here."

He trembled before her, clutching the case. "But I was hoping—"

"I will be back."

Brie blinked quickly, then snapped back to the present, doing the unthinkable and reaching out to grab Denise by the arm. "Who is that?" she asked, pointing frantically at the pair.

Denise looked, then turned back with a frown. "Dr. Matthews."

"No, I know. Who is he talking to?"

Denise glanced again, then looked at her strangely. "He isn't talking to anyone, Weldon."

Brie looked again, shocked. The blonde woman was gone.

Sherry and Brie were quiet in the car. Despite his natural affinity for investigating everything, Mike had the emotional wherewithal to let them keep to themselves. They dropped Brie off at home and waited until she opened her front door before driving off with a wave.

Cameron swept over her the moment she stepped inside. "Are you okay? I was getting worried."

"I'm sorry, there was no time to call."

"Time to call?" he repeated, placing his hands on her arms and checking her over for damage. "Are you alright? What happened?"

Brie recounted the morning's events in as much detail as possible, omitting one vital part. Cameron's eyes clouded with concern when she mentioned the man with the heart attack and grew darker still when she described what she'd seen with Matthews, the dead body, and the blonde.

"And you still have no idea who this woman might be?"

She shook her head. "The same way I have no idea why he'd be carrying around a gothic-looking, glowing sculpture to put on the bodies of the dead."

When did I start talking like this? When did this become my life?

His brow was knit together. "I have never heard of such a thing in all my days." He glanced at her face again. "But it's more than that, isn't it?"

She nodded, staring at the ground for a moment. "Cam, the conversation I overheard between them. It was on the other side of a crowded ER waiting room." She lifted her eyes to meet his. "They were close together. They were speaking softly. There's no way I should have been able to watch them or hear them like that."

She hesitated before voicing the thought that had been plaguing her the whole ride home. "No human way."

"What do you mean *you were afraid of this?*"

Cameron sat on the couch as Brie stood by the fireplace and shouted. He'd been sitting there for five minutes, regretting his initial choice of words. When she finally quieted, he chose his next more carefully, trying to pacify her as best he could.

"I only meant, as I told you before, any contact with life force energy changes you. Prolonged contact? Well, it changes you a lot. Look at me."

"Yes, but—"

"Not to mention, I think we've established that's one powerful celestial artifact you've got around your neck. We don't understand it, and we don't know the limits of its capabilities."

She stopped her pacing and whirled in a rage, pendant in hand. "It's changing me, Cameron. Turning me into something I'm not."

He was quiet for a moment before replying. "What if it's turning you into something you are?"

"Don't give me the destiny speech. I'm being mutated somehow. And the worst part is, I don't have any say in the matter. Because if I take this *thing* off my neck…" She stomped her foot in childlike fury, hands balled at her sides in fists. "This is not what I *want*, Cameron. This is not what I would choose for myself."

"Brianna—"

"No! Don't try to make this less than it is, and don't try to make it better."

"Brianna—"

"You have no idea how this feels. No idea how trapped I feel at this moment. No idea—"

"*Brianna!*"

"*What?*"

It was only then she saw him staring, horrified, at her feet. It was only then she saw that she'd stomped a deep crack straight through her living room floor.

Oh, my God…

She turned and followed the fissure as it slowly spread. It traced to the fireplace and, with a low, ominous thump, started splitting the stones apart. One after another. Cracks and dust.

Cameron was there in a flash, placing a glowing hand on the crack and murmuring something profound and unintelligible. The crack faded slightly before vanishing all at once.

He looked up at her, breathing hard. "Brianna, I say this with no intention whatsoever of invalidating your feelings: perhaps there's a way for you to experience these emotions that doesn't break your house."

◆   ◆   ◆

Brie took a bath. It was what she did whenever things felt overwhelming. She'd done it ever since she could remember.

When she was five and had to come home early from a classmate's birthday party because the excitement had been too much, and she ended up getting frosting on her party dress, the first thing her mom did was run a bubble bath and pop her in the tub.

In third grade, when Bobby Mackavoy pretended he was going to kiss her behind the merry-go-round but held up a frog instead, she ran right home after school and got into the tub.

After her mother's funeral, she spent two days in the bath.

She didn't eat or drink. She'd replenish the hot water when it ran cold. Sherry got her a toddler floatie to hold her head up when she had to sleep and stayed awake to make sure she didn't slip and drown. Her father eventually dragged her out with a strange man she'd come to know as Dr. Rogers.

Her last memory of her old apartment, her old life, was in the tub — granted, it wasn't the most relaxing experience — before she'd tried to move here to Virginia and start fresh.

What a fool's errand that turned out to be.

Just as she had that last night in her old apartment, she sank beneath the water and let the pendant float up before her eyes. It glowed softly in the fluorescence, hovering with strange precision in front of her face like it was something alive. She grabbed it between two fingers and twisted it back and forth, looking for something, anything, as though she could find a clue, a mark she'd never seen before in all her years of faithfully wearing it around her neck.

Like a millstone.

She let go and watched it drift back down to her chest, to her scar. Well, to what used to be a scar. She could barely see it anymore. She gritted her teeth together so hard her jaw hurt, and her hands balled up into fists.

It's erasing it.

It's erasing who I used to be — turning me into something else, something new.

She surfaced angrily, splashing water out of the tub.

Well, she hadn't asked to change, had she? She was just fine the way she was. Maybe she liked her scar. Maybe she didn't need some stupid magic necklace coming in and... and...

Healing your damage? Some inner voice chimed in gently. *Giving you strength you didn't know you had?*

She cupped her hands and splashed some water into her face. Things might be fraught right now, but she was not getting into an argument with herself. There were lines, dammit. There were *supposed* to be lines.

She got out of the tub and toweled off, glaring at herself in the mirror. Her eyes widened as she did a double take.

Are those abs?

She twisted around in the mirror, and there was no denying it. She was more physically fit than she'd ever been, with significantly less cause to be. Her failed attempt at a run with Sherry that morning was some of the only exercise she'd attempted in months. Back in Georgia, she was too busy completing her schooling to do anything more than a sporadic jog to the waterfall. Here in Virginia, things had been such a whirlwind, it hadn't been a priority.

Yet, here she was, muscles long and lean, curves smooth and firm. Her hair was longer, thick, and healthy, cascading down her back in a mass of chocolate curls. Her eyes were bright, her skin was clear, and her nails were strong and unbroken.

Her existential dread, her fear of loss of autonomy, and even her annoyance all gave way for a moment in favor of that powerful, most tenacious of all human emotions — curiosity.

She wondered, could she do it again?

She closed her eyes as she had in the hospital and tried to focus somewhere else. Anywhere else. She stayed this way for one minute, then two, three. Nothing happened. Just as she was about to throw on her robe and call her reflection an idiot, something happened.

She heard the squirrels from the attic. Only they weren't in the attic. They were in a tree.

She couldn't say how she knew, but she knew it was the tree in her backyard, the large beech with the wonky, low-hanging branch. She could hear them rustling around in a little makeshift nest they must have made when unwanted humans moved into their house. She could hear how many of them there were. Two larger ones and a tiny one, maybe their child.

She could hear them breathing. She could tell they were asleep.

She shook her head and glared at her reflection as though it was somehow *her* fault that all of this was happening — this alternate Brie, in her alternate world, with her alternate abs and her stupid alternate ability to... *what*, exactly? Imagine she could hear the relative age of squirrels? Spy on a coworker and a woman she was only half-convinced even existed? Break her house in half?

Great superpower, you effing walnut.

Suddenly, the weight of it all came crashing down on her. She'd erected some impressive scaffolding to keep it at bay, built largely of humor, anger, sarcasm, and disbelief, but reality is too heavy a thing to be borne up by such a structure, and it crumbled in the space of an instant.

She couldn't tell Sherry about the supernatural things that were happening. She couldn't tell Cameron about the human things she needed to talk about. She couldn't talk to a doctor, or she'd be immediately committed. She couldn't even articulate to herself what was going on because she had no earthly idea what was happening or why. There was no one in the whole world she could talk to about this in its entirety. And all she wanted was to feel like herself again.

She did the only thing she could think of. She called her dad.

He answered on the second ring. "Brianna!"

She was startled at his quick pickup. "Hi, Dad. How are you?"

"Better for hearing your voice," he said warmly. "How are you doing? How's the new place? And the new job?"

"It's... it's great," she replied cautiously. "It's all going really well. Just busy, you know." She swallowed hard. "I'm sorry I didn't call sooner. This job can get pretty dramatic."

"Sherry told me you had a rough start. I'm sorry about that. I didn't want to call in case you were still finding your feet. But I've been thinking about you a lot, Brie."

She was stunned. A part of her had expected he'd be two-thirds through a bottle at this time of night and was looking for negative reinforcement to convince herself that, yes, everything was terrible, she had made a bad decision, and this was all some punishment she deserved.

But this? This was new.

"You talked to Sherry?"

"We talk every now and again. She called to tell me why you were late getting there. I hope that's alright. She said you asked her to."

Brie nodded swiftly, still trying to catch up. "That's right, I did. You sound different. I mean, you sound great," she added quickly, trying to backtrack.

"I've been trying out some new things."

"Oh, like what?"

"Well, I've been getting up earlier, going to sleep earlier, trying to fix the house up again."

She blinked. "Oh. Well, that's really—"

"And I had a meeting with Dr. Rogers."

"What?" She sat down on the side of the bath, hard. "That's... that's wonderful, Dad. But I don't understand. Why now?"

There was silence on the other end. "I guess change is in the air," he finally replied. "It's time. It's past time, actually. Well past. I let you down by not doing this sooner. The doc says... he says better late than never."

He took in a deep breath, and she heard his voice shake a little. "I..." He coughed, clearly backing down from whatever he was about to say and choosing something else in its place. "The day you left, it shook something up in me. I knew, well, you might be moving away, but I didn't want to lose you, you know?"

He drew in another rasping breath. She could almost picture him raking back his hair.

"Anyway, I called Dr. Rogers the next day. What's that your mom always used to say? 'Make the next best decision you can,' right?"

Her throat was too thick with emotion to respond.

Now. Now you do this. After I'm already gone.

She bit her lip.

But in fairness, that is precisely what I needed to hear.

They sat in awkward silence for a minute before he coughed again and decided to change the subject to something less intense. "Sherry texted me, just so you know. Said you're dating some kind of movie star."

She had to laugh and held her phone tightly. "Well, not quite. He's probably too much of an oddball to have a future in the film industry. But I do think you'd like him."

"Oh yeah?" he asked, and she could hear the happiness in his voice. "Tell me."

They talked for another few minutes before saying goodbye. Not about anything of real consequence, not about anything supernatural or cataclysmic. Just about normal, human, everyday things. Brie couldn't remember the last time they'd spoken for so long about anything.

When it finally started winding down, she realized she was much calmer and happier. "I'll call you again soon, okay?"

"Not if I call you first. Take care, Brie."

"You too, Dad."

She hung up the phone and looked at her reflection again, this time with compassion, not blame.

"The next best decision," she said softly.

I can do that.

She put on her pajamas and stood up, squaring her shoulders with confidence. Just before she was going to leave, on a whim, she high-fived her reflection.

The mirror immediately cracked.

CHAPTER EIGHTEEN

Sunday Morning Football

The morning sun slanted in through the east window shutters at a soft angle, warm and golden, illuminating dust particles that floated lazily in and out of the light. It was still early. Too early even for Siri to wake them with her daily anguished howls. Brie stretched, then sat up with a sudden lurch. Cameron wasn't there.

Though it had been less than a week since they'd started sharing a bed, his absence nudged that place inside her where she'd held her anxiety for five years, when he'd disappeared from her life without a trace and left her with nothing but a waning conviction that he was ever real.

"Cameron?"

She made her way quickly to the bathroom, then froze the second she opened the door.

"What do you think?" he asked proudly, fists on his hips.

She gripped the doorknob, hoping it would serve as some emotional support anchor and keep her from laughing. Or swooning. While she'd slept, her guardian angel had decked himself out in full quarterback gear from the 1950s. Pads, tight white fabric, and strategically placed stripes dominated the outfit.

A helmet and mouth guard dangled from his hand.

"I asked your phone what the American football teams wore in the greatest game ever played, and it showed me photos of this." He turned this way and that, admiring his reflection in the magically fixed mirror. "I think this will help immensely in the sports rehearsal today. With so much protection, these players must never get injured."

She bit her lip so hard she almost tasted blood. "You asked about American football outfits?"

"Of course. Mike mentioned I looked like one of the people who call it that."

"From the greatest game ever played?"

He looked down at his clothes. "Do you think that was overly ambitious?"

"And it showed you a Colts uniform from 1958?"

He stared back with a frown. "I sense there's something I'm missing."

She had a heated internal debate about whether to tell him that he'd suited up for the wrong kind of game. Whether to tell him that her father had often spoken about "The Greatest Game Ever Played" when she was a girl, and she'd developed a terribly poignant prepubescent crush on quarterback Johnny Unitas while watching *SportsCenter* clips with her dad.

In the end, she decided to do the honorable thing. "Cam, we call it soccer here. This..." She trailed off as her eyes ran up and down the length of his frame. "This is for a different sport."

"Oh." His disappointment was visible. "Might this not work all the same?"

"I'm afraid not," she said with a grin, walking into the room. A wild thought raced through her brain, like a lick of fire through a dry forest. In half a heartbeat, everything was aflame. She stepped even closer, maintaining eye contact. "Though I have to tell you, this is really working for me. On many, many levels."

She hooked her fingers into the elastic on top of his pants.

New Brie. New rules.

Those heavenly edicts are his problem, not mine.

He stiffened as she drew them together. "Oh yeah?"

She nodded mutely, watching with immense satisfaction as his cheeks darkened and he tried casually to avert his gaze. Things had just reached a breaking point when she suddenly released him with a cheerful grin, pushing him towards the door. "I need to take a shower. Meet you downstairs?"

He nodded swiftly as he hurried out of the room. There was a tension in the way he was moving that betrayed any level of casual retreat, and no matter how hard he tried to stop himself, his eyes kept drifting back to her face.

"Of course. Have a good—" He let out a quiet gasp, having walked full tilt into the door frame. "Have a good shower."

She nodded lightly, already pulling off her shirt. "Remember to take off those clothes, Cam. Wrong uniform." Her eyes twinkled as she swung the door shut. "The team would never *permit* that."

◆　　◆　　◆

Breakfast was an excruciating affair. Not so much for Brie but for the angel sitting by her side.

He listened in silence as she prattled on cheerfully about anything that happened to strike her fancy. A list of top vacation spots, the list of skills she was meant to be perfecting at the hospital, the price of milk. It didn't stop when the waitress dropped off their food. It didn't even slow down.

There was a chance it might have gone on forever if he hadn't suddenly interrupted. "Do you have any idea how much I want to kiss you?" he asked quietly, freezing her in her tracks. "Do you have any idea how difficult it is sleeping beside you, night after night?"

Their eyes met, until it was finally she who was forced to look away.

"To me, you are a miracle. You are the first person who's ever been able to see me. To touch me. Do you have any idea, Brianna? *Any* idea how much I wish to touch you in return?"

Her cheeks flamed, and her gaze dropped to the table.

"I understand how it must seem," he continued softly. "And I understand the urge to push against those boundaries. *Trust me*, I do. But I don't think you understand the full consequence of where such a thing might lead. I don't think you understand the forces that stand against it. The same forces that could separate the two of us in an instant. They could make me ache for you forever..." He inhaled painfully and finished, "And make you completely forget about me."

She froze perfectly still, having never considered such a thing.

"You are a brave, intelligent, powerful, compassionate woman of surpassing beauty in body and spirit. You are everything I could have imagined, if I had ever imagined a woman for myself. If such a thing was up to me..." He trailed away with the most heartbreaking look she had ever seen. "But it isn't. Do you understand?"

It was quiet a moment, then she nodded. "Yes, I understand."

And I don't see how I'll ever recover.

She sat there another moment, then flashed a heartbroken smile herself. "Cameron, let's get you a chocolate croissant."

◆   ◆   ◆

"The *other* goal, Cameron! You're going the wrong way!"

The angel turned around and careened in the opposite direction, completely failing to take the ball along with him.

"The ball, you lunatic! Don't forget the ball!"

Cameron's research, focused on the wrong kind of football, had led to an excessive use of hands and a flagrant misunderstanding of every single rule in the game. Mike looked for all the world like one of those dads at their child's ball game who was far too heavily invested in the outcome. Brie could see a vein bulging in his forehead from halfway across the field.

Now, this is quality entertainment.

She was lounging on a lawn chair on the sidelines with Sherry, who was halfway through a glass of something called a Yellowhammer. Her insuppressible friend had smuggled a pitcher of the stuff into the McRyan Athletic Complex. Brie was immensely enjoying both the spectacle of her angel being thoroughly dominated and her best friend's gradual descent into tipsiness.

She didn't know what was in the beverage, but based on the rate of Sherry's giggle escalation over the past twenty minutes, she suspected rum.

"That is a fine-looking collection you've assembled," a cheerful voice rang out behind them. "Where's the photographer? I have to assume we're making a calendar."

"You made it!"

Rashida grinned and sank into the waiting lawn chair. Sherry lifted the pitcher of radioactive-yellow liquid in her direction. "Drink?"

"No, thank you. I'm swinging by the hospital with Brie after this."

"More for me." Sherry delightedly topped her glass off and let out a hoot, raising it in the direction of the players. "Shirts and skins, please!" she called.

"Isn't that basketball?" asked Rashida.

Brie had more pressing concerns. "Sher, that's half the police force out there. This might not be the ideal place to be drunk and disorderly."

"Who's drunk?" Sherry looked at her in mock scandal. "Brie, if you see someone drinking, you should really report them. That's half the police force out there. Noble officers who are sworn to both serve and protect me. Besides, you know I can handle my liquor better than anybody."

"You've been talking in a British accent for ten minutes."

"Sod off, ungrateful colonist. I'm trying to watch the game."

Rashida shot Brie a grin. "Is she always like this?"

"Only when there's rum involved. She turns into a gentleman pirate."

"Shirts and skins!" Sherry cupped her hands around her mouth in case they hadn't heard her the first time. Mike shot her a grin. "I see you, Mitchell. Eyes on the game."

On the field, Cameron asked curiously, "What is she yelling?"

"She wants our team to take off our shirts," Mike explained.

Cameron tilted his head in puzzlement. "Is that customary?"

"It is when my girl's involved." Mike whipped off his shirt, revealing an impeccably sculpted and blindingly white form underneath.

Sherry started laughing uproariously. "The beacons are lit!"

Mike looked over and scowled. "I'm not *that* pale."

She put on sunglasses and indicated that Brie and Rashida should do the same. "Gondor calls for aid!"

"I could have you arrested, you know."

"What was that, dear?"

"Nothing."

Meanwhile, Cameron crossed his arms at the base of his shirt and pulled it over his head. All three women pulled their sunglasses halfway down their noses to better appreciate the view.

"Damn, Brie." Rashida let out a low whistle. "You go home to that every night? How do you manage to leave in the mornings?"

Brie pushed her sunglasses back up and settled back in her chair with a sigh. "It isn't really like that," she admitted quietly.

They looked at her in surprise.

"What do you mean?" asked Rashida.

"We don't... we haven't really..."

Sherry's face cleared in a look of understanding, but Rashida was clearly shocked.

"Are you kidding me? Child, if I had something that delicious anywhere near the vicinity of my bedroom, I would take a sabbatical so we could spend more time exploring ways to corrupt each other. What's the problem? Is there something wrong with him?"

Brie shook her head quickly, wishing she hadn't brought it up.

"Of course not. He's..." She watched him catch the ball and yell, "Hike!" as the rest of the team groaned in exasperation. Mike jogged over and whispered in his ear. He dropped the ball and apologized profusely for what had to be the tenth time. "He's perfect."

It's me. There's something wrong with me.

If I were normal, I wouldn't even be able to see him. And none of this would have happened.

Neither of us would be feeling this pain.

"They're taking things slow," Sherry interrupted quickly, seeing her expression. "You can't let someone that good-looking get their way all the time, Ida. It would set the stage for a dreadful amount of entitlement moving forward. He needs to learn to sing for his supper. Besides, Brie is a woman of incomparable virtue, not a wanton harlot such as yourself."

The topic settled in laughter, and Brie flashed Sherry a grateful look.

"How's it going with that case from the other night?" she asked Rashida.

"Terrible. Worse than terrible. I've run every test and gotten everyone involved I can think of, but no matter what I do, I'm still no closer to an explanation about the cause of death. And if that wasn't bad enough, we caught another one yesterday. The bodies keep piling up, and I have nothing to tell their families." She slumped back in her chair. "At least the hospital got me a new mass spectrometer to try to help. I only wish it would turn up an answer already."

Sherry and Brie looked at each other.

"Was the one from yesterday an unexplained cardiac trauma from the ER?"

"Yes." She looked at them, confused. "How did you know?"

Brie stared out at the field, unseeing. "We brought that in."

"I thought it was your day off!"

"It was. We were out on a run. The guy just dropped right in his own driveway. We rode with the team back to the ER to try to help."

Rashida gave her a strange look. "You always seem to be right in the thick of it, don't you?"

You have no idea.

Sherry was quiet for a moment, swirling her neon yellow drink thoughtfully in her cup.

"Brie, why did you call for Cameron when we found that guy yesterday? We'd just left him back at the house, but you called out for him."

Brie was stunned for a second, before stammering, "Oh, I don't... I don't know what I was thinking. He's been there for me during a few dramatic times recently. I guess I just got used to turning to him during emergencies."

Sherry flashed her a look but said nothing.

Why does she have to be this perceptive, even when she drinks?

Just then, a wave of appreciative yells from the field caught their attention. Cameron must have finally gotten the gist of the rules because he was tearing down the field with some impressive footwork. He passed to Mike, who passed to one of his friends, who passed it back to Cameron, who sailed it into the goal with a mighty swing of his leg.

He immediately turned to Brie, both his arms raised in childlike triumph.

He was still in this pose, bathed in applause, when the goalie for the opposing team attempted to kick the ball back to him. He turned at precisely the wrong moment, and it hit him square in the nose. Blood immediately gushed forth as the goalie yelled, "Man, I'm so sorry."

He lifted his hand to the blood, glancing at his palm with an expression nothing short of delight. He flashed Brie another grin, then froze when he saw the pained look on her face.

Angelic moron.

At that point, he seemed to register that he was supposed to be having a normal human pain reaction. He stilled for a moment in indecision before throwing back his head and shrieking at an ungodly pitch that could best be described as that of a junior high girl.

The field quieted, as Sherry lifted her eyebrow slowly. "Yeah. He seems like he'd be really good in a crisis."

Not long after, Brie and Rashida left to go to the hospital. They piled into the pathologist's green sedan with plans to meet back up with the others at a pub later. Sherry promised to get Cameron to the venue and to properly introduce Rashida to their team's goalie. The two had been making eyes at one another for the past half hour, very much at the expense of his concentration, and Sherry was thrilled at the prospect of playing matchmaker.

After fruitlessly grilling Brie for information she didn't have about the soccer player she'd never met, Rashida gave up and focused on her impending introduction.

"So, I'll just change and meet you in the parking lot, okay?"

"If you want to run home, it's no trouble. I can always take a cab," offered Brie.

"No worries, I have everything I need at the hospital."

Brie looked at her sideways. "You do?"

"Of course," the woman answered easily. "I always keep a cocktail dress and heels in my locker, just in case. Doesn't everyone?"

Brie grinned. "I really shouldn't have introduced you to Sherry. You have everything in common. You're bound to run off together. I'll soon be nothing more than a distant memory."

Rashida shook her head, smiling. "Nah, that lady adores you. I've never seen a grown woman so intractably protective of another."

"What do you mean?"

"Little things. Like how she bullies and bribes everyone on the nursing staff to switch shifts with her until your schedules match up. Or when I asked you about your handsome boyfriend. She practically grabbed my shoulders and steered me in the opposite direction." Rashida laughed. "She called me a harlot."

Brie couldn't help but grin. "Well, in fairness——"

"Yeah, yeah. Laugh it up, Chuckles. The point is, I don't think there's any getting between you two." She looked over warmly. "But I am glad you have room for a third."

They drove on in silence for a while before Brie said, "It isn't for lack of trying, you know."

"What isn't?"

"Me and Cam." She fought through her reluctance and said it out loud. "The truth is I've been wholly unsuccessful in my every attempt to seduce him."

Rashida's eyebrows shot up, but she remained quiet as Brie continued.

"We come from very different worlds. And where he comes from, to be with someone like me is considered taboo. Whether or not he wants to… it isn't allowed."

Rashida considered this, then nodded slowly. "Sherry mentioned that he might be Amish when you went to the bathroom."

Brie didn't know what to do except agree. "Right. Well, the point is, being with me might destroy his relationship with his people — with his family. And I don't know if I'm selfish enough to want him to do that. But I'm afraid that I am."

Rashida was quiet for a minute. "I know exactly how you feel."

"You do?"

She laughed humorlessly. "Believe it or not, dating as a Nigerian woman in the American South hasn't always been the smoothest sailing. I've run into a few families less than thrilled to accept their son's new girlfriend with open arms."

"What did you do?"

Rashida shrugged. "The only thing I could do. The only thing anyone can do. I made my choices, and they made theirs. Sometimes, I walked away. I decided that they were too much work, and if they wanted to be with me, they'd stop dragging their feet and make it happen. Sometimes, I took the initiative. I made my feelings known, and they took that information and made their decision."

She looked over at Brie. "It's all about choices. In the end, you can only be responsible for your own."

Brie swallowed hard and looked at the road ahead. "Rashida? I'm thrilled you're our third."

CHAPTER NINETEEN

Horns of a Dilemma

"Stash your stuff. We have a bad one."

They'd scarcely walked through the door when Denise jerked her head to indicate that Brie should follow her fast and close. Brie lifted her hand to Rashida in a hasty goodbye and stashed her backpack with Cindy with a brief nod of understanding, then hurried down the hall.

They swept into a trauma room, and Brie stopped cold. A red-haired girl, no more than six, lay on the bed. Her lips were white, her face tinged with green. Her breathing was shallow, and she lay perfectly still, except when a round of convulsions shot through her like a bolt of electricity, arching her back and shaking her limbs like rubber toys.

Her mother stood in a corner, her eyes wide with shock. She was being questioned by a nurse Brie hadn't met before.

"I don't know. I don't know," she kept repeating. "She was fine when I brought her in. That doctor examined her, and she was fine. Just a fever that wouldn't go away. I only brought her in because it was so high, and our doctor is away on vacation." She looked at the nurse with tears spilling down her cheeks. "What's wrong with her? What's wrong with my baby?"

"I don't know, ma'am, but that's what we're going to find out."

"Don't just stand there, Weldon."

Denise snapped her fingers, and Brie shot back into focus. She immediately walked to the girl's side and assisted the other nurses attaching monitors, taking vitals, and taking her blood pressure. It was dangerously low, so low the machine registered an error the first time.

As Brie bent down to readjust the cuff and try again, the pendant slipped from her shirt, knocking lightly against the girl's arm. Suddenly, the shaking stopped. Green eyes flew open, locking onto Brie in an instant of sudden, inexplicable lucidity. Tiny fingers curled around her sleeve.

"Please," she whispered. "Please, help me."

A second later, her eyes rolled back in her head, and she started convulsing again.

There was a sudden commotion on the other side of the room. The nurse had dropped his clipboard. The mother was staring in complete shock. Even Denise looked rattled, planting her hands on her hips.

"Weldon, what was that?" she demanded. "What did she say to you?"

Brie stared for a split second longer, then the words burst from her lips. "It's poison."

There was a beat of silence.

"What?" Denise asked doubtfully, staring with concern. "Weldon, there's no—"

"It's poison," Brie said, louder. "Cut her clothes off, don't pull them over her head. Run fluids. A ton of them. She needs an anticonvulsant. Take vials of her blood immediately and deliver at least one of them to Rashida Botha down in the morgue. And pump some fresh air into this room. We don't know how this got into her system, but it got in while she was here."

Everyone in the room had stopped and was staring at her.

Of course they are, you lunatic. What the hell is going on?

If the situation had been any less urgent, if it had been anything less than a helpless child lying on the bed, she might have come up with some reasonable explanation. But there was no time.

Brie turned desperately to Denise. "It's poison."

Denise looked at her for a moment before nodding curtly. "Alright, you heard her. Cut those clothes off. Open that window, and pump air into this room. Make sure you're wearing gloves to handle her. Somebody wash her face and eyes and try to swab her nasal passages. I need a tox screen ten minutes ago. Someone call the lab and tell them they have an incoming priority one. Get a vial of blood to Dr. Botha in the morgue."

She rattled this off in a single breath, then turned back to Brie. "Weldon, get me ten ccs of diazepam, split into ten one-milliliter doses. Push every two to five minutes. Marcus, as soon as she stops shaking, you find a vein and run fluids right through this kid. We are not losing this little girl today, people."

"What's going on here?" Dr. Matthews stood in the door, a shocked expression on his face. "What have you done to my patient?"

Brie didn't miss a beat. She turned directly to the mother. "Tell him you refuse his care. Tell him you demand a different doctor, and he needs to leave."

The poor woman was lost in a storm of emotion, but when her eyes met Brie's, they seemed to clear. She nodded swiftly and turned to Matthews. "I demand a different doctor. I refuse to allow you in this room. Get out, and bring me another doctor. Right now."

Matthews stared at her, his face a mask of disbelief. He didn't move.

Fortunately, that's when the rage kicked in. "Get out of my little girl's room," the mother screamed, two inches from his face, "and bring me a doctor who knows what he's doing *right now*!"

He stumbled backward, white with shock. A second later, he disappeared into the hall.

◆   ◆   ◆

Two hours later, Brie was sitting on the floor of a deserted hallway, her back against the wall and her head hung low, forehead almost touching her knees. She'd spent an hour and a half working with the little girl to try to flush the toxins from her system and manage her symptoms before she was stable enough to move to the ICU. She'd spent the last half hour sitting on the floor. She was exhausted mentally, emotionally, and physically. She barely registered when Denise walked up, paused a moment, and sat beside her.

They sat in silence for a minute before Denise spoke. "It was strychnine. Well, something almost chemically identical to strychnine that the lab has never seen before. She inhaled it. It was all over her clothes, all in her hair."

Brie didn't say anything.

Denise put a hand on her shoulder and forced her to look up. "She's alive, Brie. She has kidney damage, and her liver's been through hell, but that little girl is alive because of you. We never would have caught it in time."

Brie nodded slowly as the words sank in. "She'll be okay?"

"She'll be okay." There was a pause. "Weldon, it was all over the room too. The poison. What you said about how she'd been exposed after she was admitted?" She paused again. "You saved the entire team from exposure."

Brie didn't say anything.

"How did you know? Did she say something to you?"

Courtesy of my magical necklace.

Denise leaned back against the wall. "The police want to talk to you. I told them you were under my direct supervision the entire time, and there was no information you could provide that I couldn't."

She looked at Brie. "Did I tell them the truth?"

Yes. Unless you count seeing a phantom woman who may or may not have hooves for feet blackmail that girl's doctor into attempted murder as information.

Brie looked at her and nodded.

Denise exhaled. "There's an ex-husband in the picture. No custody, very bitter after the divorce. Nobody saw him come in, but—"

"It wasn't the ex," Brie said in a quiet, flat voice.

Denise locked eyes with her and asked carefully, "You're saying that someone else was responsible for her poisoning."

"Yes."

"Someone involved in her admission or initial examination, someone who works in this hospital *deliberately* exposed a six-year-old child to an unknown, lethal toxin," Denise repeated carefully. "An action that would almost certainly have killed her and poisoned the rest of the emergency room team had it not been for your early diagnosis."

Brie's voice was a whisper. "Yes."

"Any idea who that might be?"

Their eyes met briefly.

"Yes."

Denise nodded in what looked like slow motion. "Matthews was in the showers when the police asked for him. He's still in there."

Brie found her voice. "They'll never find anything on him."

"No, they won't," agreed Denise. "Especially because this is such a bizarre, motiveless crime. He has no connection to this child that we're aware of, Weldon. This is…" She exhaled and leaned her head against the wall in a rare moment of vulnerability. "This is one of the worst, most senseless things I've seen in all my years here. I can't tell you why, but I know in my gut that you're right." She placed her hand on Brie's shoulder again, gently this time. "You'll need to give your statement to the police. Don't speculate. Just tell them what you know. But first, I want you to come with me."

Brie obediently stood and followed Denise down the hall. She didn't have the energy to do anything but follow orders. People looked at them and whispered behind their hands as they wove their way through the hospital up to the ICU and into the child's recovery room.

The little girl lay on the bed with her hair fanned out around her like a fiery halo. There were so many tubes in her arms she looked like a science experiment. Brie's breath caught in her throat, but then the girl opened those bright green eyes and focused them on her. "I know you."

Brie forced herself to smile, stepping closer. "You do?"

The little girl nodded.

Denise eased gently forward, gesturing between them. "Kylie, this is Brie. Brie, Kylie."

There was another toothy grin. "Brie, like the cheese Mommy likes?"

The two women chuckled.

"Brie, *just* like the cheese your mommy likes," Brie answered, perching on the bed. "It's very nice to see you, Kylie. I'm sorry you've had such a terrible day."

Kylie leaned back against her pillows, exhausted even by the effort it took to sit up. "The doctors said I almost died."

Brie nodded gently. "Yes, you did."

"And that you saved me."

Brie cocked her head towards Denise. "Denise over there saved you. Nobody would have listened to me if it wasn't for her."

"Yes, but you… you saw it. You're the one who saw what was bad and told everyone how to help me." Kylie reached up a tiny hand toward her. "Thank you."

Brie's throat tightened as she took the girl's hand. For a long moment, nobody said anything. They simply sat on the bed, listening to the quiet ticking of the clock on the wall.

"I'm going to go check on the mom," Denise said quietly, backing towards the door. "She's been with the police a long time. You got this?"

"I've got this."

Kylie and Brie sat together quietly for a few minutes longer.

Brie rubbed gentle circles on the back of the little girl's hand with her thumb, and a warm feeling of relief bloomed between them. It reminded her of the way it felt when Cameron touched her, or when she'd touched him in his other form, when he was nothing but energy and light.

After a few minutes, Kylie shifted around in the bed.

"Can I get you anything else, honey?"

"No, I just want to go to sleep."

"That's a good idea," Brie murmured, tucking her in. "Get some rest. Have a nice dream."

Kylie snuggled deeper into the pillows, her eyes already beginning to shut. "Brie?" she asked sleepily.

"Yes?"

"Don't let the bad blonde lady come back."

Brie's blood ran cold. "What bad blonde lady, honey?"

"You know. The one with the bad fairy dust. The one with the silver horns."

Brie didn't know where she was going.

Kylie had fallen asleep. Brie had waited for her mother to return, her thoughts racing crazily. Then she took off through the hospital, almost running, without a thought as to her destination.

She was real. I didn't imagine her.

She wanted to slap herself.

Of course she's real. How could she not be? Matthews knows who she is. He's spoken with her at least twice. That plot? The one that had something to do with a child? That was this. That was Kylie.

She'd ended up in an atrium, a space filled with plants and trees and enclosed by glass. She wondered if it was one of those meditative spaces they made for cancer patients. She sat down on the nearest bench and tried to think it through logically. If logic had any place in all of this.

By now, they've reviewed all the security cameras dozens of times. The blonde woman couldn't have shown up on any of them, or they'd have locked down the hospital looking for her. And Denise couldn't see her the other day in the ER. It wasn't that the woman left before she turned around — it was that she actually couldn't see her.

The realization struck like a ton of bricks.

She can only be seen if she wants to be.

Just like Cam.

Because she isn't from here.

A second later, she was up and running. A few minutes later, Brie burst through the doors of the morgue so suddenly that Rashida nearly dropped her test tube.

"What is it?" Brie demanded, trying to catch her breath.

"Brie!" Rashida gasped. "Are you alright? I heard what happened—"

"I'm fine," she said quickly, trying to calm her racing heart. "Ida, what is that stuff? The stuff they found in her system. What *exactly* is it?"

Rashida was looking at her like she might be crazy, but in light of recent events, it was understandable, and she certainly deserved the benefit of the doubt.

"Here," she finally answered, "have a look for yourself."

She stepped aside and indicated the readout screen of the mass spectrometer. Brie focused on the monitor and found herself looking at a series of symbols and graphs. She didn't know what any of it meant.

"Okay, new approach. Why don't you pretend that I don't know anything about mass spectrometry and explain this to me as one would explain such a thing to a small child?"

Rashida sat beside her. "Alright. The mass spectrometer identifies unknown compounds by measuring the weight of their molecules after converting them into gas-phase ions." This was met with a blank stare. "You might need to just take my word for it."

Brie nodded. "Fair enough. Just tell me what it is."

"I can't," Rashida answered. "I can only tell you what it very nearly was."

"I don't follow."

"It was almost strychnine. It was just different enough from strychnine to fool all the usual tests. I'd never seen anything like it before."

Brie absorbed this for a second, then looked up with a hint of dread. "Why do you keep using the past tense? Isn't it still in the lab? Did you send it off to the CDC already?"

Rashida shook her head. "That's the thing. The compound disappeared from every single sample you sent down. It completely disappeared before my eyes without leaving a trace."

Brie sank into a chair.

Without leaving a trace that you can see.

"So, I was too late."

"No, you weren't. I got it into the machine right away. I took a video of the tests and the results. There's a video of the substance disappearing." Rashida sat beside her. "We might not be able to study the toxin itself, but because of you, at least we have an idea of what we're dealing with. Because of you, dozens of families will get closure. And I'll send that video to the CDC first thing in the morning. They'll know what to do."

No, they won't.

Rashida stared at her vacant expression, then put her arm around her in a friendly hug. "You've had a helluva day. What do you say we go to a bar and get hammered? Maybe find me a handsomely crafted soccer player to give me a ride home?"

Brie couldn't summon any enthusiasm, but she nodded. "I need to give my statement to the police first."

"You go do that while I change. We'll meet back here when you're done. Say half an hour?"

Brie shot a look at locker number five. "Let's just meet in the parking lot."

CHAPTER TWENTY

Darkness Falls

Brie gave her statement to the police three times. Repeating it didn't help it make any sense. No matter how hard anyone tried, they simply didn't understand how she knew Kylie had been poisoned. She didn't think telling them that her magical necklace had somehow clued her in would be in any way helpful. She was seated in an abandoned conference room across from two detectives who stared at her like she was mentally disturbed. She did exactly what Denise had told her to do and stated only what she knew, which wasn't much at all.

"But, how did you know it was a toxin?"

"I have no idea. I just knew."

"You can understand why that's a woefully insufficient explanation, right, Miss Weldon?"

"Yes."

"Can you help me straighten that out?"

"If I could, I would, but I truly cannot."

Three times she relived the story. Three times she remembered how it felt to hold Kylie's hand as death tried to get a better grip on her little body.

By the time they were done, she was utterly spent. She walked out of the room and straight into Rashida, who had kindly come to wait for her to finish up with the police in her cocktail dress and heels. Together, they walked to the lowest tier of the parking lot in silence.

It was nearly eight, and the sun had dipped low on the horizon by the time they got to the pub, an Irish place called Tartarus. Rashida ushered Brie up to the bar and ordered two double shots of tequila. They licked the salt from their hands, tossed back the shots, and promptly ordered two more. As they bit into their lime wedges, they surveyed the scene.

Mike and Cameron were sitting together at a table, laughing as Sherry regaled them with a story that involved some grandiose hand gestures. The angel had two columns of bloodstained tissue jammed up his nose. The rest of the soccer team was crammed into booths and perched around tables surrounding them, laughing and chatting away.

It was a happy scene. One that Brie felt very much separate from.

"There he is." Rashida had caught sight of her goalie. She smoothed her hair and dress, casting a discreet glance over her shoulder. "How do I look?"

Brie looked at her and said honestly, "You're a vision. Go have some fun, okay?"

With a girlish grin, the woman sauntered over to the tables, pausing a moment to speak with her friends. Cameron glanced up when she approached, then automatically scanned the rest of the room for Brie. He pushed to his feet the second he saw her, but Rashida caught him by the arm.

"Give her a minute," she murmured.

Brie startled, then looked around at the general clamor.

How did I just hear that?

Sherry got up and suavely introduced Rashida to the handsome soccer player sitting nearby. He played the moment well, kissing her hand lightly while maintaining eye contact and delivering what was surely an effective compliment before offering to buy her a drink.

The lovely woman graciously accepted, and the two headed to the opposite end of the bar to get to know one another better under the pretense of ordering cocktails.

Brie watched in silence, feeling like something had stolen her breath.

They would probably hit it off beautifully. Maybe they'd get a couple of drinks and watch the sunset together before finding an excuse to meet up again. Maybe they'd spend the night together straight away. Maybe they'd end up getting married and living in a house with a white picket fence and an ancient oak in the front yard with a tire swing for their two-point-five beautiful children. They'd probably get a dog to teach the kids about responsibility when the time felt right.

The blush of a new romance, the comfortable glow of the bar lights, the laughter of friends and comrades, the general air of merriment and unconcern… Brie didn't feel like she had a place in any of it. She reached up and touched her necklace.

I'll never have it. Not if I keep wearing this. It'll just be danger and darkness. And there's nothing I can do.

A dark mix of emotions rose in her throat. She bit her lip, reopening a cut, and tasted copper. She gritted her teeth, squared her shoulders, and clamped down her jaw, trying to push the feelings back down. It wouldn't do anyone any good for her to feel them, so what was the point?

Just ignore it, right? Even her thoughts were tinged with bitter sarcasm. Her face twitched as she tightened her eyes and thinned the edges of her lips. *It's fine, right? Everything's friggin' perfect.*

The bartender placed two shots on the counter next to her. She threw hers back with abandon without bothering with the salt or citrus. She drank Rashida's too.

Then she plastered a smile on her face and walked over to join her friends.

"The woman of the hour!" Sherry raised her glass in greeting. "Ida just told us. How did you know? How could you *possibly* have known? Brie, that's amazing! Did you brush up on your toxicology studies this past year or something?"

Cameron got up from his seat under the pretext of taking her coat. "What happened?" he whispered in her ear.

She just shook her head.

"Brianna, if you want to leave, we can."

"I don't want to leave," she answered with a strangely flat affectation. "This is where I belong. Right here. With my friends. In this bar."

He nodded cautiously and took a seat, still eyeing her with concern. She ignored him. "How did the rest of the afternoon go?" she asked the group.

"Nowhere near as exciting as yours," Sherry exclaimed. "Mike's been off his phone all day, trying to rein in the screen time, so we only just heard. Do you really think there was a poisoner in the hospital? I mean, that's just insane. Do they have any idea who it might be?"

Brie finished whoever's whiskey happened to be in front of her. She answered a little too loud. "Yeah, it was super crazy. Tell me all about soccer. What happened?"

There was a split second of silence, then Sherry pushed them quickly past it. "Well, you know how Cam got hit in the face?" she began. "It happened again. Somebody had the bright idea of making him the goalie—"

Mike threw up his hands with a grin. "In my defense, I thought there was no way he'd be a worse goalie than a midfielder."

"But somehow failed to teach him how to, you know, *stop the ball*. So instead of catching it like most people, he decided to use his whole face," Sherry finished.

Of course he did.

The guy shoots lightning from his hands, but heaven forbid he catch a soccer ball.

"It turns out you're *allowed* to use your hands when you play goalie," Cameron piped up.

"Is that why you're sporting that stuff up your nose?" Brie eyed him sarcastically. "Don't you think you should take those out? You look ridiculous."

"This is a *wound*, Brianna. I've been *wounded*."

It looked like he wanted to say more about it. It looked as though, at some point during the afternoon, he'd probably transcribed the entire experience into song. But he took a single look at her face, and the words died on his tongue. A second later, he pulled out the tissues.

For the next fifteen minutes, Brie drank steadily through the banter. She let out a hard laugh when the others laughed. She smiled cheerlessly when the others did. She didn't contribute, didn't speak. What she did was throw back shot after shot until the room swayed unsteadily beneath her. Cameron monitored her with increasing worry, but she refused to look his way.

"Yeah, we should totally go. It's by this great director, a real visionary in the horror genre."

Brie clicked back into the conversation at precisely the wrong time.

"Well, there are these monsters—"

"I think they're zombies."

"Right, zombies. Well, they're trying to get away, and for a minute, it looks like they can, but then these beasts crash right through the roof of the car—"

Brie stood up suddenly. Too suddenly. She tilted precariously before grabbing the back of a chair to right herself. "I need to get out of here," she muttered.

Sherry stopped mid-sentence, half-rising to her feet. "No problem, sweetie. Let's just get you to the bathroom—"

"No!" Brie interrupted, too forcefully. "I mean, no. You stay here. I just… I need some air."

In all her life, Brie had never snapped at Sherry. Not once. Not even when they were kids. A horrible silence fell between them before she took off suddenly, lurching for the exit.

Cameron grabbed her coat and quickly followed her outside.

She burst through the doors into a welcome rush of cool air that shivered over her body and flowed through her hair. There was a second of respite, but it wasn't enough. Before she was even off the patio, she flew to the side and started retching into the flowerbeds.

Cameron was there in an instant, holding back her hair.

"Don't touch me," she snapped.

He backed away, stung, before trying to approach again. "Brianna, let me help. Let me take this away for you. It'll only take a second."

"*I don't want any more of your help!*"

She took a second to revel in his shell-shocked expression, then started pacing dizzily away from the restaurant — not caring whether he happened to follow or not. She didn't look back as she continued yelling. "When have you ever really helped, anyway? You didn't save my mother. You told me to keep this awful thing around my neck for years, and the whole time, it's been turning me into some freakish mutant. I have abs now, Cameron. I can hear squirrels. *Squirrels!* I broke my house in half, and now I'm diagnosing patients with no information because my jewelry told me to."

She whipped around and jabbed her finger at him through the air. "I thought I was crazy for five long, lonely years, and now, you know what? I wish I were. It would be easier to be crazy, than to try to make sense of any of this."

Her fingers closed around the pendant, making a tight fist. "All I want is to be normal. I want a normal, boring life. I want to be with my friends and not feel like a freak. I want my life back. I want my scar back. I don't want *this* anymore."

He approached cautiously, like she was something wild. "Brianna, don't—"

"Don't tell me what to do!" she screamed. "This is my life, Cameron. I'm taking it back."

It was over before it started, before she could really think it through. In a single drunken motion, she ripped the pendant off over her head and flung it to the ground in front of her, watching as it clattered on the pavement before going abruptly still. The sound echoed impossibly between them as the last rays of the golden sunset glinted off the shimmering chain.

She stood in perfect silence, trying to catch her breath. Then all at once, she started laughing. *Hysterically* laughing. She threw back her head and flung her arms wide.

"You see?" she gasped, oblivious to the look of horror on Cameron's face. "Nothing happened. And nothing's going to happen. This was all just—"

It came out of nowhere, a roiling grey cloud, as though dozens of shadowy, terrifying creatures had slipped through cracks in the air itself to appear as an impenetrable horde.

She barely had time to scream before they were upon her. Beneath her. Around her.

It was like watching an incoming wave you couldn't possibly hope to outrun — one that was destined to sweep you into a rough and merciless sea. It was every bit as hopeless and even more terrifying, because this sea had teeth. There was a hunger in the way the creatures came at her. A ripping, howling sound that spoke of famished, barbarian emptiness tore through the air. All she could hear was the sick, thwacking sound of leathery wings and the gnashing of faces made entirely of long, thin, inward-curving teeth. It overwhelmed her. Everywhere she looked was a nightmare. Everything she saw had come straight from Hell.

And then he was there.

He tackled her to the ground, cupping one hand behind her head to absorb the crack on the pavement. With his other arm, he sliced through the air and hit the ground, letting out a deep cry. *"Abu-nan, d-b-s'myaa!"*

All at once, the darkness shifted. The image brightened as they were surrounded by a glowing sphere orbited by intricate runes. Ancient words swirled around them in rings of protection. From the sphere's equator, an enormous scythe made of golden light and heavenly heat shot out like a blade made from a sliver of the sun, carving and burning its way through the entire horde, spinning and attacking from every direction at once. The monsters' revolting bodies froze in place for an instant before sliding apart in perfect halves. The smell that was released turned Brie's stomach before the blade of light itself splintered apart into shards. These turned of their own accord as though aimed by Heaven's archers and shot from a thousand perfect bows. They drove themselves into all that remained of the wraiths and dissolved them into nothing until not a trace remained.

Cameron pulled his hand from under her head, revealing the pendant. He stared at it a moment, then placed it firmly around her neck. Her eyes were wild, and her heart was racing. She wrapped her arms around his neck, clinging like a child as he touched their foreheads together.

They held on for a long moment. Then he spoke in a voice that left no room for discussion. "You have to keep it on."

The telephone pole on the opposite side of the parking lot made a strange, moaning sound and cracked in half where the heavenly scythe had touched it. It crashed neatly onto an entire row of cars.

Broken glass showered around them like rain as a dozen car alarms went off, filling the air with sirens of protest and a dizzying explosion of flashing lights.

The door to the bar burst open, and about twenty police officers from the soccer game flooded into the parking lot. Mike was among the first, followed quickly by Sherry.

"My Lord! What the heck happened?" he cried, surveying the damage. "Are you alright?"

Brie nodded in silence. Cameron got up and offered a hand. She took it but couldn't seem to make it past a sitting position. His palm glowed discreetly, removing the nausea and clearing the alcohol from her blood.

"I think she's in shock," he said.

"I wouldn't doubt it," Sherry replied in a strangely flat tone. Brie locked eyes with her for a moment before turning away, cheeks burning in shame.

Did I yell at her before I came out here?

"Thank God we parked on the other side of the lot." With that, Sherry knelt down and gave her a quick examination. "Follow my finger." She held up her middle finger and moved it back and forth in front of Brie's face, monitoring her pupil dilation and her ability to track it, while making her feelings known. "Are you okay?"

"I'm fine, Sher. It's just… I got a little drunk. It's been a long day."

Satisfied that she didn't have a concussion, Sherry sat back on her heels. "You've been having a lot of those lately." Her eyes drifted over the wreckage strewn about the parking lot. "What happened here?"

"I don't know."

Sherry looked at her with an expression Brie had never received. Not from Sherry. Not ever.

Suspicion.

"I saw from the window, Brie. Cam tackled you *before* the pole fell."

All the blood drained from Brie's face. "The sound," she said faintly. "He heard a sound, and I guess he just…" She trailed off, unable to think of a convincing lie in the moment.

Sherry stared a moment, then shook her head. "It's like Rashida said earlier. You always seem to be in the middle of something these days." She cocked her head and gazed intensely. "Is there anything you want to tell me?"

Yes. There is something that I very much want to tell you.

Then in a flash, she remembered Sherry's face all those years ago, right after the accident, when Brie told her what had really happened to her mother. When she stretched her arms wide to show her the size of the shard of glass that had impaled her. When she uttered the word *shadow-monster* for the first time. When she told her about the angel. Sherry hadn't said anything. She'd just tried to calm her down. She'd tried for days to be supportive, to nod and stroke her hair and affirm Brie's feelings without confirming what she saw as the delusions of a traumatized mind. Brie could tell she didn't believe her and couldn't begin to blame her. She wouldn't have believed such a thing herself. After the funeral, she broke down and moved into the bathtub. Sherry was there for her then, too.

She couldn't put her through that again.

I want to tell you. But I can't. It would break your heart.

"Yes." Her heart caught in her throat. "I'm so sorry I snapped at you before. I don't know why I did that. It's been such a terrible day, Sherry. You should have seen that kid."

Sherry's face softened, and she sighed. "Oh, honey. What in the world am I going to do with you? You must be the unluckiest… Well, never mind all that. Let's just get you home."

The rest of the police force was jotting down license plate numbers and trying to match the customers with their ruined cars. Someone was already on the phone with the electric company to get the power to the felled line turned off. Rashida and her handsome goalie were staring out over the parking lot, thunderstruck.

That's a hell of a first date.

Cameron quietly followed the girls to Sherry's car and slipped into the back seat. He wouldn't meet Brie's eyes. He wouldn't even look at her. He didn't say a word the entire way home. He just opened the door for her when they arrived and stepped back, ever the gentleman.

The second the door shut behind them, Brie ran to her room and threw herself on the bed. She needed to cry, but she couldn't. She heaved a dry, broken sob, and then another, praying that the tears would just fall already to give her some relief. But there was nothing. Nothing but that familiar ache behind her eyes. The feeling of being completely hollow and utterly alone.

For what felt like hours, she buried her face in her pillow, counting her breaths until she finally fell asleep. For what felt like hours, Cameron stood on the other side of the door, his face turned up to the heavens, dying with each passing second, counting those breaths himself.

CHAPTER TWENTY-ONE

One of the Seven

That night, Brie dreamt of the accident. The car seats stained red around her, her mother's gasp of horror. The chain placed around her neck, the miraculous healing of her wound, a beast of shadow ripping her mother away. But instead of seeing the moment of her mother's death, the wraith with its hand in her chest, the way her face had paled a moment before going forever blank, the image shifted. She found herself in a round, white room with a single painting hanging inside. She floated, as though disembodied, through the featureless expanse, for some reason trying to look anywhere except at the painting. But there was nothing else in the room — no windows, no doors — and soon enough, she found herself face-to-face with it.

It was her mom. In fact, it was an enormous oil portrait of a very familiar photograph, one she kept tucked up behind the sun visor of her car. Her father had taken it, catching her mother in an unguarded moment by their kitchen window, just turning her face to him and reaching out her hand.

Brie knew every angle and line of that photograph by heart. But the painting unsettled her somehow. Something was wrong.

Although she couldn't say why, she knew that this wasn't her mother at all.

She floated closer, puzzling over what it might be, inexplicably afraid. She lifted a hand in a gesture mirroring her mother's, stopping just before her fingertips touched the canvas.

All at once, it clicked. The eyes. Those weren't her mother's eyes.

One was green, and one was blue.

As she leaned in to take a closer look, they moved, flashing to the right and staring straight at her. Then a hand made of oil paint reached out of the canvas and grabbed her wrist.

She let out a wild scream.

The eyes followed along as she tried to stumble backward. The painted hand stretched and twisted with her attempts to escape. But there was no escaping that iron grip, and there was no containing it. The paint began to spread up her arm and down her hand, covering her like a second skin in colors of flesh and light. She struggled uselessly against it, but it was like trying to escape her own body. She cried out and tried to tear it off with her fingernails, only to find her other hand trapped in the oil as well.

The rest of the painting started to melt into a hateful tar, dripping and spreading across the floor. The drops grew into dark, dense pools where they fell until the whole of the room was drenched, and it threatened to swallow her up. All the while, those eyes glinted and followed her.

"Please!" she screamed, over and over. "Please!"

When she woke up, she was still screaming.

Cameron was there, trying to calm her down.

She gasped for air and raked her fingernails down her arms. Angry, red scratches appeared for a moment before immediately healing themselves. He drew closer and held her as her eyes flew wildly around the bedroom, latching onto every familiar sight and possession to reassure herself it was only a dream.

"It's alright. It's alright." He chanted it over and over like a soothing mantra, holding her against the steady beat of his heart. It took a few minutes before hers began to match the rhythm. It took another few minutes for her to catch her breath. When at last she was quiet, he glanced down at the top of her head.

"Was it the girl?" he asked quietly. "The girl from the hospital?"

She remained silent.

"It's enough to give anyone nightmares," he murmured, tightening his grip. "Just knowing there's someone in your hospital, someone you work with, who would poison a child like that." He shook his head and held her closer still. "Such an evil, arbitrary thing to do."

Her blood ran cold as she realized that in all the drama and madness of the evening, she hadn't even told him yet. So much had happened, it didn't even feel like the same day.

She pulled away slowly, gazing up at him. "It wasn't the girl," she said. "And it isn't someone in the hospital."

He frowned. "What do you mean?"

"It was the woman, Cameron. The woman I saw," she clarified, "the one who was talking with Matthews. The girl saw her, too. Only..."

"Only what?"

"Only Kylie said she had silver horns."

Cameron tensed for a moment, before paling with a look of irrepressible dread. When he finally managed to speak, it was in a voice so quiet, Brie could barely hear. "I need you to tell me *exactly* what happened at the hospital today."

◆ ◆ ◆

"Tell me again."

Brie was sitting at her kitchen table, a mug of basil root tea untouched before her. Cameron paced frantically around the kitchen island.

"Which part?" she asked wearily.

"All of it." His voice had taken on a wild tremor she'd never heard before.

"I think that Kylie saw the same woman I did," she repeated for what had to be the tenth time. "She said she used 'bad fairy dust' to make her sick. I think it's the same person I saw talking to Matthews. I don't think anyone else can see her, and I don't think she shows up on cameras."

He stopped pacing and sat in the chair before her, leaning forward and gripping both her shoulders in his hands. "Tell me exactly what she looks like, Brianna. *Exactly.*"

"She's tall. Thin. Ice-blonde and gorgeous. Bright green eyes. Too green. You could cut a diamond on her cheekbones, and she has perfect taste in shoes."

Brie paused, trying to think of anything she might have forgotten. "Oh, and she may or may not have hooves. And silver horns."

The angel sat back in his chair. "Why didn't you tell me any of this before?"

"I did."

"You didn't tell me you thought she had *hooves*, Brianna. That didn't strike you as being particularly relevant information in light of recent events?" he demanded. "I thought she was an entitled hospital donor who gave you a bad feeling. A human woman who had you spooked. You didn't think that telling me the woman might have *hooves* would be pertinent?"

Brie drew back, stung by the accusation in his voice. "I didn't know if any of that was real. I've spent the past five years thoroughly convinced I'm crazy. Five years of a highly reputable psychiatrist telling me that I suffer from a combination of PTSD and a vivid imagination. *Hooves?* Forgive me for erring on the side of self-effing doubt."

He stared at her a moment before pushing to his feet. "It doesn't matter anymore," he muttered, raking back his hair. "The woman you're talking about isn't some low-level wraith, and whatever she's up to, whatever plan she's trying to bring to fruition, you can be absolutely sure you don't want to be anywhere near this place when she finds out that *you* are the person who got in her way."

Brie shivered in spite of herself, wishing he would sit back down. "I don't understand. You know her?"

"Everyone in my world knows her," he replied without thought. "Everyone in Heaven and everyone in Hell knows her." He stared out the window as though she might be standing right on the other side. "She's a Knight of Hell, Brianna. She's one of the Seven."

"The seven what?"

"The Seven Fallen Ones. The Seven Deadly Sins. Whatever you humans call them in your grotesquely inaccurate mythologies. Though I can promise you, nothing that has ever been written even comes close to conveying the depths of depraved power they wield." He started pacing, then turned back all at once. "And she, your blonde woman, is one of the worst of them."

A crow flew past her front porch. Cameron was at the window in a flash, pulling back the curtain and looking out on high alert, as though any movement might be a harbinger of doom. It was nearly dawn. The sky was full of clouds, and a dim light had just begun to filter up from the horizon.

"I can't imagine what she's doing here," he muttered. *"Here,* of all places. *Here,* of all times."

"Who is she?" Brie's voice was barely a whisper.

"Mammon." He turned to face her. "Greed. She's Greed, Brianna."

There was a beat of silence. "I don't know what that means."

"Think of it this way," he began, "everything humans pour their energy into, everything humans worship with their time, their money, their love… every single act of devotion makes the thing they're worshiping more powerful." His eyes burned into hers. "How powerful do you think Greed has become after all these centuries? How powerful, after all these generations, all these billions of humans slicing and sacrificing one another for a fistful of coins?"

Brie realized she'd forgotten to breathe. "Why does someone — *something* — as powerful as all that need someone like Matthews to do her dirty work?"

"She doesn't," Cameron replied. "She can kill with a thought. Why she's meddling around with humans? Why she needs a child sacrifice? I have no idea." He paused, then continued in a rush. "And I cannot have you anywhere near this place until we know."

In a flash, he was kneeling beside her. "Brianna, I know you don't want to, but you must trust me. You *have* to trust me. You need to come to Elysium. Whatever's going on here, it isn't a coincidence, and it isn't safe."

His hands reached for hers for a moment before dropping helplessly to his sides. "I know you don't want any of this. You've made your feelings very clear. Everything you said back at the pub was true," he continued softly. "I haven't protected you. I haven't helped. Since the moment I've come into your life, it's been filled with chaos. I saw how much it hurt you to lie to Sherry and how much it hurts you to feel isolated from your friends. I couldn't save your mother, and I don't know if I can keep you safe. You must think I'm a curse." His eyes tightened for a ghost of a second before locking onto hers. "But please, I beg you. Let me protect you from what's coming." He reached out and took her hands after all. "You must believe me: once it is upon you, there will be no escape."

She looked at him, heart heavy and throat thick with emotion.

He's right. And he's wrong.

It's already upon me. And there is no escape.

She nodded. And with that simple nod, she relinquished all hope for a normal life.

"Alright," she murmured, taking a breath to steady herself. "I have to go back to the hospital first. I need to tie up some loose ends."

"Absolutely not."

She glanced up in surprise, thinking the hardest decision had already been made.

"I *have* to. Sherry and my dad…" Her voice broke. "I need to give them a good story, Cameron, or they will *never* stop looking for me, and it will *ruin* their lives. I will not ruin my best friend's life, and I will not put my father through that kind of uncertainty and pain."

He opened his mouth, but she stepped right in front of him. "I can't. I won't."

He slowly nodded, planning on the fly. "You'll need to be quick. When you took off the pendant—"

She gasped in comprehension. "They saw the light. They'll be coming. She'll be coming here, to Yorktown."

He shook his head grimly. "You can be assured they are already here." When she started to hyperventilate, he was quick to add, "They can't see you. When you're wearing the pendant, the darkness *cannot* see you. I'll come with you to the hospital. If you wish, I can take a different form to stay out of your way." There was a slight pause. "I only wish to help. I've never wished to do anything more than that."

She looked at the floor. It was too much to process, but his abject hurt was impossible to ignore. "Cameron, what I said back at the bar. I was drunk. It's been an insane day. I'm so——"

"Please, do not apologize to me," he interrupted swiftly. "I already have infinite regret for the way my influence has made you feel and what my presence has done to your life. If you feel any guilt or responsibility for my feelings on top of everything else, I will not be able to bear it." He squared his shoulders. "I'll come with you in my Elysian form."

She looked at him. His face was like a door closing.

I can add him to the list of everything I've lost today.

She cleared her throat. "Whatever you need to do."

She looked around the little house, at the books on the shelves, the coffee mugs hanging on their little hooks, and the toaster that had captured the fascination of her celestial guardian. Her eyes rested for a heartbreaking moment on her miraculously revived plant, then the picture of her mother and father holding her as a baby.

I've barely been here a week.

How is it POSSIBLE it's only been a week?

A knot rose in her throat as she wondered what her life might be like if she could choose the path *she* wanted. If she could wake up every morning in the arms of a man she could actually be with. If she could go to work every day and do her best, and her best would be good enough. If she could come home every night and relax with her friends, safe in the knowledge that this was the life she had chosen. If she could rebuild her relationship with her dad now that he was finally ready.

But here she was, with a chain around her neck —— ruled by fate, about to say goodbye to everything familiar. About to say goodbye to her entire world, to run from a danger she scarcely understood, into the unknown… a place that would not return her remotely the same, if it returned her at all.

She stood abruptly. "I need a moment."

He nodded, turning away. "I'll send a signal ahead to let them know we're coming."

He knelt to the floor, and a wide circle of ancient lettering began to glow red around him as he murmured something in a language she didn't understand. She stared for a moment, then turned deliberately away and headed up the stairs. There was no time for wonder, no time to process.

Soon, that will be the least shocking thing I see.

She sat at her desk in her bedroom and wrote two letters on the stationery she'd bought herself on her last birthday. One for Sherry. One for her dad. Something about how it was all too hard, and she was going to take a leave of absence and stay with Cameron's family for a while. In Europe. Croatia. Something about how she didn't want them to worry. Something about how she was sorry this was so sudden. Something about how she'd get in touch soon.

Pretty lies, so when they pictured her, they'd think she was somewhere beautiful. She'd rather they were stung by her selfishness, than terrified for her life.

By the time she was done writing, she could barely drag in a full breath. It felt as though there was tremendous pressure on her chest, a stone monument to everything she was losing.

She walked back into the living room and placed both letters on the mantle as Cameron stood by quietly. Then she took a last look around the lovely place that could have been her home.

"I'm ready."

CHAPTER TWENTY-TWO

Mammon

"I don't understand." Her unit manager stared at her in confusion. "You just got here. What do you mean you want to take a sabbatical?"

Brie took in a deep breath, repeating herself for the fourth time. "With everything that's happened, I need to take some time away. A leave of absence." The accusatory gaze of a white kitten hanging from a branch over the words *Just Hang in There* loomed at her from the poster on the opposite wall. She stared at a paperweight on his desk, unable to meet either of their eyes. "I can't stay here. I wish I could."

"You haven't even finished your orientation yet."

"I know."

"Denise is going to be furious. And you're going to *Croatia*?" He sat back in his chair and frowned. "This is highly irregular, Ms. Weldon. This isn't college. This is a competitive program at a prestigious hospital. You can't just take a gap year."

"I know."

A golden glow emanated from Brie's purse, one she was certain only she could see. As if on cue, the expression on her manager's face started to change. He struggled for a moment before the lines on his forehead smoothed, and a blissful, vacant expression graced his features.

"Of course, you've been through a lot," he said vacantly. "You should take some time off. Relax. Get your head straight. I'll do the necessary paperwork. You are welcome back at any time. Have a lovely day, now." He turned to his computer and started opening his files.

She slowly rose to her feet, darting doubtful glances his way. "So, is that it?"

"That's it," he murmured to her dreamily, inputting her information into his computer. With just a few taps to his keyboard, he placed her on leave. "Have a safe flight."

She stared for a moment, then grabbed her purse and walked out of his office. It wasn't until she was safely back in the hall, away from prying eyes, that she looked down into the bag. "That was you, right?"

Silence.

"Cameron, would you get out here, please? I don't want my last memory of this place to be me walking the halls, talking to my purse like a maniac."

In a brief golden flash, he was beside her. "Is that better?"

She nodded, then gestured back at the office. "Thank you. Thank you for that."

"Of course."

"I need to check on Kylie and leave a note for Rashida."

He nodded in agreement, and they started pacing silently through the halls, pausing more times than Brie was fully aware of, letting her eyes drift wistfully over all those suspended dreams.

How long did I work just to get here?

"I'm going to miss this place," she murmured, trailing her fingers along a desk. "I barely got to know it. I don't even know why it's called Daya."

He threw her a peculiar look. "It means compassion."

"Oh. That's… that's really nice."

Her heart caught in her throat as she walked on.

He moved his hand as though to take hers but decided not to. "It's a leave of absence, Brianna. Not a death sentence."

She looked at him sadly, wondering if he genuinely believed that. "Of course."

With that, every light in the hospital went out.

"It's okay. It's going to be okay. Are you okay?" Cameron asked in a panic-laced voice.

"I'm fine. Stop saying okay." Brie hissed back in a whisper.

I am so effing far from okay.

They had both instinctively frozen, their backs pressed against the wall, his arm flung protectively across her chest. The lights were still out, casting the hall in an eerie glow from whatever laptops happened to be running on batteries. But that was the least of her problems.

"Um, Cam?"

"What is it?"

"You're crushing me."

His arm dropped immediately. "Sorry."

They inched along the wall, closer to the ICU, then started walking again, their path lit by the flashlight on her phone as they waited for the backup generators to come on.

Both were determined to play it off as casual. Both were entirely incapable of doing so.

"This isn't right. The power should've turned on by now. We have people on ventilators in here." She shivered. "Something isn't right."

That's when she ran into someone.

"Oh, excuse me," she apologized, before realizing something was wrong. There had been no give. Their body hadn't responded at all. She reached out a finger and touched them before shrinking back in alarm. "Cam?"

"What is it?"

"I'm hoping you can tell me," she said, full of dread.

It was a nurse Brie had seen around the hospital during the past week. He was absolutely still, midstride, his weight already shifted over his front foot at an angle that would have been impossible to maintain if physics had been working properly. He wasn't blinking, wasn't breathing.

She circled him in terrified fascination, waving her hand in front of his face. There was no reaction.

Holy Freddy Mercury… we're in trouble.

Cameron froze in a split second of shock, then nodded his head curtly. "Right," he said shortly. "I need to get you out of here. Immediately. Now."

She stared a second longer, then shook her head. "I have to check on Kylie first. They came for her before. For all we know, they might be coming for her again."

His hands clenched in scarcely contained exasperation. "Brianna, I don't know what more could possibly happen to convince you that we are far, far out of our depth here. Your safety is my top priority. We need to *leave*."

"And the safety of that six-year-old child is *my* top priority," she insisted, breaking into a sprint. "I can't just leave her here. Not without making sure she's okay."

For the first time since opening its doors, the chaotic halls of Daya Memorial Hospital were quiet and still. Brie passed dozens of human statues on the way, coworkers she'd barely begun to know by name, frozen in time. Coffees halfway to their faces, orders half-typed into computers, eyes half-closed in a blink. One of them was in the process of trying to use the broken stapler from the pediatric nurses' station. Her brow was creased in frustration as tiny metal flecks glittered in suspension around her hand.

Brie ran without stopping. She ran until the sudden sound of voices stopped her cold. The angel was beside her in an instant, cupping a hand over her mouth to stifle her instinctive scream.

Of course it's you. Of course you're the only ones not frozen.

Matthews and the blonde woman were standing in the atrium she'd stumbled upon just yesterday. She could see them reflected clearly in the window across the hall.

"My dear Jonathan, I thought we talked about this."

Mammon, or Greed, as Cameron had called her, made a tsk-tsk sound eerily reminiscent of a snake, ticking her index finger back and forth in time with the click of her heels as she advanced on the doctor cowering by the foliage. He was clearly terrified. Every part of him was shaking in fear.

But at the same time, he seemed to have come to a decision. As the tip of her shadow reached him, he drew in a faltering breath and shook his head.

The strangely shaped briefcase levitated towards him through the air as the woman pouted in a mocking sulk. "Just this once, Jonathan. Just one little minute of your time. Only your time, I might add. I stopped everyone else's." She gestured around her in false benevolence. The lights flickered back on, illuminating the still-frozen people. "Now you'll have no interference. No excuses." Her eyes flashed with what Brie could swear were emerald-green sparks. "Why don't you get on with it, Mister Matthews? The sooner you do, the sooner all your dreams can come true."

She let her arms drop by her sides as she walked forward, and showers of golden coins streamed from her fingers. Fountains of incalculable wealth clinked and clanged to the floor, rolling every which way. Then she raised her arms, and the coins on the floor multiplied until there were piles of gold and treasure on either side of her path, crushing the plants beneath their weight, reflecting every ray of light.

"I'll even kill her if you like. You only have to collect."

Brie's eyes widened in panic, and she struggled to get away. She might have even managed it if Cameron hadn't tightened his grip upon her, silently begging her to be quiet and still.

Matthews was staring at the piles of gold on the floor, the sheen reflected in his eyes.

"Think of it," Mammon purred, gliding towards him with a terrifying gracefulness. "You could acquire anything. Possess anything." She laughed, and a shudder ran down Brie's spine. "Everything you could possibly want on this godforsaken rock can be yours. I'll take care of that meddlesome mortician. She'll be dead the moment she walks in the door. Nobody will ever know what happened. All you have to do is stop all this useless moralizing and bring me what I want."

Matthews slowly turned away from the riches to face her, tears streaming down his face. "It isn't worth my soul."

Mammon stopped her advance. The strange black suitcase fell to the ground with an unceremonious thump as her eyes narrowed.

Behind her, the piles of golden coins transformed into a horde of vicious, jewel-toned crabs that writhed on the floor in giant heaps of dizzying motion before vanishing in a flurry of popping and ten thousand wisps of red smoke.

She tilted her head. "Your soul, you say?"

Matthews nodded, pale as a bone.

She let out a frustrated sigh and opened one of her palms. There was a sickening sound, like a watermelon being smashed by a sledgehammer. Matthews' eyes widened. He gasped, clutched his chest, and dropped to his knees. There was a brief moment of silence before he fell forward. His face hit the floor with a hideous crunch.

Brie sucked in a silent breath. She didn't understand what had happened. Not until her eyes traveled slowly back to the woman.

She was holding a still-beating human heart.

"What an inconvenient time to find out you had one of these." The woman glanced uncaringly down at the prone figure of the fallen doctor, lifting the heart to her lips and taking an absentminded bite as if it were an apple.

Brie screamed soundlessly into Cameron's hand as he started to pull her away, easing them from the wreckage and toward the opposite end of the hallway. She closed her eyes, chanting inside her head. *The darkness can't see me. The darkness can't see me. She can't see me. She can't.*

"Excuse me, dear."

The voice came from directly behind them. Brie turned and screamed out loud. Greed had stuck her head through the wall as if it didn't exist, and they were now eye to glittering green eye. She smiled at them as they scrambled backward, blood dripping down her chin, and stepped the rest of her body through the wall.

"I'm not sure who you're trying to convince, little one." Her heels clicked like a metronome as she advanced upon them. "But I see you. And it's frightfully rude to run off before we've been properly introduced."

CHAPTER TWENTY-THREE

The Battle of Daya Memorial

She took another bite out of Matthews's heart. "I'm Mammon," she said, around a mouthful of his left ventricle. "What's your name?"

Brie was frozen in absolute horror, but her angel had seen such things before. He threw his body in between them with a frantic shout. "Run! I'll hold her off."

A wave of heavenly fire poured from his hands, but for possibly the first time, it glanced off Mammon as harmlessly as if it were a snowball. Then, with the tiniest flick of her finger, Mammon sent him flying into the opposite wall. He struck with a gasp. A spiderweb of cracks haloed around him.

The woman tilted her head with a childish giggle. "That's funny. Tell another one."

Instead of letting him answer, she lifted her finger once more, and he was dragged roughly up the wall, pinned and thrashing, as though someone was holding him by the throat.

"Stop it!" Brie screamed. "Let him go!"

Mammon tossed her hair with a shrug, and the angel dropped back to the earth, clutching his throat and gasping for breath.

Brie raced towards him, sliding to a stop at his feet. "Are you alright?"

"Brianna," he rasped. "Get out of here!"

"Brianna," Mammon threw the heart backward over her shoulder and peered at Brie with sudden interest. "So *that's* your name. What's wrong with you, little one?" She squinted and tilted her head. "There's something out of phase about you. You're blurry, and I can't see your light. Not quite in this world, not quite in the next." She considered this a moment. "Have you, perchance, recently died?"

Cameron shook his head desperately, a terrible bruise spreading across his neck. "Don't answer her. Don't say any—"

But then he could speak no more because, within the space of a second, his mouth abruptly vanished — closed over with smooth skin.

Brie watched, frozen in horror.

"Now, now. Manners," Mammon chided, considering him at the same time. "There's something wrong with this one, too. Human, but it's been marinated in something else for a very long time." She looked back at Brie, amused. "Any other misfit toys running around the hospital you'd like to introduce?"

Brie stood up slowly. *Keep her talking. You aren't dead if she's talking. Cam isn't dead if she's talking.* "Mammon, was it?"

Greed gave her a congenial nod.

"My companion tells me you're a powerful player in certain circles," she continued shakily, glancing back at the angel the entire time. "What brings you to my neck of the woods?"

There was a burst of dark laughter, like shards of glass falling on stone. "*Keep her talking. You aren't dead if she's talking,*" Mammon parroted in a singsong voice.

Brie's mouth went completely dry. *Well, that's a neat trick.*

Greed bowed with a grin, then stopped short. "What is that?"

Faster than thought, she crossed the space between them. Cameron struggled helplessly in the background, chained to the floor by an unseen force, as Greed bent to examine Brie's pendant.

Her face lit with fascination. "So *you're* the one all the fuss is about." Her green eyes danced with a spark of anticipation. "My, my, my. You've no idea the sorts who are out looking for you, little one. Dastardly fiends with horrible plans." She grinned. "You're actually lucky I'm the one who found you. May I?"

Without waiting for an answer, she reached out a finger to touch the delicate teardrop. A fountain of sparks and white lightning lashed through the air, and she jerked back her hand as if she'd touched an electric fence. There was a gasp of delight, and she caught her breath excitedly.

"Oh, it's everything they say it is, isn't it!" she cried. "That almost hurt! My goodness. What's a pretty little thing like you doing with a powerful relic like this?"

Brie didn't say a word. There was a chance she couldn't.

Mammon rolled her eyes, then flicked her fingers up and down once more. Like a weightless doll, Brie slammed first into the ceiling, then the floor. She cried out in pain, and Cameron let out a stifled moan behind her, straining against whatever invisible force had him trapped.

Brie lifted her head a few inches off the tile, then started scrambling backward towards the atrium and Matthews's crumbled form.

"Let's try this again, shall we?" Mammon reached up and pulled a slim, serrated metal board out of thin air and started filing her nails into points. "Where did you get that marvelous little bauble? And try not to lie," she added lightly. "It's so boring."

Brie continued her breathless retreat, backing away on her hands and knees.

"Are you trying to get away?" the woman scoffed. "Really?"

With a careless toss of her hand, she sent Brie careening backward at top speed, crashing through a planter box and coming to rest beside the corpse of Dr. Matthews. She blinked away stars and tried to pull in a breath, but the wind had been knocked clean out of her lungs. She clutched her chest and tasted blood as she struggled to inhale.

Mammon continued her slow advance, filing her nails all the while. "They say the key to good eavesdropping is not getting caught. I'd say you're rather an object lesson in that little truism at this moment. Wouldn't you agree?"

Brie could only gasp in pain.

"At any rate. I don't know how much you overheard, but suffice to say, my patience has been tested quite enough for one night. And I'm not generally known for that virtue in the first place." She tossed back her hair, suddenly brusque. "So why don't you hand over your shiny little locket, and we can all get this over with? I've long wanted to add this to my collection."

Brie glared up at the beautiful woman, helpless yet enraged. Her focus narrowed, and she felt something hot and powerful start to grow within her. Her pulse quickened, and her breathing slowed.

She stared levelly at Greed. "You can't have it."

Mammon smiled chillingly. "Can't I?"

Horns split their way out of her forehead, silver stained with black. They curved backward and up again. She seemed to grow taller at the same time, her body elongating with an unnatural, animalistic quality. She threw her nail file without looking, burying it deep in Cameron's shoulder.

His eyes cried with pain. Brie felt it in her very soul.

No!

With few options and even less time, she scrambled further into the atrium, groping blindly on the floor, before she found the thing she'd been looking for. Her body angled instinctively to hide it as she fumbled with the clasps behind her back.

"Why do you want it?" Mammon reasoned. "What use could someone like you possibly have for it?" She paused, eyes shining in amusement. "Or do you even know what it's for?"

Brie said nothing. Another burst of laughter crackled between them, like ozone during a lightning strike.

"Keep the guardian in the dark. Well, it's a strategy, I guess. The Bright Ones have always been notoriously poor at communication." She clapped her hands twice, as if drawing a room to attention. "Come now, no more of these games. Hand it over willingly, or I'll kill the other one."

Inch by inch, the file started to drag toward the center of Cameron's chest. The clear agony in the twists and turns of his body was unbearable. For all the things her angel could do, all the hellish nightmares Brie had seen him defeat, he was helpless against such powers.

She glared at Greed with a hatred more profound than anything she'd ever felt before, then looked at Cameron with a protectiveness that ran deeper still.

So, you can hear my thoughts, can you?

"That's right, dear." Mammon inclined her head sympathetically. "I know. It hardly seems fair, does it? But then, what in this wretched world does?"

Well, hear this.

Their eyes locked.

I'm going to absolutely destroy you.

"Oooh. Kitty's got claws." Mammon grinned, showing all her teeth. "I'm trembling in my boots." Her legs elongated, and her feet transformed into black, cloven hooves. She stomped the ground, preparing to charge. She threw back her head in laughter.

It was the moment Brie had been waiting for. The second Mammon's throat was exposed, she grabbed the strange wooden sculpture from Matthews' briefcase and launched it like a discus with all her newfound supernatural strength directly at the Fallen One.

It sliced messily through her neck, sizzling where it touched, and cut off her laugh with a horrible gurgling sound before burying itself in the wall behind her. No blood issued from the wound. It merely bubbled black, as though touched by acid. Mammon's head swung back at an impossible angle before rolling off her shoulder and dropping on the floor with a clatter of horns on tile. The rest of her started to shrink back down to a human size, and her hooves became feet again. Her body instantly knelt to the ground and started feeling around for her head. It lay several feet away in a pool of ice-blonde hair, blinking in surprise.

Brie didn't hesitate. She sprinted forward and pulled the file from Cameron's chest. A second later, she grabbed her pendant and pressed it to the wound. It started to seal before her eyes, and his mouth reappeared.

He sucked in the air like a man half-drowned. "Brianna," he gasped. "How did you—?"

"There's no time. I need to warn Rashida."

She helped him up, and the two staggered down the hall to the elevators, making a conscious decision not to glance back as the headless body dragged its way across the floor.

The doors slid shut behind them, and a cheerful male voice floated down from the speakers, crooning about raindrops falling on his head.

They shared a silent look as they both struggled to catch their breath.

"Are you alright?" she finally managed.

"I will be," he panted, "thanks to you. I just need a minute."

She stared straight ahead for a second before saying, "By the way, since I'm probably about to die and all... I'm halfway in love with you. I didn't mean any of the things I said back at the bar. Not even a little bit."

He looked at her, shocked.

"I was having a moment." She raised her eyes to the ceiling, refusing to meet his gaze.

"Brianna, I—"

"It's fine," she interrupted. "You don't. You *can't*. I get it. I just thought you should know."

They stared in silence a moment longer, then the elevator opened, and they sprinted down the hall to the morgue. Brie rattled the doors, but they were locked. They did not survive her attempts to open them. She and the angel peered curiously at her handprints indented in the steel.

"Well, that's one way to keep her out of there, I guess," he said.

"She'll be getting here soon," Brie answered, still breathless. "She's probably in the parking lot. We have to get there first."

A second later, they were running again, this time to the lower lot where Rashida always parked. They weren't counting on what greeted them on the other side of the door.

Oh, no... Please, no...

Sherry slammed the door of Mike's squad car so hard it was

a miracle the window didn't shatter apart. She caught a glimpse of them by the elevator a moment later. She froze in fury, then stormed towards them, waving a familiar letter in the air.

"What in the name of *Hecate* do you mean you're moving to Croatia?"

Brie had never seen her so angry. Her eyes widened in horror. "What are you doing here?" she gasped. "You have to go back. Sherry, get back in the car."

Sherry was enraged. "Don't you dare push me away, Weldon!" she cried. "Is this him? Is this his doing?" She looked at Cameron like she was trying to light him on fire with her mind.

"No, you don't understand." Brie pleaded. "This isn't—"

"You are damn right I don't understand!" she raged. "I've tried to take this on good faith and just go with it, but enough is enough. You can't throw away your whole life to run off to Europe with some guy you hardly know. I won't allow it."

Rashida's green sedan pulled into the other end of the lot.

Mike appeared and tried to throw a little diplomacy on the situation. "Ladies, is there any way we could try to take this somewhere else?"

"*No!*" shrieked Sherry.

"*Yes!*" yelled Brie.

"What's all the yelling about?" called Rashida. She'd parked and was getting out of her car a few rows down, never seeing Brie's desperate look.

"Ida! Listen, you have to—"

She cut her sentence short as Rashida's expression froze. She looked down at her sweater. What started as a dot of red quickly expanded into a pool of blood.

She fell without a sound, revealing a towering blonde woman with silver horns behind her, pulling a long, silver file out of her back.

Brie's anguished scream echoed into the brimming dawn.

Mike immediately drew his weapon. "Get down on the ground! Drop your weapon and get down on the ground!"

When Mammon didn't comply, he fired. Five shots rang out in rapid succession. Every one of them hit their mark. Not one of them made the slightest difference. They ricocheted, bouncing into cars, the walls, the ceiling.

Mike lowered his gun and stared at her uncomprehendingly. "What the hell—?"

Mammon let out a roar and, with a flick of her hand, sent him flying across the parking lot into a support pillar. He crumpled to the ground and went still. Sherry screamed in terror, dashing towards the elevator.

"Yes, run!" Brie cried. "Keep running!"

Cameron knelt to the ground, summoned the last of his strength, and flung scythe after scythe of that heavenly light. They bounced off harmlessly, vanishing in a golden mist.

Mammon's feet became enormous hooves. Her nostrils flared with rage. She pawed the ground and started stomping toward them through the cars. The ground beneath her feet crunched and sizzled with every step. The paint on the cars blistered from the hellish heat radiating off her body. With every step, she seemed to grow.

"Have you had enough yet?" she roared as she closed in. "Is all of this—?"

She stopped short with a sputtering cough when she was abruptly covered in foam.

Sherry hadn't run away. She'd grabbed the fire extinguisher from the wall and was now emptying the entire canister over the ancient, demonic woman. A woman who was frozen in utter disbelief. It seemed to last for an eternity until the stream of foam eventually slowed to a flaccid trickle. Mammon glared at Sherry, who was too terrified to break eye contact. When the last of the fire retardant fizzled out, they stood there in silence for a moment, Sherry holding the empty extinguisher with a look of dread, facing off against what looked like a fire-eyed abominable snowman.

Run! You need to—

Mammon flicked her finger and sent Sherry flying into the same pillar that had felled Mike. There was a sickening crunch as her head hit the cement. Brie let out a breathless scream as her body slid gradually towards the pavement before going still.

But Mammon wasn't done. A wave of heat burst off her, singeing everything in its radius and blasting her free from the foam. She jabbed her index finger towards Cameron, who gasped as though he'd been impaled, then crooked it back and dragged him towards her like she had a hook in his spine.

"I'm going to skin them, you little bitch." She locked eyes with Brie, malevolence radiating from her like a black sun. "I'm going to make you watch me turn them inside out."

That was the moment something cracked open inside Brianna Weldon. Something old faded into memory. Something new and powerful rose in its stead.

A roar grew inside her like a tsunami, gathering tones like a wave gathers water. Light flickered beneath her skin like golden electricity as her body started to glow. Not a golden light like Cameron's. This was pure and white. Blinding white. She levitated off the ground as the roar burst forth from her mouth, from her soul. At first, it was only incredible. In the space of a heartbeat, it was unbearable. Lightning cracked and whipped around her, forming itself into a dome of light. Her eyes, her pendant, and the inside of her mouth shone like a supernova.

Not so helpless after all.

Mammon took a step back and dropped Cameron. She lifted her hand reflexively to her ear, but it was no use. The roar surrounded everything, washed over it, pulsed through it. After a few seconds, she let out a shriek and tried to turn away, but no sooner had she taken a step than she was rooted to the spot by bands of light pouring forth from Brie's hands.

Parts of her face and horns started to chip away, like a puzzle losing its pieces, as the still-rising sound tore through her. She started to scream in earnest, struggling against those glowing ropes, but it wasn't any use. Her hooves turned back into feet, and her legs kept morphing between those of a woman and those of a goat. Her face remained a woman's, screaming in pain.

In a merciless rage, Brie pulled on the ropes, forcing the creature one torturous step at a time into the dome of light. The moment she crossed its threshold, she started burning. Her ice-blonde locks sizzled and vanished. More puzzle pieces of her flesh disintegrated.

Brie pulled her closer still, until the two were standing eye to eye. At the last possible second, she grabbed Mammon's face with both hands and spoke in a voice that was not her own.

"Go. Back. To. Hell."

There was a violent explosion, a hailstorm of light. Then Mammon imploded in on herself like a black hole, ripping into itself until nothing remained.

The light vanished, and Brie dropped, senseless, to the ground.

CHAPTER TWENTY-FOUR

Out of the Frying Pan, Into the Fire

"Wake up! Please, please wake up!"

Brie opened her eyes and saw a fuzzy version of Cameron floating above her, his face half-covered in blood, his eyes shot through with agonized worry and filled with unshed tears.

"Cam?" She blinked once, twice, trying to get her bearings.

"You're alright!" He crushed her to his chest in a breathless embrace, squeezing the air from her lungs. "Oh, thank God. Thank you, God…"

She relaxed into his arms.

This is nice. Much nicer than whatever I was doing before.

What was I doing before?

It hit her. "Sherry!"

She broke from his arms and raced to where her friend lay, prone on the ground. In a flash, he was right beside her, watching as Sherry stirred with a quiet groan.

"Are you okay? Are you alright?"

Brie took her pulse and checked her all over for damage. Cameron did the same to Mike, pressing a glowing palm to his skull and healing his wounds.

"Sherry, can you hear me? Say something!" Brie cried.

There was no response.

"Love, can you hear me?"

Silence.

It was time to pull out the big guns. She leaned in close and whispered in Sherry's ear.

"Audrey Hepburn is an overrated fashion icon, and Givenchy overuses pattern."

A hand slapped blindly into the air, making weak contact with her cheek. "Blasphemy."

It was barely a whisper, but it was enough to get a choked sob of joy out of Brie. She gathered the woman into her arms, rocking her gently. "I'm so sorry, Sher. I'm so, *so* sorry."

"Mike's alright," Cameron interjected quietly. "Just asleep. Sherry should sleep too, Brie. For a moment." He touched Sherry's shoulder with a glowing hand, and she went limp in Brie's arms again.

Brie whirled on him. "Why did you do that? If she has a concussion, she shouldn't—"

"She isn't the one we need to worry about right now," he answered softly.

It took a moment to register. When it did, all the color drained from Brie's face.

Rashida.

They left Mike and Sherry propped up against one another, then turned and walked across the parking lot. There was no longer a need to run. Brie sank to the ground between the rows of cars without a hint of expression, staring down at her friend. She lay in a halo of her own blood, eyes open, an expression of permanent confusion splashed across her lovely face.

"No," she whispered, touching a finger to her cheek. The angel looked on helplessly in the background, but for once, she didn't need his help. She spoke again, louder this time. "*No.*"

Without a moment's pause, she lifted Rashida's hand and placed the pendant between their palms, lacing their fingers together so they were holding it between them.

"What are you going to do?" Cameron whispered.

Brie's fingers tightened. "The same thing you do when you need something. Pray."

She bowed her head and closed her eyes, asking with all her heart that her friend, her wonderful new friend who did not deserve this violence, be put back together and given the life that had been stolen. She repeated the silent plea over and over, kneeling there for what felt like a long time, but was really only a harrowing minute. Then, all at once, her earnest request was interrupted.

"Girl, what the hell are you doing? And what happened to my sweater?"

Her eyes flew open to see Rashida staring up at her, those beautiful eyes wide with confusion and concern.

"Oh, thank goodness," Brie cried, throwing both arms around her neck. "I thought it wasn't going to work. I thought... I thought we'd lost you."

"Lost me?" Rashida repeated, attempting to pull herself free. "What in the world are you talking about? Brie, what is this? What worked? Why am I all sticky?"

Brie merely tightened her grip, her eyes closed in relief.

Cameron was simply astounded and perhaps borderline sick. When Rashida held up a bloody hand, lips parting in alarm, he reached quickly for her arm, putting her to sleep as well.

"Would you stop doing that?" Brie exclaimed when her second

friend went limp in her arms. "Don't you think we should keep her conscious? Since she just, I don't know, *died*?"

Cameron looked around the parking lot. "I'm not saying you don't have a point, but..."

She followed his gaze. "Oh."

They stood up and turned together in a slow circle. There were enormous hoofprints embedded in the asphalt, bullet holes where the ricochets had pierced cars and walls, and a giant circle, still glowing like magma, burning around the place where Brie had sent Mammon back to Hell.

Brie shook her head, exhaling a slow breath. "What happened?"

Cameron looked at her, astonished. "You don't remember?"

She shook her head. "The last thing I remember, Sherry hit the wall, and I screamed..." She trailed off, unable to recall a second more. "What killed her? What did you do?"

There was a beat of silence. "What did *I* do?"

She turned to him, annoyed. "Look, I'm sorry I didn't see your glorious moment of triumph or whatever, but I was busy blacking out from all the unspeakable trauma I've experienced over the last week, and frankly, I don't think it's fair that you... Why are you looking at me like that?"

He took a step closer, eyes burning with intensity.

"Seriously, what's wrong?" She threw a glance over her shoulder, aware of the very real possibility that one of the daughters of Hell had come back to life. "Are you hurt? Do you hear someone coming? *Why* are you staring at me like that?"

He crossed the distance between them, looking rather wild. It was an expression she had never seen before, one that caught her breath and stirred her blood at the same time. He was so close she could feel his heart beat faster and faster, could see as deep as she'd ever seen into the oceanic pools of his dilated eyes. Her heart ached; her limbs felt weak and light all at once. Time would have stopped, if it hadn't already. They hovered on the agonizing edge a moment longer, waited to play the note they knew would ring forth forever and challenge their destiny.

Then they made a fateful choice.

His hand brushed lightly down her cheek. She lifted without thinking onto her toes.

"I should have done this a long time ago," he murmured, slipping a hand into her hair.

She froze instinctively, forgetting to breathe, gazing up at him.

"I should have done it every day since."

He leaned closer, so close she could feel the warmth of his breath, and before either could resist, their lips pressed into a delicate, passionate kiss.

It escalated without warning, without restraint. And once it started, it became abundantly clear: there was absolutely no stopping it.

They came together as naturally as a sunrise, as effortlessly as water flowing to the sea. It was as though both of them had been born for this very moment, in different places and in different times, waiting for countless centuries until they could fit themselves together once again.

She ran her palms over his chest. He cupped the small of her back, pulling her deeper into his arms. He moaned softly into her mouth, and his hand gripped a silken fistful of chocolate curls. Their lips mashed together; their tongues tangled, touching and exploring with a desperate, unending passion. She stood on her toes and circled her arms around him. Forgetting how to breathe. Forgetting her own name. There could never be enough of this feeling. There could never be enough of this moment.

They finally broke apart, but they didn't detach. He merely tightened his grip around her. She rested her cheek on the steady pulse of his chest. They lingered there longer than either of them realized before she peered into his eyes. "I thought it wasn't permitted—"

He silenced her with another kiss, long and slow and utterly worth the wait. When he pulled back, there wasn't any caution or fear — nothing but tenderness dancing in his eyes. "Brianna, if I'm to be damned for this, I want to deserve it."

Their foreheads touched together when a throat cleared suddenly nearby. They whirled to see a man standing behind them, if you could call such a person a man. He was beautiful, bare-chested, and enormously tall, with golden eyes and hair in black braids that hung to his waist. Except for some ancient-looking golden wrist cuffs, he was also completely naked.

His arms were crossed over his chest, and he had a look on his face like they'd just insulted his mother. Brie stared in shocked silence. Cameron immediately turned a noxious shade of green.

"Damned, you say?" The man's eyes flashed with heavenly light. "You seem well on your way."

EPILOGUE

The fox watched impassively from the base of the tree outside the parking lot as the demonic, horned woman continued to disintegrate into nothingness. She was of no concern. She'd bounced back from worse. What held its attention was the girl.

She levitated like a human crucifix, blinding light beaming from her eyes, her mouth, and her necklace. The pendant shone on her chest like a pulsar, annihilating whatever darkness it touched. The fox paced to the other side of the trunk to get a better look. A second later, the girl pulled Greed close with ropes of light and said something. The fox watched the Fallen One's eyes grow wide with terror and heard the echoes of her screams as she disappeared.

Back to the Father, I suppose.

What happened next was unexpected. After passing out, and after that goody two-shoes revived her and nearly cried like a baby, the girl checked on her friends. Then, she brought one of them back from the dead.

Bold move. I wonder if she understands the implications.

But it was what happened directly afterward that made the fox chitter with excitement and nearly give itself away.

He kissed her.

And not a chaste, heavenly kiss, but one that bespoke a deep and passionate love.

Well, I'll be damned. If a fox could grin, this one would be ear to ear.

He loped off into the forest, eager to share his discovery with his Father.

His eyes sparkled with excitement.

One green. One blue.

Coming Soon ...

The Forbidden Tears Series - Book Two

THE PENDANT
AND
THE PROPHECY

Sam Withrow
&
Amelia Pinkis

PROLOGUE

"They've promised that dreams can come true, but forgot to mention that nightmares are dreams, too."
Oscar Wilde

The screaming was growing tiresome.

The blistering Judean sun glinted off the speartips of the Roman centurions. The three wooden crosses atop the highest hill cast long shadows across the eastern valley. Soldiers picked at scabs and fidgeted in their armor. Wails of women filled the air. The center crucifix's silhouette reached toward the mouth of the cave like an outstretched finger.

Inside the cave, a creature, in appearance like a man, but yet not a man, extended his hand forward to touch the shadow.

He was too tall and too beautiful to be human. It was as though starlight had been braided into the very core of his being. He looked ancient, yet still young, frozen for eons in the perfect blush of youth. His hair fell long and white to his waist and shimmered even in the dark, as did the rest of his perfect form. His ice-blue eyes gazed at the cross' shadow with a kind of hunger. He stretched his fingers toward it, to the line of daylight dividing the cave from the sun.

Another piercing cry tore through the air. Behind him, a woman with black-tipped silver horns and a mutilated face broke into a series of pathetic sobs and whimpers. She was attended by three gorgeous, waif-like creatures. Two of them held her down while the third dabbed a foul-smelling potion on her wounds. Her face sizzled with each touch.

The man sighed in irritation, retracting his hand. "Asmodeus, can't you do something about that?"

The three lovely creatures nodded in eerie unison. One passed its hand over the woman's mouth, which sealed shut with skin. Her eyes still screamed and streamed with tears, but the cave was blissfully silent.

Another man stormed up to the cave's entrance, this one black-haired, wearing full armor and a scowl that seemed permanently etched into his otherwise imperious and handsome features.

"Why must we always meet here?" he growled, glowering at the white-haired man. "Every angel in the host must be crawling all over this moment."

"That's why this is the very last place they'd ever think to look."

The black-haired man pulled a gruesome-looking knife from his belt and twirled it at dizzying speed. A vein stood out in his forehead, and he clenched his jaw. "I still don't like it. What if Michael—"

"Shh, listen." The white-haired being held up his hand for silence, and the two turned their faces to the crosses on Golgotha across the ravine, listening to the distant conversation with perfect hearing, hanging onto every agonized word.

The man mounted to the crucifix on the right gasped through blood-filled lungs, "Yeshua, remember me when you come into your kingdom."

There was silence for a moment. The white-haired man's eyes shone, and he mouthed in perfect sync with the Son of God when He replied, *"Amen, I say to you, today you will be with me in Paradise."*

He leaned back, shaking his head. "Today. He'll let him in today."

The black-haired man scowled. "Why do you do this to yourself? You must've watched it ten thousand times."

The white-haired man turned and walked deeper into the cave. "You know why, Azazel," he said mildly. "To remind myself of the injustice we fight to rectify. To remind myself, there is no other way to reclaim that which is rightfully ours." He walked over to the horned woman, still silently screaming in pain, and cupped her remaining cheek with his hand. "He forgives a condemned thief without a thought. Meanwhile, see what becomes of us. His first children. Those with whom He shared all things."

He softly caressed the woman's disfigured face before turning to the rest of the cavern. "Mammon's failure is merely a setback. We have contingencies in place for such events. Belphegor's device will succeed. It is only a matter of time."

A figure in dark jeans, sunglasses, and a hoodie pulled down over his face flashed a thumbs-up and continued napping, leaning against an enormous, scale-covered wall that shifted ominously as though it was breathing.

"What about the girl?" Azazel glared accusingly. "She burned our sister to a cinder. Surely you don't consider her to be merely a setback."

"The girl was unforeseen, to be sure. But she's nothing but a mortal, subject to the same weaknesses and failings as all the rest."

"If she has the Tears–"

"If what she has is indeed the Tears, so much the better. We will add their power to our cause. Our asset will be with her soon, watching her closely. When the moment presents itself, she will offer them to us freely. She will beg us to take them."

Outside, the sun went black, and a tremor shook the earth. The cries of frightened mortals rang out as they went scuttling around the hillside like so many ants.

The beautiful white-haired man paused, thoughtfully. "Of course, there's never any harm in hurrying things along." He looked toward a dark corner of the cave. "Baal?"

In answer, the air filled with a terrifying noise. It started softly and quickly crescendoed into a cacophonous buzz as a swarm of hellish, metallic insects rose like a dark cloud and formed a face. It hovered there a moment, then twisted itself into a monstrous smile.

The white-haired man smiled in return.

"Are you hungry?"

ABOUT THE AUTHORS

Shirley "Sam" Withrow grew up in Gloucester, Virginia. She spent eighteen years as an emergency room RN until a bizarre dream shifted her timeline, and she set out to write her debut novel, now a series. She watched her wild imagination come to life, and her humor with the world shine through. She currently lives in Cape Coral, Florida, with her husband and bearded dragon, Iggy.

Amelia Rose Pinkis was born in California. After her time at the University of California Santa Barbara, she married her college sweetheart, began writing and editing professionally, and now lives near Lake Geneva with her husband and their four beautiful children.

Made in the USA
Middletown, DE
22 August 2024

59545051R00189